OMEGA PLAGUE

COLLAPSE

P. R. PRINCIPE

Published in the United States of America by Grey Mountain Press

First edition 2015

ISBN 978-0-9963264-1-4

Edited by M. J. Hyland and Trevor Byrne
Cover design by Ivan Zanchetta

Visit www.prprincipe.com

To my family

PROLOGUE

Bruno Ricasso gazed at the husk of a once-proud city. What was he thinking, coming back here? He must be out of his mind. The only sound he heard was the wind and the sea and the gulls behind him, and the pounding of his boots on the cobblestones. The late summer sun, while already past its peak, still shone brightly and cast sharp shadows. With the strong headwind, it had taken much longer to cross the bay than he had anticipated, and he needed to hurry. Bruno didn't want to be caught outside at dusk. Or dawn. He had made a point never to be out at those times. Which is probably what had kept him alive this long.

The pistol and baton strapped to his side were the last vestiges of a uniform long abandoned. He wore sweats, and had cinched his sleeves with rubber bands over his light leather gloves and tucked his pants into the boots. While chafing and hot, he much preferred being uncomfortable to risking exposure to infection. The black leather of the gun belt around his waist contrasted with the dark-blue fabric underneath. Had anyone else been there to observe, they might have noticed the grey hairs beginning at his temples and shading down into his beard, uncommon for a man in his early thirties—but perhaps not so uncommon for anyone who had managed to survive the past year.

Bruno paused for a moment to get his bearings, the sunken blue eyes behind his dark sunglasses surveying the scene. Ever-present to the southeast, the volcano menaced the city, its grey rock slopes stark in the daylight. He stood on the long road that meandered along the seaside, concrete and stone piers stretching behind him. Vulgar graffiti decorated the façades of the long, stone buildings that lined the street in front of him. A steamy breeze blew trash back and forth at his feet. The breeze carried the smell of the sea with it, but it was also tinged with the damp scent of ashes from fires that had long ago burned themselves out. The state of the city reminded him of how things had been after a garbage strike, minus the syrupy stench of rotting food. Now, the public bins were filled with refuse so old they smelled mostly of dust, not decay. Bruno peered into one of the bins. There was little point in rummaging; anything of use had long since been scavenged.

And he'd left paradise for this?

But there was no point in dwelling on what he'd left behind just across the bay. Unwisely or not, he was committed. If, against all hope, what he searched for was still here, then he would find it and get out. He headed east. While it wasn't the most direct route, he wanted to stay on main avenues, for fear of losing himself in the warrens of streets.

Cars and *motorini* with flat tires were scattered here and there. He moved briskly, but stayed as close as he could to the left side of the street: concrete barriers topped with translucent plastic screens along their lengths bordered that side, with a row of regularly planted trees behind. Beyond the trees, cranes and other construction equipment rose over an open pit. He watched for movement. Passing the half-excavated construction site, he noticed a sign on the building to his right. "Centro Storico." Good. He was headed in the right direction, towards the city center.

The street opened onto a large square with an overgrown park in the middle. As Bruno entered the square, he paused and took a wide look around. He remembered this place. It had once been lively, full of people laughing, talking, complaining. In all its long history, the city had never been this empty, this barren. He looked north and saw the trattoria where he and his father had celebrated the good fortune of his assignment so close to his father's town. The tables and chairs that had once been arranged on the sidewalk surrounding the eatery now lay mostly upturned, like fantastic four-legged creatures, dead on their backs. The long terracotta pots defining the outside dining area were filled with dry scrub weeds. He thought of the city as it had been, and continued northward.

The two-lane street lengthened into the distance and veered left, rising beyond his sight. Bruno walked on the low concrete divider between the lanes, four times the width of a normal curb. He wasn't sure if it was better to try to stick to the sides of the street, where there was more cover, or remain on the straight, unobstructed path of the divider, where he was less likely to be surprised. He decided to opt for speed over stealth, as a quick glance at the sun told him he had spent too long drinking in the sights, wasting precious time.

There were far fewer vehicles on the street than he might have otherwise thought. Before he arrived here, he had steeled himself for scenes like footage from a World War II documentary, with bodies lying naked in the streets. But he saw none. Made sense, he supposed, since most people had tried to leave the city if they could. Or they would have died at home; maybe there were tens of thousands of desiccated cadavers hidden away, unseen, all around him, lying in their beds. He tried not to dwell on that thought.

The low-rise stone and concrete buildings on either side all had balconies facing the street. The shops and storefronts on the ground floors were either empty, ruined, or locked down behind steel *serrande*. Black streaks ran up the outside of many of their windows, and many of the buildings were charred. A few buildings were relatively intact, and some of the balconies had overgrown plants spilling out. Some looked like pear trees. He took out a small pad from his sweat top and wrote down the street and cross street. Perhaps something to remember for the next time he came into the city. *If* he came back.

He reached the end of the divider and the street curved sharply to the left. The street opened onto a wide intersection of three other streets. The buildings facing the intersection terminated not in hard angles but were rounded, softening the otherwise sharp architecture. He scanned the corners of the buildings in front of him and spotted the street name on a concrete plaque mounted on the building to his right. Via Monteoliveto. Street of the Mount of Olives. This was it. He quickened to a jog.

Finally, Bruno arrived at a small intersection. A gridiron-style building rose almost directly in front of him. The streets continued sloping upward, rising sharply around the gridiron building, and they met in a triangular intersection with a similarly shaped fountain in a pedestrian square to his left. He recognized this place instantly. He had lingered many a time at that fountain, reading a magazine and smoking after his shift. With its white marble eagles, tapering up to an obelisk crowned by a bronze Spanish king, the fountain seemed defiantly elegant in the ruined silence, even though the marble lions had run dry. When water had poured into the basin, the air about the fountain had always been crisp. But now it was filled with stagnant rainwater the color of seaweed. It was not somewhere to linger anymore.

Bruno walked past the fountain and into the small square. On the left side of the square was a green metal newsstand still plastered with tattered posters and full of the last newspapers and magazines ever printed. The square itself sloped gently upward, ending in a long, three-storey building arranged perpendicular to the square. Arches framed the tall windows and stretched along the ground floor. Two navy blue vans were parked nose-to-nose across great, wooden double doors, as if to provide cover for them. The back doors of the van to his left were flung open. He approached the van with caution, drawing his pistol in his right hand and cutting a wide angle around the door, controlling his breathing as best he could. The van was empty, except for a thick, brown streak framed with handprints that stretched from the middle of the interior to the lip of the door, a gash in the otherwise white space. Dwelling on the streak and what had happened to make it would do him no good. Keeping his pistol ready, he searched the other van and found registration and insurance paperwork, in the glove compartment, and a small penlight with an LED that gave off a feeble, but still usable, white glow. He slipped it into a pocket.

Bruno turned now to the building looming over him. The wooden doors stood directly in the middle of building's façade, framed by the tallest arch. Above the arch, affixed to the second-storey balcony, were two fraying flags on masts reaching into the square. One was *il Tricolore*, the national flag. The edges of the faded red end flapped over his head. The other was the Flag of Europe. He had known as soon as he came to the square with the fountain that he was in the right place. The flags, marking a government building, only served to confirm what he already knew. There was a gold-plated plaque streaked with grime mounted just to the right of the door. He read the words: "Commando

Provinciale: Napoli." Bruno pulled the large steel ring that served as a handle, but the doors stood firm. He holstered his pistol, lowered his backpack to the ground and, after first removing and stowing his gloves, pulled out the crowbar, then began to pry the seam. He worked the tool back and forth until the wood began to give and finally, with a sharp retort, a chunk of the door flew out. The crowbar fell to pavement with a clang that reverberated around the square. He had hoped for speed and stealth during this trip back to the city, but he felt sluggish and loud. He looked around before reaching in and turning part of the mechanism that was now exposed. He heard the scrape of metal on metal and the bolt withdrew into its housing.

He remembered the courtyard of his old duty station well, and knew exactly where to go. The rational part of him knew that what he sought was probably long since removed or destroyed, but the other part smoldered with hope that what he might find here would provide him with answers—maybe even *the* answer.

He slid his pistol from its holster and stepped into the courtyard.

***

Hours later, he emerged back into the square. He paused in front of the door he had broken. His t-shirt was stained with moisture, but it wasn't from exertion. Each time he had pried or broken open a door, window, or cabinet with the crowbar, the noise had made sweat pop out from under his arms. Yet, against all hope, there it had been, sitting intact in the electronics storage cabinet, gleaming, almost waiting for him. He knew that it probably would not work, for any number of reasons: it might be broken, it might not be the right kind, it might simply be beyond his ability to use. Yet the weight of it in his backpack comforted him.

In the square, everything looked the same. The blue vans, their doors still open, were as he had left them. The sun, though, was now low in the sky. He was not sure how much time he had. He moved forward with haste, thinking only of the sea, where he would be safe. He made it only as far as the middle of the square when a long, low growl froze him in place.

He turned to his right and saw, emerging from behind the remains of the newsstand, an emaciated dog. It was a feral mongrel and looked like a German shepherd mixed with a wolf. The dog crouched slightly, its hackles raised, and began to bark. For all Bruno knew, it may never have seen a human before.

He did not want to use his pistol as he was afraid of who might hear the gunshot, but there was no way he could outrun the dog, not weighed down like he was. He eased his baton from his gun belt.

The dog stepped towards him and Bruno leapt towards it, swinging the baton. The backpack unbalanced him and he only just managed to clip the dog's snout. The dog staggered, blood staining its teeth, one of which was now missing, an incisor. Bruno dropped the baton, drew his pistol, and the dog leapt at him as he fired.

He backpedaled almost to the vans without realizing it, his ears ringing with gunfire. He stared at the dog, lying on its chest with its legs splayed out.

With a loud exhalation, Bruno released the magazine, dropping it into his left hand. He had shot three rounds. As he swapped the magazine for a full one, he reflected that his firearms instructor—God only knows what had happened to him—would probably have berated him.

He shoved the full magazine into the grip and re-holstered the pistol, then found the baton and hurried back into the square, past the fountain.

As he was turning right to head back down the Via Monteoliveto, he spotted two figures at the top of the street, past the gridiron building. His stomach tightened. He was in the middle of the street, exposed. They were not much more than two hundred meters away from him; they must have been drawn his way by the gunfire. For an instant he hoped they hadn't seen him. Then he heard what sounded like a referee's whistle, and he turned and ran back down the street, towards the seaside.

He darted down a narrow side street, which wound around and opened onto another four-lane street heading north-south. He crossed the wide avenue into a warren of narrow streets laid out in a grid pattern. He knew exactly where this was. I Quartieri Spagnoli, the old Spanish Quarter, named for when Spain ruled this city. Most of the streets were only three meters across. Tattered clothes still hung from rusting balconies, and leftist political posters, their vibrant reds long faded, hung in shreds from the sides of stone buildings. Once a breeding ground for poverty and crime, the Quarter's run-down apartment buildings now stood only as a reminder of an infamous past. He made his way through the streets, dodging around cars and overturned motorbikes and zig-zagging south, back towards the sea and salvation.

Bruno hoped the lack of a long field of view would give him some kind of advantage. He took cover behind a delivery van that had been turned over on its side. The van cut across the small street, nearly blocking it, rear doors butting right up to a building. After his breathing slowed he could hear no movement, but he wanted to make sure he had lost them. He held onto the van's undercarriage and leaned just around the front bumper. With the detritus of the city cluttering the street, he could only see three blocks behind him. But he saw no one. And the only whistle he heard now was the wind through the streets. The rush of adrenaline from the chase ebbed from him, leaving him spent. His legs felt like they were weighed with cement as he continued to trudge his way south, half-expecting to hear the sound of a whistle coming from one of the buildings around him.

At last, Bruno exited the Quartieri, the street opening up into a large square. He stayed in the shadows, making sure the square was clear, before covering the distance. He realized he had come further southwest than he'd intended. He found himself on the edge of a large open space covered in cobblestone, the Piazza del Plebiscito. He skirted the piazza, hugging the wall of the old Royal Palace, and emerged near a small park.

Bruno picked his way through the tall grasses and bushes that had grown up between the palm trees until he reached the edge of the park. He knew he was not far from where he had left his motorboat. He squatted down and slung his pack behind a palm tree; it hit the ground with a metallic clank. Bruno cursed his own carelessness. Though it was built to mil-spec standards, it could still break. And if it did, this trip would be for nothing.

He pushed himself into a thicket of bushes from where he could survey the scene. The street was flat, with three lanes; the outside lanes were for cars, while the middle lane bore the long scar of trolley tracks. He could see a long, narrow pier stretching into the sea, and just beyond it, the Beverello Pier. His motorboat was on the other side of some buildings on that pier, a relatively short and square wharf compared to some of the others that stretched hundreds of meters into the bay.

Bruno took some deep breaths, forcing himself to calm down, but as he did he saw a pair of figures walking the *lungomare*, the street that hugged the shore behind the piers. They had just emerged from around the building on the Beverello Pier. Beyond them, he thought he could see movement, maybe two or three more figures. They must have realized that they would never find him in the remnants of the city; there were simply too many places to hide. So, they made the gamble that he had come in by sea, and tried to cut off the most logical escape route. He prayed that they hadn't noticed his motorboat, pulled up on some rocks just below an overhang.

He was able to get a better look at the pair closest to him. Two men. Their clothes were loose, everything greens, blacks, and greys. Each wore netting around their head that obscured their features, and each carried weapons. The rifles they carried stood out above all: they weren't automatic weapons, but looked like scavenged long guns, made for game hunting.

The two figures were moving down the street towards his position. He crouched low, leaning his left shoulder against the tree. The sun was in descent behind him, and with luck, he'd be lost in the glare and vegetation. Slowly he retrieved his pistol from its holster with his right hand.

The first time he had ever fired a pistol, the instructor had told him the exact moment of the shot should surprise, so you don't anticipate the recoil and pull the shot off the target.

They were getting closer . . . one hundred meters . . . fifty meters . . .

He tried to slow his breathing.

. . . Thirty meters . . .

He brought the pistol to bear, holding it with both hands, trained on the slightly farther of the approaching figures.

. . . Twenty meters . . .

If he made a mistake he would be dead, or worse than dead.

He squeezed the trigger in a slow, even motion, and was amazed at the amount of blood and brains. The man died before he hit the ground. The second man froze, and Bruno fired twice; the man dropped, clutching his gut, and began to scream.

Bruno snatched his backpack and ran towards the screaming man, who was writhing now on the ground. He fired one more shot, and suddenly everything was silent. There was no time to linger. Bruno grabbed a rifle and ran towards the square pier, rounding the squat buildings and reaching the far corner. Before taking the stairs down to the water, he peered over the side of the cement railing, onto the rocks below where he had left the motorboat.

But the boat was no longer there.

PART I

CHAPTER 1

September 19

Bruno leaned against the doorway, captivated by the scene on the flat screen above the bar. He wore a light-blue shirt with epaulettes and dark slacks with a brash scarlet stripe down the side of each leg. A white leather bandolier lay across his chest, and his gun belt was weighted with the usual law-enforcement gear: pistol, handcuffs, and baton. His uniform marked him as a member of the *Carabinieri*, an arm of Italian national law enforcement with both military and police duties. Many of its members had been deployed abroad for missions that straddled peacekeeping and the fighting of wars. There were fewer of them than local cops. They were better paid, and they unquestionably held more prestige than many of the other overlapping national law enforcement agencies. None of that, however, kept the telling of irreverent Carabinieri jokes from being a national pastime.

A taller, lanky man wearing the same uniform appeared in the doorway. "Why the hell are you watching this crap?" said Cristian Di Cassio. Cristian swallowed off the end of his words, typical for someone born and raised in Rome. He was angular, with a hawk-like nose and a sparse beard running along his jawline.

On the television, throngs of people followed a procession of priests and bishops into a cathedral. One of the priests, in red and white vestments, carried what looked like a thick mirror on a long, silver handle. Upon closer inspection, however, it was clear the object was not a mirror; rather it was a round container, a sandwich of glass, and between the glass was suspended a clear phial of what looked like black powder. After arriving at the altar of the cathedral, the priest turned toward the crowd and thrust the object into the air. The audience erupted into applause and the perspective on the screen shifted, focusing on the phial within. The substance did not seem to move, and a murmur went up from the crowd. The priest began to pray. Two grey-haired men sat at the bar, laughing together, paying no mind to what was going on over their heads.

"It's the festival of San Gennaro," said Bruno.

Cristian laughed. "Of course, your patron saint! You Neapolitans love your pagan rituals, don't you? The ancient blood becomes liquid again!"

Bruno looked up at the screen. "Doesn't look like it turned to liquid this year. And I'm from Nusco, not Naples."

"Well, if it didn't turn to liquid, then bad luck for Naples. Guess they'll lose their next five games against Roma," said Cristian. "Forgot you were from Nusco. Isn't that a little piss-hole of a town outside the city? You bang sheep there, no?"

Bruno had met Cristian his first day on duty on the island last year, after his assignment from their regional headquarters in Naples. Cristian was the type who had no problem telling you what he had for lunch and what it looked like coming out the other end. A few minutes after they'd first met, Bruno discovered far more than he wanted to about Cristian's divorce (it was her fault), his seven-year-old daughter (now living with Cristian's parents), and how many foreign tourists he'd bedded since being stationed on the island (a lot). Nevertheless, Cristian had a malicious charm. He'd only slightly toned down his self-aggrandizing profanity since he'd started dating Bruno's older sister, Carla, a few weeks ago. But that didn't deceive Bruno; he knew Cristian was still full of shit.

"Come on, Bruno. If you watch too much of this stuff, you'll go, from this," Cristian held his finger up, "to this." Cristian dropped his finger down, limp and lifeless.

Bruno smiled and gestured with head. "All right, let's go," he said.

Though he was happy to joke with Cristian, Bruno in fact took no solace from the feast days of the Church's beloved saints. The death of his mother and little brother seven years ago had left him cold. In fact, in the months following their deaths, he had ceased to believe in God at all. He had even toyed with joining a group that had paid for slogans on the side of city buses in Milan that read: "Bad News is, God doesn't Exist—Good News is, You Don't Need Him." It had caused quite a stir. But while he may have agreed with the sentiment, Bruno realized that associating with those mildly subversive types would invite heightened scrutiny from his superiors. Not to mention what he knew his mother would have thought. So, mostly, he kept his opinions on religion to himself. Following their mother's and brother's death, Carla had returned to Naples from her teaching position at San Raffaele Hospital in Milan, and had just a few months ago taken a position at the hospital on Capri. Carla and Bruno were already planning a surprise visit to their father at Christmas. Bruno turned and walked back into the square, and Cristian followed.

The late-afternoon sun shone brightly, and they squinted their eyes on emerging from the bar into Capri's main square. They had spent the better part of the morning reviewing intelligence on a gang in Naples running drugs and arms to Serbia, so they were happy to be outside now enjoying the sun. Their boss told them that after they signed off on the reports, they could patrol until the end of their shift. Taking full advantage of the opportunity, Bruno and Cristian wandered about, nominally on patrol, but in reality simply taking in the beauty of the scenes before them. It was the middle of September, but on Capri, the promise of many warm fall nights lingered well into November.

From just off the main square the view was spectacular. The marina rested at the bottom of rocky slopes, dotted with rich, verdant vegetation and orange terracotta roofs on whitewashed houses. Figures below bustled along piers where boats were coming and going. Beyond the marina lay the semi-circular Bay of Naples, and beyond that, looming over the shore in grey haze and terrible splendor, stood the cone of Vesuvius. The volcano served as a reminder that Naples lay under a delayed death sentence. Someday it would erupt again, and hundreds of thousands would face evacuation or suffocation. Bruno had heard a scientist on the news mention an increase in tremors over the last few months, enough to raise some concerns among volcanologists. He had even read on a British website once that if an eruption from Vesuvius were large enough, it might devastate the climate around the world for decades, even centuries. It had happened before in prehistory, long before there had been people to bear witness. Now the same event might cause civilization to crumble. If there were ever a serious eruption, Bruno had heard that the government's evacuation plans called for cities and towns all over Italy to take in refugees. But in an emergency like that, what were the chances anything would go as planned? Zero, he thought.

Out in the bay, Bruno could see vessels steaming towards the city. He noted the massive bulk of an aircraft carrier with another vessel behind it. From this distance, they looked the size of children's toys. Ships from the US Navy's Sixth Fleet, headquartered in Naples, were probably coming back now from a deployment on the open sea. No doubt the sailors would be happy to hit the streets of Naples, causing more work for his colleagues tonight. Bruno smiled to himself. The only crime they saw on Capri was the occasional inebriated tourist pissing in some alleyway. And anyway, on the island, the municipal police handled the drunks. There hadn't been a serious crime in years. Even then it had been jewel theft, nothing violent. Bruno had plenty of time for musing while on patrol.

The contrast between Naples and the island of Capri, the jewel in the bay, always amazed Bruno. Less than an hour's ride by hydrofoil from Naples, Capri seemed worlds away from the city's chaos, noise, and delinquency. He wondered if it was the same when the Romans had built their villas on Capri. Had Naples been hot and sullied then, as now?

Cristian had wandered back into the main part of the square, packed with foreigners, and Bruno quickened his pace to catch up. This time of year, the island was still teeming with tourists from Europe and Asia. Lately, Bruno noticed more Chinese than Americans roaming in the piazza; the Great American Debt Crisis a few years back and subsequent Chinese bailout had taken their toll on America's economy, and the United States was still digging itself out of the hole it had dug for itself. Bruno and Cristian picked their way through the crowd. Tables and chairs from the restaurants were set out in the square, and waiters buzzed back and forth. Though it was late afternoon, many patrons were still lingering over the remnants of lunch. Cristian nudged Bruno when he spotted a woman walking through the square.

"She's taken, I think," said Bruno, as the woman gave a decidedly non-daughterly hug to a man who was old enough to be her father.

"Who cares?" said Cristian. "I'm just looking. He's just some rich old fart." Cristian's voice took on a longing tone. "She's a dark angel, for sure; good to look at, but maybe dangerous to touch." Then as if realizing the ridiculousness of his own serious tone, he chuckled.

"You're dating my sister, remember."

"Don't worry! I said I'm just looking!" laughed Cristian. "Actually, I prefer older women doctors like your sister. And president of the hospital, too. A rich older woman—I *really* like those!"

Bruno said nothing.

"Oh, come on! I'm just joking, Bruno. You're so uptight! You need another woman."

"How much longer will I be the only one who has to listen to your shit? When do you think Marco will arrive?" asked Bruno, changing the subject.

"Il Maresciallo said he'd be here in about two weeks. Could be longer. You know how slow they can be at headquarters." Bruno knew exactly who Cristian meant by "il Maresciallo." There was only one Marshal with the Carabinieri on the island: Bernardo Veri, their boss.

"Maybe we should dump all our shit cases on Marco when he gets here," laughed Bruno.

"I'm sure Veri would get a kick out of that," said Cristian. "What about that shit case of yours, that weird pirate radio thing? Wasn't the broadcaster some kind of conspiracy nut?"

"Oh yeah, that guy was transmitting all sorts of tinfoil hat shit, then just stopped. I talked to a few amateur radio geeks, but they're pretty tight-lipped. Not many of them on the island. If they know anything, they're not telling. Fucking nutters, the lot of them."

"What a waste of time."

"Yeah, whoever it was hasn't broadcast for months. I'll probably just recommend closing the case," said Bruno.

"How did you end up with it?"

Bruno shrugged. "Dunno. I guess when they referred this case to us, someone at the Provincial Command remembered I spent six months working as a communications tech."

"Well, I'll tell you how to find out who's broadcasting," said Cristian. "Find the geekiest ham radio guy, the kind who couldn't get laid in a bordello. That'll be your man."

"What a brilliant strategy. Clever aren't, you? Like Sherlock Holmes."

"Nah, I'm more like that TV cop—what's his name?" Cristian paused, then snapped his fingers. "Commissario Montalbano! Smart *and* sexy."

"You're a bloody idiot," said Bruno.

Their meanderings had brought them full circle, and they were standing in the entrance to the bar again. The same two old men were lounging about, still paying no mind to the screen overhead. It was a few minutes after the hour, and the voice of a female news presenter caught Bruno's ear. "In other news, the Minister of Health in Rome will honor a group of ten doctors, including three Italians, from the charitable group Médecins à l'aide des autres, who are returning from West Africa today after a twenty-one day quarantine. The honors are in recognition of their assistance in containing the latest outbreak of Ebola, as well as fighting mosquito-borne diseases. They will continue on to . . ." the news presenter's downy voice faded into the background as a group of bustling Japanese tourists led by an Italian guide carrying a sign on a stick moved past them. Bruno found it curious that the Japanese still liked to have a live tour guide, unlike most of the English speakers, whose various devices constantly droned on wherever they went.

Cristian looked up from his phone. "Hey! Carla just texted me. She's got a friend who wants to meet you."

"Really?"

"Oh yeah! She's a nurse—works at the hospital with Carla. I think Carla's her supervisor, actually. And I bet she's hot!" Cristian laughed. "Come on, you want to meet up tonight?"

Bruno shrugged. "Why not?"

Cristian clapped him around the shoulder. "Now that's what I like to hear! Don't worry, after tonight, you won't even remember your ex—what's her name? See, I can't even remember!"

"Good. You watching the game tomorrow?"

"Napoli-Roma? Of course, we're going to kick your asses!"

"Did you hear what happened to your captain?"

"Manelli? Is he injured?" Cristian's face grew dark with concern.

"While he was driving around Paris in his Porsche, a bunch of thieves busted his window and stole his girlfriend's purse, right in front of him. You know how sensitive he is. That'll wreck his game for sure."

"Good thing he wasn't in Naples," said Cristian with a smirk. "In Naples they'd steal the Porsche, but leave the purse."

CHAPTER 2

October 2

Bruno raised his right hand, steadying the earpiece and pushing it deeper. The orange sun lingered over the ocean on the western horizon. He was enjoying the still-warm air as it settled over the island. Bruno was at the marina, watching the crowd queuing up for the hydrofoils and ferries to Naples. He scanned the people in front of him, his face blank as he spoke to his sister.

"Did you see the video?" said Bruno, just loud enough for Carla to hear.

"Yeah, I saw it," said Carla, her voice loud Bruno's ear.

"Is it fake? The sores on that guy looked pretty real."

"I've been talking about it with some doctors here," said Carla. "We think somebody's just trying to get famous off this new Ebola scare."

"Well, this virus—or whatever it is—has got someone in the Interior Ministry scared. We've been placed on alert. And why hasn't anyone seen those doctors who were in Africa? Where are they?"

Carla did not answer.

"Are you still there?"

"Yeah, sorry, just got an e-mail." Carla paused again. "The Minister of Health is convening a conference call with the presidents of all hospitals nationwide in one hour."

"That doesn't sound good," said Bruno. "The news said there are people in London, Paris, and Rome that are showing signs of sickness."

"Oh, the call's probably just routine information sharing, or something like that. For sure, this thing's not Ebola. It's probably just some weird flu strain. And you know how people are; they hear something like this, they get a runny nose, and think they're going to die." There was a pause again. "Listen, Bruno, I've got to go. I won't be able to meet you and Cristian tonight. Tell Cristian I'll try to see him tomorrow, okay? Bye."

Bruno started to talk, but realized he was talking to dead air. Carla was already gone.

For a few minutes, Bruno scanned the crowd. Then Cristian returned from his patrol of the other side of the marina. Veri had sent the two Carabinieri to the marina to back up the municipal police.

"How goes it?"

"People are on edge," said Cristian. "Guess Veri was right to be worried, but there aren't any problems yet. You saw the video?"

"Yeah, Carla thinks it's fake," said Bruno. "So do the other docs at the hospital. But take a look around. Some people are already wearing masks. And I don't think it's a coincidence that the people who had close contact with those damn doctors are in quarantine."

Scores of people stretched along the piers and back into the buildings along the water, more people than usual waiting for the ferries and hydrofoils. They were jostling and talking more loudly than normal. Some foreigners wore makeshift masks made of handkerchiefs and clutched at their suitcases. The natives yammered away on their phones, whether unconcerned or in disbelief about what might be happening, Bruno could not say.

Two municipal police officers made their way towards Bruno and Cristian. Their arrival at the marina meant they had come to relieve the two Carabinieri. They conferred briefly. Bruno and Cristian let the new arrivals know that people were on edge, then they departed for their station.

At Cristian's suggestion, they decided not to take the funicular up the side of the slopes leading to the main square, choosing instead to walk through the winding stairs and narrow streets between houses. Though the daylight faded, they took their time.

"How's your family doing?" Bruno knew Cristian's family lived near Rome.

"For now, fine," Cristian replied. "Just talked to them yesterday. Someone had the sniffles in my daughter's class, and they closed the whole school." He laughed. "My daughter loves it. She's home with my parents all day." Cristian's face clouded. "Guess they don't want to take any chances with kids. I hope there's nothing to it . . ."

Bruno didn't reply. They kept walking in silence for a time, then Cristian said, "Anyway, I've got leave scheduled next week to go see them."

"No doubt they'll be happy to see you." Now that the Interior and Defense Ministries had put everyone on alert status, Bruno knew there was no way leave would be permitted anytime soon, but he didn't have the heart say it.

The sun had just disappeared into the sea when they arrived at their station, just off the main square. They entered a confined waiting area with four low chairs and a small round table, magazines with ageing celebrities and scenes of Mediterranean islands on their covers strewn about. The area was stark, with off-white walls and a sad potted plant in the corner. Directly in front of them was a thick glass partition with an opening at the bottom, like a teller's window, and a black steel door to the right of the partition with a small square window. Beyond the glass partition a stout, uniformed, grey-haired man with a white goatee sat on one corner of a low metal desk. There were two other desks. All the desks had monitors on them. Veri was reading, a sheet of paper in one hand and a cigarette in the other.

As they opened the outer door a chime rang in the back. Veri looked up and waved his cigarette at them in acknowledgement. The steel door buzzed along with the sound of electromagnets unlocking. Bruno and Cristian walked in and the door clanged shut behind them.

"Ah. Good evening, lads. No problems on your shift?" Veri had a raspy voice from a few too many years of smoking.

"It's more crowded than normal at the marina, Maresciallo," said Bruno. "And a little rowdy. But nothing too bad yet." Cristian nodded.

Veri snuffed his cigarette out in the ashtray on his desk. Judging by the pile of butts, he cared not a whit about the "Vietato

Fumare" sign just past the inner door. The man moved around his desk and sat down. His eyes were bloodshot as he looked back and forth from Bruno to Cristian. "Well, get ready, gentlemen. I think we're about to have a real shit-storm come down, and soon." The stout Veri would never be confused with a movie star. Carved in his face were decades of law enforcement time. But while he could be brusque to the point of rudeness, both men had benefited from his willingness to bend the rules to support them, instead of acting like a rigid martinet. In return, Bruno felt loyal, even devoted, to Veri.

Veri called them "gentlemen" only when he was about to inform them of some particularly vexing request from their regional command. Bruno braced himself as Veri motioned for the two of them to gather around his desk. "All right," he began. "I've just received message traffic from Regional Command in Naples. First, all transfers and leave have been cancelled. No surprise there. So, it looks like our additional officer, Marco, won't be arriving here anytime soon." Veri then picked up another sheet of paper. Bruno smiled to himself; Veri was so old-school, he still liked to print things out. "I also received these orders, maybe an hour ago. Let me read them to you." Veri looked up. "I think you'll find them . . ." he paused. "Well, I'll just read them and be done with it."

"'In light of the emergency conditions commencing as of this date and in order to maintain public order, pursuant to Chapter 5, Article 40 of the Code on Public Security, all civilian permits for firearms possessed by individuals are declared null, void, and are hereby revoked, effective 72 hours from the time of promulgation of this order.'"

Veri put the sheet of paper down. "There's more, but the bottom line is that we are supposed to help our friends in the national and local police confiscate all legally owned weapons on the island. And of course any unregistered ones as well. All the regional commands received this order straight from Headquarters. Apparently our government is nervous that things could get bad—and soon. This order will be made public tomorrow."

Bruno shook his head. "That's the stupidest fucking thing I've ever heard. This is just like the Ebola shit a few years back. Panic for nothing. And taking peoples' legal guns? This is the first thing the government worries about? That doesn't make sense."

Cristian scoffed. "Are we supposed to confiscate knives and forks, too?"

Veri reached for three sheets of paper on his desk and held them up. "Gentlemen, here is the list of individuals on the island with legally registered firearms. It's got to have around a hundred people on it." Veri paused, lit another cigarette and took a drag, then held the papers over his cigarette. Within seconds, the corners began to smolder, and flames began to lick the sheets of paper. Veri turned in his chair and dropped them into a metal wastebasket behind his desk, where they continued to burn.

Veri finished his cigarette in silence. Smoke from the wastebasket rose from behind him. When the smoke dissipated, Cristian finally spoke.

"We're going to tell the higher-ups we don't know who has guns now because you burned the list?" Cristian said. "What, it's not on the computer?"

"No," replied Veri, taking him seriously, despite Cristian's manner. "We're not going to plead ignorance. Quite the opposite, actually: we're going to tell Headquarters we've followed their order."

"You're just going to lie?" said Cristian. "You're going tell them we've confiscated the weapons?

"That's exactly what I'm going to do."

"Now, wait a minute. What if an inspector comes to check on the weapons? And what about the Questura, the local police office? They're the ones who issue firearms permits in the first place. They won't simply look the other way."

Veri leaned back in his chair. "I've already spoken to Commissario Esposito in their office here on Capri. He thinks this is a bullshit order too, and is in full agreement."

"So, what, that means you can just ignore it? Sir, do you know what they'll do if they find out? They'll crucify you." Cristian gestured towards Bruno. "And probably us to boot!"

Veri stood up, walked around his desk, and put his hand on Cristian's shoulder. "Of course, I will take full responsibility for this decision." Veri's gazed shifted to Bruno. "I would never hang you lads out to dry. Anyway, trust me, no one is going to check. The chain of command has more urgent things to deal with than watching us. Besides, if this sickness turns out to be nothing, the worst that will happen is a reprimand." He chuckled. "Don't know about you young bucks, but at my age, I'm sure I can handle a sternly worded letter. And if the sickness is real . . ." Veri paused for a moment, considering his words. "If it's real, then the last thing anyone will care about is whether or not we followed this order."

"Sir," said Bruno, "if it ever came to it, the higher-ups aren't going to believe we didn't know what was going on. Even if they did, we'd certainly be considered derelict, at least, for not knowing about something this—this—" Bruno struggled for the right words.

"It's fucking insane," said Cristian.

Veri ran his fingers though his cropped hair. "Look, I understand what you're saying. But you both know history—think of it like the orders our military got when they were in Croatia back in World War II. The military didn't obey, because the orders they got—those orders were wrong. They were evil. These orders are wrong, too."

Bruno understood Veri's point, but he doubted orders to round up innocent Jews for slaughter constituted the moral equivalent of this firearms confiscation order, and he was certain their superiors would not think so.

"Gentlemen," Veri continued, "our duty is to protect our citizens, not to put their lives in jeopardy. In thirty years as an officer, I have never done anything to put a civilian's life in danger. But that is exactly what this," Veri pointed to the smoldering trash can, "preposterous order does. It turns law-abiding citizens into criminals, overnight. It takes away their right to defend themselves. I want no part of it. I can't stop this order everywhere, but we can at least stop it here, but . . ." Veri paused. "I can't do anything without your support."

Bruno considered the request. If he acquiesced, it would, at best, mean the end of his career. He did not want to think about the worst that could happen. Even so, the words were out of Bruno's mouth before he could stifle them: "All right. Fine. I'm in."

Cristian shook his head. "I thought I was the stupid one," he said, and laughed. "I guess you've got this all sorted out, sir." His tone suggested that he thought the exact opposite. "I hope you're right, for all our sakes."

Veri nodded, but said nothing.

***

Later that night, Bruno lay in his bed, staring at the ceiling. He looked at his watch. Only 23:16. The long depths of night still stretched before him. He flung the bedsheet off and sat up. The crescent moon was surprisingly bright, lighting up Bruno's one-room flat. He stood, opened the glass doors, and walked, naked from the waist up, onto the balcony. The slight chill in the air was refreshing. He looked down towards the village of Capri and beyond it to the dark sea below. Living in Anacapri, the less tourist-saturated village above Capri, was the only way he could afford to live on the island. He had no desire to brave the twice-daily ferry commute to and from Naples like Cristian and Veri. Though it was late, lights twinkled against the velvet dark of the sea. The beauty of it captivated Bruno, distracting him for a moment from thoughts of cover-ups, deception, and disobedience.

A light on his neighbor's balcony came on and the glass door slid open. A white-haired man in a robe stepped out, a half-full wine glass in one hand. The man's face was weathered like the rocks of the island's Faraglioni. Bruno had always thought he looked more like a sailor than a priest.

"Buona sera, Father Tommaso," said Bruno.

He saluted Bruno with his glass. "Bruno, good to see you."

"Haven't seen you for a week. You've been traveling?"

"I got back from my brother's place in Salerno last night. Retirement has its perks, travel being one of them. And I only have to say Mass once in a while now."

"Right." Bruno nodded and looked back over the water. He drummed the railing with his fingers as he stared at nothing. They stood there in silence for a while. Then the priest spoke.

"How are things at work?"

Bruno continued tapping. He didn't answer right away. "Good question. Could be better, I guess."

"You all right? Something bothering you, Bruno?"

Bruno stopped tapping. He looked over at Father Tommaso. "You ever do something you think is right, but it breaks the rules?" He enjoyed talking to Father Tommaso about Napoli's chances of winning the Scudetto this season and the region's Roman and Greek roots, but Bruno seldom spoke about religion. And he almost never requested advice from the priest, but tonight was an exception.

Father Tommaso swirled the wine in his glass. "Don't we all do that sometimes?"

"So how do you know what's the right thing to do?"

"You've got to have faith, Bruno. Faith that your heart will guide you."

"Faith?" said Bruno. "What if you don't have it?"

"We all have it. But sometimes we forget it's there."

Bruno didn't respond. He looked back over the water into the night and started tapping the railing again.

Father Tommaso stood there for a moment and then spoke again.

"I'll leave you to your thoughts."

"I'm sorry, Father, I just—"

"No worries, Bruno," said the priest as he went back into his flat. "If you want to talk, please, just knock anytime. Buona notte."

As he stood there alone in the cool evening, Bruno's thoughts returned to cover-ups, deception, and disobedience. This is how a republic ends, Bruno realized. Even though he agreed with Veri, he sensed their insubordination might represent the beginning of something insidious. Local needs might override decrees written by some distant, unseen official. Expediency might replace principles. The rules that kept nations intact might fray, and eventually snap. Yet as he thought about the possible unraveling to come, he realized that he was wrong: this wasn't the beginning of collapse—in truth, it had already started. The useless politicians in Brussels had already begun their blathering about coordination of efforts, sharing information, and "solidarity," but from what Bruno understood about human nature, things could very quickly become every country, every city, even every man, for himself.

Bruno did not sleep well that night.

CHAPTER 3

October 9

Bruno could see the lights dotting the coastline through the mist even before they were halfway across the bay, but the rest of the world around him floated in inky darkness. The choppy sea that night made Bruno acutely aware of every handhold on the patrol vessel. He stood in the glass-enclosed cabin, Veri in front and Cristian across from him. The cabin was small enough that there was only an arm's length between Bruno and Cristian. In front of the cabin, the patrol boat captain peered intently at the control panel and listened with headphones to radio traffic, oblivious to his passengers.

The blue light from the instrument panel provided the only illumination. Bruno glanced at Cristian, whose face looked sickly in the pale light.

"Hey," said Cristian as loudly as he dared, not wanting the boat captain to hear. "How the hell can he drive this damn thing without lights? I know we're trying for stealth, but it's pitch-black!"

"This is a Model 800 motovetta. It's got enough radar and IR sensors to see a match flame five klicks away." Bruno gestured toward the captain. "He probably drives better in the dark than he does during the day."

Bruno returned to his own thoughts. There must be more to what they were doing tonight

Veri turned facing outward so he could talk to both of them. The rough sea made him keep both hands on the railing running along the cabin. With the glow of the light and his goatee, he looked menacing.

"All right, gents, you know what's going on. The confiscation order is a week old, and we've all seen what it's done."

Bruno reflected over the last week. When enforced, the resistance to the confiscation order had turned violent in a few of the major cities, catching the government flat-footed and serving as a costly distraction from disease monitoring and containment, as more cases began to pop out in Rome. Why resistance had been a surprise to the morons running the Ministry of the Interior was unfathomable to Bruno. And with seven million registered firearms, Bruno was certain that the government's efforts would ultimately be futile.

There had been little reported violence in the rural areas, particularly in the South, leaving Bruno to wonder if they weren't the only ones who had disregarded the order. When Bruno had asked Veri what he thought, Veri had just smiled, saying cryptically that he had many friends in the service who thought being far from the provincial commands makes many things easier.

"Still," said Veri, "I think the Interior Ministry is using what's going on as an excuse for something bigger. Not that I have a problem going after this particular bunch of thugs. But we'll see if I'm right when we get the expanded mission brief."

Veri shifted position, leaning forward. "Keep your ears open. The rest of the squad will meet us on the dock."

The boat slowed noticeably now; they had begun to maneuver up to a long, concrete pier with no illumination save for the lights of the city. Two people moored the boat and returned to the pier. Once the boat was secure, the captain indicated it was safe to disembark.

As they left the boat behind, Veri, Cristian, and Bruno secured their facemasks. They had already started to ration their surgical masks, stretching their life over more than the recommended one day. The masks were becoming grimier by the hour. Bruno hoped that, no matter the shade of grey, they would still provide some kind of protection.

The revelation that the doctors were not in quarantine in London, but were actually dead, had caused a firestorm. Even the notoriously lurid British media refused at first to show pictures of what the doctors looked like after death. But then the pictures leaked out, circulating first on people's phones, then throughout the commercial media. Diseases like flesh-eating staph, Kaposi's sarcoma, and necrotizing pneumonia had consumed the doctors. In the media, some medical professionals theorized that whatever it was must have ravaged the victims' immune systems, leaving them vulnerable to opportunistic infections. Like they all had "hyper-AIDS," one said. British, French, and Italian authorities tried to quarantine everyone who had come in contact with the doctors. The media said it would be too late—quarantine hadn't worked during the swine flu pandemic that broke out in Latin America a number of years back, and it had barely stopped Ebola in Europe. The doctors had come into contact with hundreds of people during their European travels, including, of course, high-level government officials. While there were no reports of the disease outside of London, Paris, or Rome, Bruno knew it was only a matter of time before it spread.

The two who had moored the boat joined the three figures standing on the pier. In the semi-dark, Bruno couldn't make out their faces, other than to see they, too, wore masks. There was enough light to see their uniforms, which were the same as worn by the trio from Capri. The Carabinieri had abandoned their cheerful blue attire for dark navy tactical uniforms. They were thick and practical, complete with helmets and body armor, and black boots heavy on the feet. All of them carried 9mm submachine guns slung across their chests.

As the two groups of officers approached, they all held their hands out with palms down, as if showing their nails to each other. No one shook hands.

"Good," grunted Veri. "Everyone's clear." Given that no one was exactly sure of the disease's incubation period, a hand check wasn't perfect, but it was a quick method to see if anyone had tremors, the initial symptoms of infection. Yet Bruno wondered whether they should even bother, since no one was sure if people were contagious even before the tremors began. Maybe the real purpose of the check was to give people a false hope that let them continue to function. Otherwise, no one would set foot outside their home, and then things would really go to shit, and fast.

One of the five stepped forward. Bruno thought he had met him before, the bright-blue eyes standing out even in the shadows against the man's tan skin, but it was difficult to tell with everyone masked.

"Veri, good to see you again," he said. He motioned toward a waiting blue van.

"Lieutenant Colonel Costa." Veri nodded in acknowledgment.

The back doors of the van were open, and all eight of them entered, the last person shutting the door.

Bruno now remembered Costa, the provincial commander in Naples. Bruno surmised that if lieutenant colonels were out doing real operations instead of signing reports and giving orders, law enforcement truly teetered on a razor's edge. Costa's head, shaved bare to the skin, glinted from the small light in the van's ceiling. They sat on the bench that ran along the inside of the van, while Costa stood stooped in the middle, bracing himself on the walls with both hands. He knocked on the panel immediately behind the driver and the van's engine turned over twice before coughing to life. Then the van moved slowly off the pier.

"Thanks to our colleagues from Capri for coming," Colonel Costa began, raising his voice to be heard over the engine. "I'm glad the island is calm enough for you to assist us." His face grew grimmer. "I wish I could say the same for Naples. We've been stretched thin already—most of my officers are guarding critical infrastructure, not kicking in doors. The Camorra clans have been active, taking advantage of the fear of this outbreak, whatever it is."

Costa continued, briefing-style, all business.

"So here's the sitrep: Coordinated raids on organized crime cells are taking place all over the country tonight, on direct orders of the Commanding General himself." Costa paused to let the import of his words sink in before continuing. "Every major city in the country has at least ten squads making arrests tonight. There are twelve other squads in Naples alone. In Rome and Milan, there are even more. Tomorrow morning, the PM is going to announce this initiative to enforce the weapons confiscation order and smash organized crime once and for all." Veri exchanged a knowing glance with Bruno and Cristian.

Costa's voice grew severe. "But back to our business tonight. Our targets are these six individuals—two Bosnians, and four Camorristi—they're holed up at this address." Costa pulled out a flat screen pad from a deep pocket in his jacket and handed it to Veri. "Here are pictures of them and a schematic of the building and their flat." Veri studied it, swiping through each photo, and passed the pad along.

As they looked at the pictures, Bruno eyed his colleagues in the van, wondering when the last time was any of them had been on a raid. He recognized a couple of them, like Marco, who was supposed to have come to Capri but instead ended up stuck in Naples. Marco and a few others looked like they had just started to shave. The rest of them teetered on the edge of what should have been a lengthy, well-deserved retirement. Bruno hoped they hadn't gone too soft from years of riding a desk. This whole damned operation struck Bruno as futile. Why go after a few thugs now? What good would it do, with some sort of unknown virus spreading?

Costa continued to talk as each team member looked at the pad. "This bunch crawled out of some shithole more than a year ago, and their gang's been terrorizing the Quartieri Spagnoli worse than any other Camorra clan."

Costa paused, giving time for each team member to study information on the pad. "Note that two of the Camorristi are brothers. They're probably the most dangerous. These two and their crew have muscled the Russo clan out of their territory. And I don't have to tell you what a bunch of savages that lot was. These brothers have both done time for assault with a deadly weapon and extortion, and are implicated in the killings of five rival clan bosses. God knows what else they've done that we don't know about. So be careful." By the time the last person handed the pad back to Costa, the van had come to a stop.

Costa looked at the men arrayed around him. "No doubt some of you are wondering why we are bothering with this scum at a time like this. Keep in mind, this is a nationwide, coordinated effort. Like I said, there are twelve other squads in Naples taking part in raids tonight, not to mention in Milan, Palermo, Catania, Rome, Bari—I could go on." His eyes now shone with emotion as he spoke. "If we can take down the leadership, in one blow, then we cripple organized crime nationally. And maybe keep Naples that much farther from falling into anarchy."

"Falling into anarchy?" said Cristian sotto voce to Bruno. "Naples is *always* in anarchy." While Bruno considered whether

Cristian was being serious or just trying to be an ass, Costa's eyes narrowed and he looked straight at Cristian.

"You! Di Cassio, isn't it? Is there a problem?"

"No, sir!" replied Cristian in his best military voice.

"Good. Keep it that way."

Bruno felt Costa had answered his unspoken question about the reasons underlying these raids. But judging by how deep into the pool of manpower they dove to get enough people for the raids, they'd be lucky if none of them got hurt.

The van came to a halt. Costa opened the doors and the squad tumbled out, two at a time.

"We've parked two blocks away. We're on foot the rest of the way, so with luck, we won't be spotted."

As they assembled near the back of the van, the team began to check and double check their main weapons and sidearms.

Veri leaned over to Cristian and swore under his breath. "Cap'e cazzo! Can you not control your mouth even for a second?" Cristian didn't say anything, but from the look in his eyes, Bruno knew that under the mask, Cristian sported a shit-eating grin.

Bruno looked around. The dingy apartment buildings and uneven cobblestone streets meant they were in the heart of the Quartieri. Bruno glanced at his watch. The luminous analog display showed 01:02, well past the newly-imposed nationwide curfew of 22:00 hours. Anyone out and about now risked arrest. Bruno looked up and drank in the night air. Silence blanketed the warren of narrow cobblestone streets. The only noise rippling in the night was the distant sound of what to Bruno sounded like gunshots. Things were indeed falling apart.

After a final review of the schematics and discussion of tactics, the team began to quickstep as quietly as they could toward the entrance to the apartment building. The streetlights cast pools of light here and there, illuminating the mist in the chill night air.

Bruno went over the plan again in his head as they approached the entrance. Third floor, Interno 3A, down the hall on the right. He could feel adrenaline surge as the group paused just before the entrance, in a line with backs against the wall of the low, stone building.

Cristian and Veri were together, but Bruno's assigned partner was a fresh Academy grad, a kid named Gianluca. Bruno glanced to his left to check on his partner. Gianluca's hands trembled slightly as he checked his weapon one last time. Bruno reached over and touched him on the arm. "Hey," whispered Bruno, "it's all right. Stay right behind me and follow my lead."

Gianluca nodded. "Right. Don't worry, chief. I've got your back." Bruno imagined that under his mask, the kid smiled a pale half-smile.

Bruno patted him on the shoulder. "I know you've *got* my back—just don't shoot me *in* the back, okay?" Bruno joked. But the teasing and confident gesture belied Bruno's true thoughts: Old men and boys. Already that's all we've got left.

Finally, each man gave the ready signal and they slipped into the building entrance; on cat feet they walked up the flights of stairs. The light in the stairwell flickered on and off, the old fluorescent lighting in desperate need of an upgrade. The two lead team members stopped as they arrived at the landing. The door to Interno 3A lay just to the right of the stairs. The two lead officers stopped, and they readied their battering ram. The team dotted the stairs, winding partly down almost to the floor below, as there was not enough room on the landing for them to fit single file. Bruno and Gianluca stood almost at the head of the pack. From where he stood, Bruno could hear men shouting or arguing over the buzz of a television. They're awake, he thought, and cursed to himself. On a silent count of three, the lead officers swung the ram, powering through the door with the sound of rending wood and metal.

The team poured into the apartment one behind the other, shouting "Police! On the ground!" Bruno felt his partner's hand on his shoulder as they stomped into the apartment. Scenes of upturned tables and men with hands in the air flashed into Bruno's vision, but he focused on his own part of the mission, heading to the right, down a short hallway, and through an open door.

"On the ground!" Bruno shouted as he saw the bald-headed man standing in the middle of the tiny bedroom. The man wore jeans, but no shirt. Bruno entered the room, focusing on the man, while his partner followed right behind him. "On the ground!" Bruno repeated. "Face down, hands behind your back!" The man dropped to one knee upon Bruno's second command, but Bruno noticed the man's head flick to the right. The dingy room had a cot, table, and lamp as furnishings, but nothing more. Bruno noticed the large tattoo on the back of the man's head as he moved to cuff him. But as Gianluca called "Clear!" Bruno realized the room had not truly been cleared. He looked to the man's right, realizing that what looked like a solid wall actually had a knob in the middle.

"Cuff this one!" shouted Bruno. "We're not clear!"

Gianluca moved to the stocky bald man, snapping handcuffs on one wrist, while Bruno transitioned to his sidearm to gain more maneuverability. The closet was the folding-door kind, spanning almost the entire length of the right wall. Pistol in his right hand, Bruno yanked the knob and the door folded open like an accordion.

Something in the closet rustled, Bruno saw movement, and the crack of a pistol—Bruno's own pistol—rang out. A figure from the shadows fell forward through hanging clothes into the room, almost at Bruno's feet, twitching as soon as it hit the floor. Bruno had shot the man in the head.

Before Bruno could say anything, something bashed him into the wall. The impact knocked the breath out of his body. Stunned for a moment, Bruno watched while Gianluca wrestled the partially handcuffed man to the ground and Veri stormed into the room.

"He came at me!" shouted Bruno. "I saw him!"

The bald man, now beneath Gianluca, began to wail.

"He—he came at me!" said Bruno. "Trying to grab my pistol!" Then he turned to Gianluca. "You saw, didn't you?" Bruno heard a tremor of fear in his own voice, the sound of a schoolboy caught starting a fight.

As more officers poured into the room Veri stared at Bruno, but said nothing.

***

Bruno spent the rest of the night at the Naples Provincial Command Headquarters answering questions from the investigators and filling out forms. The questions were as predictable as the forms. When they finally let Bruno leave just before dawn, Bruno saw Veri on the steps outside of Headquarters, cigarette in hand. The streets were empty.

"I fucked up, I . . ." said Bruno, his voice trailing.

Veri gazed at Bruno, then took a long drag before responding. "That garbage made a grab for your weapon. I saw it."

"But Gianluca, he saw—"

"Gianluca didn't see anything. He was busy with the brother. I was first in the room. I told them what I saw. And that's that."

Bruno didn't know what to say.

"That guy you shot—*that* guy deserved exactly what he got. Anyway, we found weapons hidden all over that place. Who knows if that piece of trash had one stashed near him." Veri paused, dropped his cigarette, and snuffed it out. "Of course, under normal circumstances, you'd be suspended until the investigation is concluded. But things are already starting to get bollocksed up. They need every available officer right now. So, they've suspended the investigation, pending discovery of additional evidence, which I'm happy to say is bloody unlikely."

"Look, I don't know if—"

"That's enough talk, Bruno." Veri patted him on the shoulder. "You *did* fuck up. But you're a good officer, Bruno. Now don't ever bring this up again, understand?"

Before Bruno could react, Veri walked off, leaving Bruno alone with his thoughts in the cool air.

Bruno knew he should just leave, let it go; but something made him go back inside Headquarters. He had unfinished business. After calling in some favors and telling a few more lies, Bruno got permission to go down to the holding cell.

Bruno found the bald man standing alone with his back to the cell doors. Bruno studied him through the bars. The dark tattoo looked almost three dimensional in the fluorescent light. Bruno donned his mask. Although Bruno could tell the bald man had heard him talk to the guard just outside the anteroom to the cell, the man continued to stare at the wall, not acknowledging anyone else. The four other men in the cell also ignored Bruno's presence, remaining on the bench, talking in low whispers to one another.

Bruno stared into the cell. Then he spoke. "I think I recognize your tattoo. It's a double-headed eagle, no?"

Without turning around the man replied, in perfect TV-announcer Italian, "Yes—from the Serbian flag."

Bruno nodded. "I've read your file. I have one question. Why? Why the Camorra? Why get involved with that lot?"

The bald man laughed softly. Then he turned and strode up to the cell door and stared at Bruno across the bars, black eyes burning. "They're my family," the man stated. Bruno stood nearly eye-to-eye with him, but the bald man's bulk made Bruno happy a cell door stood between them.

Bruno's words, though, betrayed no such fears. "Family?" said Bruno. "Your mother was from Naples, but your father was Serbian. You were born and raised here I know, but that wouldn't matter to the Camorra, now would it? You must know that to them, in the end, you'll always be Il Serbo. Isn't that what they call you?" Bruno smirked. "Definitely limits chances for advancement, doesn't it?"

"Tell me something," said Il Serbo, cocking his head to one side. "Did that other pig cop lie like you did about killing my brother? Did that other pig cop lie to save your ass?"

Bruno paused before he spoke. He ignored Il Serbo's question. "I also read your brother's file. He spent time in jail for armed robbery and multiple assaults. He nearly got charged in the killing of a rival boss in another clan and the rape of the dead man's wife." Bruno shook his head. "But she was so scared to say what happened that he got away with it. So, you'll forgive me if I don't shed any tears that I had to shoot him during a raid. I can't think of anyone who deserved it more." Bruno smiled. "Except maybe you—but you must be the smart one, right? You didn't try to grab anyone's weapon . . . like your brother did."

Il Serbo took one step closer to the cell door. "You lying piece of filth!" Grasping the bars with both hands, he growled, "You think you know a lot about me, don't you? Well, let me tell you something else—something that's not written down." He paused, then looked all around as he spoke. "All this—you see all this? This is coming to an end soon, very soon, and when it does, Signor Ricasso da Capri, I assure you I will come for you on your pretty little island, you murdering little shit-sack, and I'll tear your liver out."

Even through the mask, Bruno felt as if the other man's hot breath shrouded his face. Bruno shifted his weight back.

Il Serbo laughed. "What's the matter? Scared? Are you surprised I know your name?" His voice dropped again. "Yes, I know you're on Capri—our clan has good ears." He glanced around at his cellmates. "Oh yes, even in this shit-hole. But don't worry, you've got time. I'm going to gut that old bastard that lied about what happened first. Then it will be your turn."

Bruno turned sharply and strode to the door leading to the antechamber.

"Or maybe your sister's turn," said Il Serbo. "I've always had a thing for doctors, you know."

Bruno froze. But he did not turn around. He hit the intercom to summon the guard to let him out, the laughter of Il Serbo filling his ears. After an age, the door buzzed open and he burst out.

Il Serbo shouted after him, "We're safer in here than you lot are out there! You'll see!"

The laughter still rang in Bruno's mind long after he left the cell behind.

CHAPTER 4

October 12

Bruno thought about the weather, hoping they wouldn't get caught in the rain, and trying to fill his head with thoughts other than worry about his sister. He had ridden on his motorcycle with Cristian when their shift was over, after neither one could get Carla on the phone and the hospital had told both of them she wasn't there.

Cases of the disease were now being reported from Rome to Florence and Milan, and cities outside London and Paris as well. People who'd had no known contact with the doctors were falling ill. All Western European governments had declared states of emergency. That meant schools were shut and recommendations were to stay at home. It also meant military mobilization and troops with automatic weapons on the streets of every European capital. People hunkered down. Some older people who had got the disease had already died, and hospitals were being flooded with people who were sick or thought they were sick. The island, as yet, had avoided infection. Over the protests of businesses, Capri's mayor and municipal council forbade the landing of any ferries carrying passengers to the island, in an attempt to prevent its spread. People could leave, but they couldn't come back. But the island lay only a few kilometers from land. A small boat could almost certainly make landfall on the island undetected. Bruno believed their efforts to stop the disease's spread to the island would fail.

Carla lived in one of the nicest parts of Capri, not far from the main square. There were a few people walking here and there. Most of them wore a mask of some kind.

Bruno walked stiffly, his neck and back still sore from the raid two days ago. "If she's not there, I'll—"

"Don't worry. It's Saturday afternoon, you're overreacting. I'm sure she's around somewhere. If I know her she just forgot to charge her phone," said Cristian as they approached her apartment building.

Cristian pulled out his phone. "Hold on. Wait a sec." He tapped Bruno on the arm. "The website's back online—I can finally download the video—the guy with the Shakes! Christ! Bruno, you've got to see this." Cristian handed him his phone, the video already playing. Bruno didn't look.

Cristian told Bruno about an infected Irishman living in London who had taken pictures and video of himself and uploaded it to YouTube. They pulled the video, but not in time to stop it from going viral. The man calls his tremors "the Shakes," saying it was like what happens the morning after a night of binge drinking. The British media loved the name, and it stuck.

"It just came out yesterday," said Cristian.

"I don't want to watch it," said Bruno.

"Come on! This disease is insane, look what it does!"

Bruno relented.

The man in the video sat shirtless in front of the webcam. Pustules oozing blood covered the man's face and chest. Bruno could hear the man wheezing, trying to talk in English about the disease's symptoms as his lungs filled with fluid. Listening to the man describe what was happening to him made Bruno regret being able to understand English.

"Christ, do you know what kind of panic this will cause?" said Bruno. "You think this is a fake one, too?"

"Even if it is a fake, it could still cause complete chaos," Cristian responded. "I spoke to some friends in Rome yesterday. Stores are already having problems keeping food on the shelves. And open air markets are closed."

"This one looks real. And if they can't contain the disease, panic will only get worse," Bruno said.

Cristian shook his head. "They kept rabies out of Britain for one hundred years—too bad they didn't keep out Médecins à l'aide des autres while they were at it."

They approached the entrance to Carla's apartment building and walked in.

"Hey listen, Bruno, I'm sorry about what happened on raid. I know it wasn't your fault. I can only imagine how you feel, and—"

"Thanks."

"If you ever need to talk about it, just—"

"I really don't want to talk about it," said Bruno as he climbed the stairs up to Carla's third-floor flat.

Bruno knocked on the door. No one answered. "Carla, are you there?" No response.

He glanced at Cristian. "You have a key, don't you?"

Cristian rummaged around in his pocket and produced the key. He paused. "In case you're wondering, I sleep in the other bedroom when I stay here, so don't think that I—"

"Just shut up and open the door."

Cristian opened the door. Carla's flat was considerably larger than Bruno's but the layout was not so different. In the foyer, a suitcase lay near the door. At the other end, through the glass balcony door, Carla stood looking out over the sea. They walked in. There was a flat screen mounted on the wall in the main living area, with the news humming.

Carla turned around, saw them, and came inside.

"Ciao," said Carla, giving Bruno a hug and Cristian a kiss on the cheek. She was a petite woman with dark hair pulled back in a ponytail.

"We were worried about you. Your phone went straight to voice mail and the hospital said you weren't there," said Bruno.

"Sorry, the phone ran out of charge, and I've had barely a minute to think. It's been so busy."

"Why the suitcase?" asked Cristian. "Where are you going?"

"I'm going to stay at the hospital for a few days. They need me there."

"Did you see the latest video? Is it real?" said Bruno.

Carla took a deep breath. "Yes, we think so."

"Christ," said Bruno.

"Look." She spoke to both Cristian and Bruno. "You should stockpile some supplies; food, water, whatever you can. There are going to be shortages. At least that's what the pandemic models predict."

"We will," said Bruno. "But what about you?"

"The hospital is probably the most prepared for this kind of thing. We've trained for pandemics. We're ready."

"All right, well—" started Bruno, but then the news caught his interest.

A reporter he recognized from one of the national networks stood in front of the UN building in New York City. The tall steel-and-glass building reflected the light of early morning, and the sun was just rising. "We can now confirm cases of this new disease outside the UK, Italy, and France. It has now spread to New York, Cairo, Berlin, São Paolo, and Madrid." She spoke with authority.

"I've got to go," said Carla. "Stay if you want, but lock up after you leave." She hugged them both and left, pulling the wheeled suitcase behind her.

Bruno and Cristian stood in the middle of the room. Bruno wondered what to do next. The reporter went on talking, but Bruno did not listen.

CHAPTER 5

October 15

Bruno woke with the sounds of the TV still in his head, and found that he had forgotten to turn it off. He rolled over and looked at his phone on the nightstand. 0625 hours. The sky was pale with pre-dawn light. He sat up and swung his legs out of the bed and faced the TV screen hanging on the wall. The island still had not seen the turmoil that infected the major cities. It was calm here; so far, at least. But it wouldn't last. In Bruno's mind, once it spread to the island, all bets were off. He rubbed his lower back as he caught up on what had happened overnight.

Reports proclaimed that in America, the Centers for Disease Control had jointly confirmed with the European Centre for Disease Control and Prevention in Sweden that the disease was indeed an airborne strain of the AIDS virus, but much more fast-acting and lethal. And the disease finally had a name: Type I Hemorrhagic AIDS Variant, or HAV. Rumors had been flying in the old broadcast media and on social media for days about the mysterious spread, not just from person to person, but to people who had no contact with the infected. Now maybe an answer: unnamed sources in the American government stated that they also discovered that this HAV could be spread by mosquitoes, explaining why people who had never come in contact with the infected had fallen ill. European governments as yet had no comment on the mosquito hypothesis. The news presenter declared that worldwide shortages of netting, insecticides, and some medications had already been reported, even before the official announcement late last night, New York time. Speculation was that the US Department of Defense (and maybe its British counterpart) had bought those items in large quantities in the hours before the information was leaked. Although the United States denied those accusations, nations around the world condemned it nonetheless. They were all hypocrites, these countries, Bruno reflected. Any one of them would have done the same, had they found out mosquitoes were carriers before anyone else did.

He grabbed his mobile phone. When he found what he was looking for, he pointed the phone at his TV and swiped his finger towards it. A map of Italy color coded by regions appeared on the screen. On his phone, he touched Campania, the region containing the city of Naples. Naples was the largest city in the region, but the administrative province of Naples covered a large part of land outside the city itself. Touching the province of Naples brought up a more detailed map of the major towns in the Naples area where the illness had been discovered. Finally, the Ministry of Health bureaucrats had done something right with their website. Bruno scrutinized the text and the colors of the map. Capri was not listed and was still colored white. On the webpage, the Ministry of Health asserted it was getting the infection data directly from reporting hospitals, with a delay of only hours between reporting and posting. Even if Bruno believed that (which he didn't), looking at all of the areas to which the disease had spread, he understood it was now only a matter of days, maybe even hours, before someone fell ill on the island. And given the incubation period of the disease, coupled with whatever reporting delays there might be, for all he knew, it may already be here.

When the first reports of HAV spreading from person to person began, Bruno had steeled himself for what he feared may come. After Carla had urged them to stock up on supplies, he and Cristian had made a shopping run, which consisted mostly of buying extra food, bottled water, and medicines. Of course, they had looked for surgical masks, but in vain. Bruno had also stocked up on batteries, bars of soap, and toilet paper. The old lady at the cash register had given him quite a look when he walked up with a basket overflowing with nearly fifty bars of soap, the entire inventory of the store, and thirty rolls of toilet paper. Cristian had made things worse telling the poor woman that the soap "was made from *peeeople*," in his best Heston impression. But Bruno had figured if there were some things he might be hard pressed to make or find in stores soon it would be soap, batteries, and toilet paper. "Well," Cristian said, "if the zombies come, at least you can still wipe your ass in style."

Now Bruno scrambled around his flat, taking stock of what he had, in addition to his most recent acquisitions. Some items were stored under his bed, some in his only closet by the front door. The island depended entirely on supplies from Naples, from the food in the stores, to the wine in the restaurants, to the designer purses in the storefronts. Bruno feared there would surely be critical shortages soon, since the disease showed no signs of slowing its spread. At best he had three, maybe four weeks of food and less water. Bruno didn't have nearly enough supplies, nor the room to store them, nor enough time to find more of either. He knew he would have to make do with what he had now and whatever he could manage to scrounge in the future.

As for weapons, there, too, he wished he had more. He had no rifle. The 9mm pistol might be sufficient for close-in fighting, but for serious combat, for ranged combat, if it ever came to that, his pistol would not nearly be enough. The arms locker had two PM 12 S2 9mm submachine guns, but they were under biometric lock and only Veri could access them.

Bruno had a few folding knives, but his favorite was a fixed-blade knife, a commercial version of the one carried by the paratroopers in the Special Forces. That knife was a gift from his father. He rummaged underneath his bed and his hand felt a long, rectangular shape. He took the box out and opened it. His knife was still in its original black box, embossed with gold letters, the company's Latin motto resonating with Bruno now more than it ever had: "Last Resort." Bruno gripped the knife; it moved with ease in his hand. The color of charcoal, the blade was partially serrated, with a small guard where it met the handle. The knife was long enough for stabbing and slashing, if need be, but short enough to be carried comfortably on his person in its belt and sheath, which was made to lay vertically in the small of the back. Seeing the combat knife reminded him of his father. At least his father lived well outside the chaos of Naples. If it all fell apart, he would have a better chance of making it than anyone in a large city, far better than Bruno himself would have if he were still stationed in Naples, and maybe even better than being on the island of Capri itself. Bruno promised himself he would call his father after his shift today. He strapped on the knife directly against his skin, resolving never to be without it from now on.

Bruno's most critical need was ammo. He wasn't sure how much the station had, and there were strict limits on the amount of ammo any one individual could own. Bruno had never thought that would be a problem, until now. He had been sorely tempted to steal as much ammunition as he thought Veri wouldn't notice, rationalizing that there was nowhere to buy ammunition on the island. Not that Veri could say a fucking thing. After the lies about weapons confiscation, Veri was hardly in a position to complain about Bruno taking a box or three of 9mm. Still, while he knew his own preparations were inadequate, Bruno would never do that to Veri; not after what he had done for Bruno.

While preparations were on his mind, he decided to look for a basic survival manual. As he scrolled through what he found online in Italian, it was mostly new age crap about living in harmony with nature, or disconnecting from society and living in the mountains somewhere. He didn't want any of that. Then he noticed that someone had translated the US Army Survival Manual into Italian. Perfect. Though years old, it was free, and it was time-tested, exactly what he was looking for. He printed the document in case things really took a turn for the worse. It had been so long since he'd printed anything he wasn't sure his printer still worked until, down there in the far corner of the room, it finally hummed to life.

While the printer hummed on, page after page, Bruno stepped outside onto his balcony. The azure sky promised a cheerful, crisp day. The breeze from the sea chilled him as he looked northeast towards the still mist-shrouded shore. Father Tommaso stood on his own balcony watching the water.

"Buon giorno, Father Tommaso," said Bruno.

"Buon giorno, Bruno. Looks like it will be a lovely day today."

Bruno nodded towards Father Tommaso's glass. "A little early for wine, wouldn't you say?"

Father Tommaso laughed, making his face even more craggy. "Who says? Can't hurt to start the day with a little wine, like the Romans." Father Tommaso sat down on a chair, turning it toward

Bruno. "I'm celebrating Mass at Saint Sofia's on Sunday. Will I see you there?"

"Maybe," lied Bruno, hoping the priest would talk about something other than Bruno's attendance at Mass. But Father Tommaso was relentless.

"I think you might enjoy my sermon this week. It's about celebrating mortality."

"Doesn't sound very uplifting. And especially with everything that's happening, do you think anyone will show up?"

Father Tommaso leaned forward. "Now it's more important than ever for people to remember their faith. How could we really appreciate our mortal life if it went on without end?"

Bruno opened his mouth to argue, but his phone began playing the national anthem. Bruno knew exactly who was calling.

"I've got to take this," he said, stepping back into his flat.

"Sure, we'll talk later, Bruno," said Father Tommaso as Bruno shut his balcony door.

Bruno answered his phone. "Yes, sir, what's going on?"

Veri's voice was taut, whether from jogging or fear, Bruno couldn't tell. "I know your shift doesn't start for two more hours, but there's already a crowd gathering at Farmacia Nazionale on Via Madre Serafina. People are looking for insect repellant, medicines, God knows what else. You can imagine what might happen if the pharmacy runs out. The municipal police are there now, and I'm on my way on foot."

"You're on your way?" Bruno wondered how Veri could have arrived at the island from his home in Naples so quickly.

"After our little Naples adventure, I changed my mind and came back to the island—slept at the station last night—or rather this morning, I should say. I'm going to stay here until things calm down. My wife thinks I've lost my mind. She's gone to stay with her sister and—"

"I can be there, no problem. I was already awake. Maybe ten minutes?"

"See you there."

There were only four or five pharmacies on the island, and Bruno knew exactly how to get to National Pharmacy. Living in a place that was only ten kilometers square meant nowhere on the island was distant. Bruno ran his fingers through his hair then put his uniform on with haste. Still strapping his gun belt to his waist, he made his way out of his apartment, down the stairs, and onto the sidewalk.

His eyes fell on his Moto Guzzi Griso 850. It crouched along the curb, black and silver shining in the early dawn light. Though an older model, for a small island the motorcycle was seriously overpowered. On Bruno's salary, he'd had to scrape together every last bit of extra money to pay for it, but to him it was worth every Euro. Bruno jumped on and the motorcycle roared to life. He headed down the winding street.

As Bruno rounded the last corner before the pharmacy, the street straightened. The sun had just broken over the horizon, illuminating the scene. He could see the green neon cross hanging above the entrance about a hundred meters distant. What shocked him was the number of people milling about, blocking the street. He came to a stop and parked his motorcycle on the sidewalk. While there were few private cars on the island, small buses and three-wheeled delivery trucks had already begun to back up on both sides of the street. The sound of horns blaring rose over the crowd.

Slipping on a surgical mask, Bruno half-ran toward the green neon cross looming over the pharmacy entrance. Scores of men and women milled around the pharmacy, and more were coming every minute.

The small parking lot across the street from the pharmacy entrance was overfilled with people. Their desire to obtain items to repel or kill mosquitoes must have overwhelmed their fear of getting the disease from being in a crowd. Still, most of them wore something over their faces; masks, bandanas, or simple pieces of clothing. A few weeks ago, Bruno imagined that these people were probably enjoying an evening walk in the main square. Now they were queuing at a pharmacy for supplies, a desperate gleam in their eyes. Actually "queuing" was the wrong word. The way people were bunched reminded Bruno of a scrum in a rugby match.

Through gaps in the crowd, Bruno saw eight or nine municipal police officers standing in a semi-circle around the entryway. Two tall windows flanked the glass door at the entrance. Emblazoned in green letters across the windows were the words "Farmacia Nazionale." The crowd maintained a distance from the officers, none of whom wore riot gear. Bruno spotted Veri talking to one of the officers standing directly in front of the door and made his way through the crowd as politely as he could, saying, "Excuse me," more times than he could count, and trying not to jostle anyone too badly. In a situation like this, he knew better than to needlessly antagonize anyone. Things could get out of hand quickly. Veri noticed Bruno coming through the crowd and gestured to him.

"Good, you've made it." With the noise of the crowd and his mask covering the lower half of his face, Veri's voice was hard to hear, even though he was speaking directly into Bruno's ear. Veri motioned towards the crowd. "They're looking to buy insect repellant and anything else they can get to kill mosquitoes. You've heard about the mosquitoes, right?"

"Yeah. Bad news travels fast," Bruno said.

"Well, it's not supposed to open for another hour, but we called the pharmacy owner and he's on his way." Veri looked over Bruno's shoulder towards the crowd. "I'm going to let them know what's going on."

Veri turned, raised his hands, and walked a few steps, right to the edge of the crowd. "All right, everyone!" Veri's voice approached a shout. "Calogero DeLuca, the owner, is on his way—he's going to open early, so everyone please stay calm!"

"When will he get here?" someone in the back shouted.

"I just spoke to him a few minutes ago, and he should be here very soon—perhaps ten minutes." Veri stepped back towards the pharmacy entrance, terminating the conversation before some wise-ass asked any more questions. "Thank you all for your patience."

Bruno watched the people react to Veri's statement. People were talking to each other, the tension easing a bit. He hoped it would last. Two police officers took advantage of the lull to break from their line in front of the entrance to shepherd people out of the street. The traffic congestion began to ease, but there must have been over one hundred people arrayed on the sidewalk around the pharmacy's entrance.

Veri took a few steps back toward the entrance, where Bruno had remained.

Bruno glanced around at the number of law enforcement officers, counting off in his head. Eight, plus the two of them. Not good odds. Then he looked at Veri.

"Don't we have any more officers coming? More local police at least?"

"The other police organizations are busy guarding the other pharmacies and God knows what else." Veri spoke to Bruno, but kept his eyes on the crowd. "For a potential riot situation like this, I'd usually call the Regional Command, and they would have sent a squad in full riot gear. They'd normally be here by motovetta in a half-hour." Veri's voice was just loud enough for Bruno to hear. "But no one is coming. I talked to Colonel Costa on the way here—they've got their hands full in Naples. After the mosquito announcement, there's already looting breaking out all over." Veri gritted the words through clenched teeth, only now looking directly into Bruno's eyes. "Costa said we're on our own."

Bruno nodded in silence. *On our own.* The words weighed on Bruno, but he didn't have much time to ponder their ramifications. One of the officers who had been keeping the traffic flowing now walked toward Bruno and Veri. A lean, balding man with wispy, white hair accompanied the officer. The man wore a tweed coat and striped tie, accentuating his tall, professorial look. To Bruno, from what he could see of the man's face not covered by the surgical mask, he looked quite pale, and his hazel eyes stood out against his skin. The police officer held the older man by the elbow, half-pushing him forward. The man's eyes darted back and forth between Bruno and Veri.

"This is the owner," grunted the officer, letting go of his elbow.

Veri nodded and gestured toward the door. "Ah, Signor DeLuca, yes, glad you are here. As you can see, there are many people who would like to make some purchases—and I don't think it would be wise to keep them waiting."

DeLuca glared at Veri. "You didn't tell me there were this many people here," DeLuca hissed. "Look at them! They'll ransack my store!"

Someone in the crowd shouted, "Is that the owner?" Bruno could sense the crowd's impatience growing by the minute. Others began shouting in response. The crowd pressed forward, surging into the street once more, close to the officers arrayed around the pharmacy.

Bruno muttered to Veri, "This is about to get out of control."

Veri turned to DeLuca. "Signore," Veri began, "there aren't enough of us to stop them. But if you let them in a few at a time, we can keep order. We *can* protect your store, but only if you help us." Bruno had never heard Veri's voice tinged with fear before. DeLuca looked at the crowd, then back at Veri. As Bruno had hoped, DeLuca saw reason and relented. "Only ten at a time. I won't let this rabble destroy what I've spent my life building. And they can only have one can of insect repellant per person."

Veri nodded. "Thank you."

DeLuca moved toward the door. "Before I open up, I need to get some cash out of the safe. Banking networks have been overloaded, I suppose." DeLuca took out a key ring with a large, square key. "Just keep them out for another two minutes." DeLuca opened the door and went in, shutting the door immediately behind him.

Veri turned to the crowd. "All right, everyone! Signor DeLuca has gone in to open up his store. People will be let in ten at a time and are limited to the purchase of one item of insect repellant per person."

The crowd grumbled, but began to form something resembling a line.

Two minutes came and went. But there was no sign of DeLuca, and the door remained closed. Veri tried the door, but it was locked. The scene being played out agitated the crowd.

Then someone cried out, "The British Prime Minister is dead! It's on the news! He just died!"

Something shifted. Bruno could feel a new dynamic in the air, as this news shocked the group from crowd into mob. Two or three hundred strong by now, they began to shout.

Veri yanked on the door one last time, then turned back toward the mob, hands raised, shouting. Bruno couldn't tell what exactly he was saying; the noise overwhelmed any one voice. Bruno stood at the apex of the semicircle of officers, with Veri directly to his left in front of the shop window. By now, the mob was pressed up against the officers arrayed around the entrance.

Veri shouted toward Bruno, "Get that door open, I don't care how!"

Bruno backed up toward the glass door. He didn't know what Veri thought he could do. He didn't know how he was going to get the door open. Bruno turned his back to the crowd and pulled out his pistol, trying to shield it from view, but meaning to shoot off the lock.

Without warning, the mass lurched forward. Bruno, standing in the doorway, saw the front of the crowd surge into two officers. Bodies crashed through the plate-glass window, screaming, cursing. One officer twisted towards his left side, avoiding the brunt of the mob's force, but the other, with arms flailing, fell backwards, like someone who'd been pushed without warning into a pool. A tangle of limbs kept Bruno from seeing who was on the bottom.

Bruno pointed his pistol and pulled the trigger, aiming over the heads of the crowd into the stone building across the street. Bruno's ears rang. Another officer, too, had shot over the heads of the mob. The mob pulled back, piling up into the ones behind them, the front line now seeing the downed officers and pile of bodies and retreated, fearing for their own lives.

Bruno turned to his left and saw shattered glass where there had once been a window. After the din, the silence itself felt oppressive. People were on the floor of the store. One got up, clutching at a bleeding gash on his head, looking stunned. A second officer sat staring at the shards of glass in his shoulder and arm. The other lay on his back, behind the remnants of the window. The downed officer was quiet, yet Bruno could see his legs trembling.

Bruno moved out of the doorway toward the fallen officer. A jagged shard of glass stuck out the left side of Veri's throat and crimson blood poured onto the tile floor.

Bruno dropped to his knees, laying his pistol by Veri. He pulled Veri's mask down to help him breathe and cupped his hands around his neck to staunch the blood flow, applying as much pressure as he dared. Bruno's hands trembled as he looked into Veri's eyes. They were bright and piercing against his pallid skin. The pain and fright Bruno saw made tears spring to his own eyes. Bruno was aware of movement around him and heard someone call for an ambulance, but he couldn't break eye contract with Veri.

"It will be all right," Bruno reassured. "An ambulance is coming."

Two other officers approached with gauze and pads they had taken from the pharmacy shelves and handed them to Bruno. Bruno pushed them against Veri's neck gently, not wanting to make anything worse. The whine of an ambulance filled the air.

Veri spluttered, as if to say something, and Bruno bent down closer. Frothy blood coated his lips and splashed onto Bruno's face as Veri tried to speak.

A fierce tremor rocked Veri's body and his eyes rolled back into his head.

"No, stay with me—" Bruno said.

After a few seconds, Veri's rigid body went limp. His eyes were wide open, glassy. Bruno let go of Veri's hand and it fell to the tile floor. A halo of blood now surrounded his friend's head.

Two paramedics kneeled on either side of Bruno and Veri, and a third gently moved Bruno to the side. They began to work on Veri, but Bruno knew it was too late.

Bruno scooped up his pistol, stood up and surveyed the scene. Bloody glass was strewn about the floor. The paramedics hunched over Veri's body were still working. The crowd had begun to disperse, though some were detained by officers who were trying to take statements from witnesses. Bruno had no hope that anyone would say anything of value. No one saw anything, no one knew who pushed whom, and everyone would blame someone else, some unknown troublemaker.

Bruno didn't much care who in the crowd had done what. His eyes fell on DeLuca, standing two or three meters from Veri in the middle of his store. DeLuca simply stood there, staring at the tiles on the floor, fidgeting with the keys in his pocket. Then he started scratching his arm. To Bruno, DeLuca looked like he wanted to sink into the floor, to hide, but didn't know how. A detached part of Bruno noticed that DeLuca looked like he was in shock. Bruno couldn't have cared less about DeLuca's mental state. He stiffened and moved towards DeLuca, but one of the municipal police officers put a hand on Bruno's arm, as if to lead him away. Bruno shrugged it off. DeLuca stared at his own feet, at nothing.

"I—I'm sorry." DeLuca's voice sounded flat and emotionless.

Even though DeLuca slouched as he stared at the ground, he still loomed over Bruno. Bruno grabbed his shirt and yanked him down to his level, and DeLuca stumbled forward.

"You piece of filth!" Bruno spat. "This is your fault!" He kept hold of DeLuca's shirt with one hand, and tightly gripped his pistol in the other.

Finally Bruno let go and DeLuca took a step back. Bruno reached up towards DeLuca's face, and DeLuca flinched as Bruno almost tenderly pulled DeLuca's surgical mask down around his chin. Bruno left a crimson stain of Veri's blood on the mask's white fabric. Bruno stared at him. "Imagine what I'll do to you if I ever see you again," Bruno whispered.

DeLuca simply stood there, repeating the words, "I'm sorry."

Bruno turned away without another word and walked over to the paramedics, who were lifting Veri's body onto a stretcher. One of the paramedics pulled a white sheet over Veri's head as they stepped over the remnants of the window and back onto the sidewalk. Bruno followed them. All he could do was look at the blood congealing on his hands.

***

By the time Bruno returned to the station, hours later, Cristian had already been on conference calls with their superiors. He was still on a call in what used to be Veri's office when Bruno walked in. While Bruno waited for Cristian, he called his sister. She didn't pick up her mobile phone. But to his relief, she picked up her work phone.

"Hi, Bruno," she said.

"Carla, Veri's dead. The British PM is dead. I don't know what to . . ." his voice trailed off.

"I know about both. And I'm sorry about Veri. But, the government's got everything under control."

"Under control? They don't have a fucking thing under control! If the head of the British government can die from this HAV, who's safe?"

"There are contingency plans, Bruno. Everything will be okay. I have faith in the government's response."

"Faith? You have faith . . . in the government?" He wondered who this person was on the other end of the phone. She'd never had any confidence that their government could do anything right. "Are *you* all right?"

"Don't worry about me. I'll be fine. You and Cristian take care of yourselves. Don't come to the hospital, Bruno . . . it's . . . not safe for nonmedical personnel."

"Not safe? What the—"

"We know how to take proper precautions. You don't."

"But—"

"Listen, I have to go. I'll contact you when I can. I love you. Tell Cristian I love him too. Ciao." The phone went silent.

Bruno spent the rest of the day at the station staring at his desk. The one clear memory Bruno had of the remainder of that day was hearing the screams of Veri's wife, even though Cristian spoke to her over the phone from Veri's office.

After Cristian had finished dealing with higher-ups, other officers, and God knew who else, it was early evening. Cristian walked out of the office in the back, over to Bruno's desk, pulled up a chair, and sat down. Their masks dangled around their necks, a breach of the anti-infection protocols, but neither of them cared.

"You know, he hated to use his office," Cristian said.

Bruno nodded. "He always wanted to be out here with 'the lads,' said he felt like an arrogant ass when he had to stay back there." Bruno rubbed his eyes with the heels of his hands. "It was terrible to see him like that."

Cristian looked down. "I can't imagine what it was like. I'm so sorry I wasn't there. I was still on my way from Naples—"

"How could you have known what was going to happen?"

They could spend all night talking about what happened, about how much they would miss Veri, Bruno knew. He also knew that they needed to press on.

"Look," Bruno started, then paused. "I guess . . . well, what's next?"

Cristian didn't respond. He leaned back in the chair. After looking at the ceiling for a moment, Cristian leaned forward.

"It seems I'm officially in command here, at least for a while."

Bruno wasn't surprised. Cristian had a number of years more experience than himself.

Cristian continued. "And I spoke to Commissario Esposito. He's quite happy continuing Operation Whisky-Tango-Foxtrot. He's already had to deflect some inquiries from his own higher-ups."

Bruno gave him a puzzled look.

"Oh, come on," Cristian responded. "You know—the weapons confiscation order."

Bruno still looked puzzled. "All right, but why 'Whisky-Tango-Foxtrot'?"

Cristian laughed. "I thought our little deception needed an appropriate military designation: Operation W-T-F. That's the English abbreviation for 'Ma Che Cazzo!'"

Bruno shook his head, with a pale smile playing around his lips. Cristian did his best never to take anything too seriously, not even the end of civilization.

Bruno straightened up in his chair and turned on the monitor at his desk, swiping his fingers on the screen and ignoring the keyboard. Cristian brought his chair around so that he could see the screen.

"What are you looking for?" asked Cristian.

Bruno didn't answer immediately, nor did he look up at Cristian. Instead, he continued to swipe.

"This," said Bruno, pointing at the monitor.

The monitor displayed a map of the Naples region. Bruno's finger hovered over the island of Capri. It was now the color of night, as was the entire coastline.

"Christ," said Cristian. "It's finally spread to Capri."

Bruno stared at the monitor and nodded his head. "It's here."

"So, what do you think will happen?" Cristian asked, a quiver in his voice. "The British PM is dead. The government has called up all military reserves. What's next?"

Bruno shook his head. "The ruin of everything—the ruin of it all."

CHAPTER 6

October 25

Bruno's boots pounded on the street. Veri had been right. No one cared about enforcing the weapons confiscation order anymore. Cristian followed behind him as they chased three men through Capri's main square, out onto a side street.

Bruno stopped short when the three figures darted out of their sight, deciding not to pursue them down the narrow alleys in the fading light. If he had continued, he would have shot them all.

Cristian jostled into Bruno as he looked down the street where the looters had fled.

"What? You're letting them go?"

Bruno didn't look at Cristian, thinking it best to keep both eyes where the looters had run, until he was quite certain they were gone. "We'd have to shoot them if we caught them. I didn't get a good look at them. I think they were just getting food." He looked at Cristian. "They didn't deserve to die." The order to shoot looters on sight had come down two days ago as chaos grew in the major cities.

Cristian shook his head. "I can't fucking believe they emptied the prisons last week!" Cristian gestured in the general direction of the thieves. "This is what happens!"

Bruno holstered his pistol. "Could've been worse, though. They might have tried to fight."

"Well," Cristian responded, holstering his own pistol. "I doubt the only ones released were the so-called 'nonviolent' offenders."

"I bet the real reason they released so many is because there aren't enough prison guards left now."

"Exactly. Sick, or dead, or even more likely, just AWOL," Cristian said. Then he patted his pistol. "Good thing we can do something about it."

"For now," said Bruno. "That is, until we run out of ammo." In the fifteen days since the Naples raid, so many were sick, or afraid of getting sick, that the networks most people in the cities relied upon for their survival teetered on the edge of total collapse. Too many people sick and not working led to fuel shortages, which led to transportation problems, which led to shortages of goods, and on and on and on: cascading failure. Things unraveled faster than Bruno could have believed possible.

Cristian shrugged. "I don't know how many hundreds of rounds we have in the station. Enough to last quite a while I think."

"You can never have enough bullets. Not now," said Bruno.

"Could be worse. Unlike real zombies, this lot doesn't need a head shot to stop them. One or two in the chest should do it."

Bruno grunted in response as he turned his back on the narrow street and broke into a brisk walk. "There's no one else here. We should go back to the station. It's been warm the last few days, and I don't want to take any chances with mosquitoes either."

Bruno looked around at the piazza as they made the short walk back to their station. The fading light rendered the scene before him all the more cheerless. The boarded-up shops and restaurants contrasted sharply with the sparkling nightlife only weeks earlier.

"How many people are left on the island, I wonder," said Bruno, more to himself than Cristian, as they made their way back to the station.

"Who knows, really. There might still be quite a few holed up here and there."

Since the disease had spread to Capri, the trickle of people leaving for the mainland had become a flood. They left by motorboat, rowboat, or any other means they had. Over the last few days, Bruno and Cristian watched people spill all around the piers and docks of the main marina, most with suitcases, clothes, anything they could carry that they thought had value.

Bruno shook his head. "Those people who left, they should have stayed put, here. I guess they thought their chances were better with relatives on the mainland."

"Maybe," said Cristian. "But with all the military checkpoints, if they got stuck in Naples, they're as good as dead."

"True. And not just in Naples," responded Bruno. "You've heard the reports—all over the country, people are trying to leave the cities—trying to leave death behind."

Cristian built on Bruno's glum assessment. "Seems like the only ones left are the ones who couldn't or wouldn't leave, and the ones who prey on anyone left."

They walked together in silence for a few moments. Something had been gnawing at Bruno since yesterday, and now that they could take a breather he asked, "Have you heard from Carla? She's living at the hospital full-time. We texted a few days ago. We were supposed to meet yesterday, but she didn't show up and I can't get through to her. If I don't hear from her today, I'm going to the hospital."

"Don't bother. I tried to get in the hospital to see Carla, but they have guards there, and they wouldn't let me in," said Cristian.

"But that's impossible. You're a Carabiniere. They *have* to let you in."

"Didn't matter that I was a Carabiniere. They said they're operating under some kind of emergency regulations. No one gets in."

"Cristian, I've got to get to her. I've tried text, phone, e-mail. Nothing. When we spoke last she sounded strange, like—"

"Like what?"

Bruno shook his head. "I'm not sure. She sounded like—" But the thought he was about to vocalize sounded as crazy to Bruno as the ham radio guy, so instead he shrugged and said, "Guess it must be stress from dealing with everything. But as soon as the station is squared away and my shift is over, I'm going to the hospital. At least there are guards there. She should be safe, right?"

"Of course she's safe. Hope you have better luck getting in than I did," said Cristian as they arrived at their station. They entered, and promptly barricaded the outer door and the inner door with tables as they passed through.

They pulled their masks down as they entered the main office. The overhead lights blinked on in response to their movements. "Good," said Cristian. "The power's on." In the last few days, the power grid had teetered on the edge, with rolling brownouts, then blackouts. With mobile phone networks and the Internet sluggish and unreliable too, old broadcast radio surpassed streaming media for obtaining information.

Cristian went right to the desk in the middle of the room, and while donning his headset, began to dial the landline telephone. He stood with his arms folded at his chest, his leg bouncing with impatience. Then without warning, he threw the headset on his desk.

"Fucking voice mail! I'm trying to call Esposito at the police and all I get is voice mail? We need to tell them about those three thugs. Where are the police?"

Bruno's face showed no emotion. "Deserted—or dead."

"Well, turn on the radio—let's at least see if we can find out what the hell is going on."

Bruno turned on the small radio on the desk in the middle of the office. The voice sounded soft and lilting:

"We must have faith that through this darkness a light will shine. We must trust that God's plan will see us through to the other side of these trials. We must pray that—"

"Please!" Bruno groaned as he slapped the radio, turning it off. "Who wants to hear that?"

"That's the Pope!"

"So what? Please, don't tell me you actually believe anything he says."

"At least find another station! We need to hear what else is going on."

Bruno brought the radio to life again and hit the scan button immediately. He didn't think he could stand another second of the Pope. The radio settled on the next strongest broadcast: the all-news channel.

North Africa burned from Cairo to Marrakesh, with governments in full collapse, chaos in the cities, and refugees seeking escape from the disease. The news in Europe, too, painted a grim picture. The rest of the Old Continent staggered in various states of strife, some places worse than others. France, in particular, suffered. The news reports Bruno heard froze his blood. The turmoil in most major French cities made the austerity riots from a few years back look positively mild in comparison. Looters and rioters torched the city centers of Lille, Marseille, Nantes, Lyons, Nice, and parts of Paris. Bruno feared the last images in his mind of the City of Lights would be smoke choking the Champs-Élysées. The Brits had already clamped down London tight before France went up in flames, and the Bundeswehr flooded the streets of Berlin, too. But Bruno wondered if anything would be enough.

Cristian brushed off the bleak news with a wave. "I don't give a damn about France. I want to know what's going on here."

Italy seemed to have weathered the death of its prime minister better than France had dealt with the demise of its president. Never before had a French president died in office, and shock gripped the nation. Ironically, having a revolving door of prime ministers for decades meant that the Italian Prime Minister's death didn't cause nearly the kind of turmoil there as the same event caused in northern Europe. Hell, we even had an ex-PM kidnapped and murdered in the '70s, Bruno recalled from a school history lesson, and the country went on.

Bruno touched the scan button again and the radio found the next station. Whatever station this was overflowed with commentary on what was left of the American military and its withdrawal from all over the globe, including from Italy and the rest of the Western Alliance. The two male commentators' attitude rang clear: "good riddance."

They ranted that it was one thing for the American president to condemn but tolerate a state like Montana's secession, but it was quite another to let Texas get away with seizing oil wells just before cutting ties to the US government. The commentators agreed that the President couldn't just stand idly by—she had to take action now, and the remnants of American armed forces had to be called home.

Whoever these radio morons were, they proclaimed that many people in Europe were happy to see the Americans go. They claimed the social media were in "a lather," churning with the notion that the Americans were behind HAV. The commentators, for their part, blamed either the Americans, the Russians, or the Chinese (in that order) for the outbreak. How could something this deadly be natural? they asked. How could this thing not be genetically engineered, a bioweapon, either out of control or deliberately released? How could anyone believe the American line of bullshit that the disease was either a mutated natural strain of the AIDS virus or a terrorist enhanced one?

The Americans' exodus brought to mind the ancient Romans forsaking Britain, abandoning the periphery, in hopes of protecting the core of the Empire. But their withdrawal only delayed the inevitable, and the Romans and their Empire ultimately faded to dust. Still, Bruno was convinced that without the Americans, the only thing keeping war from sweeping from one end of Eurasia to the other was the virus itself. It spread so quickly and so many were sick, dying, or absent, that there were not enough numbers left to mount any major military campaigns. And so none of the major (or even minor) powers had used nukes—at least, not yet anyway. What would be the point? Even the crazy leaders understood that. Or so Bruno hoped.

"The news is worthless—pure propaganda!" Cristian exclaimed. "Did you hear about Lampedusa?"

"Yeah, that's where they're putting all the Libyan refugees."

"But what's *not* on the news is that they've evacuated all Italian nationals from the entire island. It's just one big refugee camp. The Guardia Costiera is just dumping anyone they intercept trying to get to Italy and letting them fend for themselves."

"Jesus. But how do you know?"

"That's what my friends in the Guardia told me. And I believe them," said Cristian.

"But how can they keep it a secret?"

"Who's on Lampedusa is the last thing anyone cares about right now." Cristian wandered off to his desk and stood in front of his monitor. "I'm going to see if we have any message traffic."

Cristian's finger traced patterns on the monitor. Then he abruptly stopped and backed away. Bruno was wondering what was on the screen when Cristian waved Bruno over. "You'd better take a look at this." Bruno turned the radio volume down, and the raving morons faded to a low buzz.

Cristian pointed to the monitor. "Look at this."

Bruno pulled up a chair and sat down, all the while reading the information. "They can't do this!"

Cristian's response was definitive. "Oh yes they can. We're to initiate shut-down procedures and lock this place down. The speedboat will pick us up at 22:30 hours tomorrow at the Marina Grande. End of story."

"We can't. We might be the only cops left here on the island!"

"Don't you get it? They need reinforcements in the big cities, since, on top of everything that's going on, the idiots in the Ministry of the Interior let out these supposed 'nonviolent' prisoners for 'humanitarian reasons.' Now look around—it's chaos—and Naples . . ." Cristian's voice trailed into silence before quickly regaining its strength. "Naples will burn! The small stations—this island—they're nothing."

Bruno pondered Cristian's words. He stood up from the chair and turned to him. "I'm not leaving the island. At least not until I talk to Carla again."

Cristian turned his back to Bruno, walking away from the desk. "You can do whatever you want," said Cristian. "I'm leaving. But not with the Carabinieri."

"What the hell are you talking about?"

"I made arrangements this morning with a friend in Naples. He's got a small boat, and he's agreed to pick me up and take me to Naples in exchange for a fee. I've got my gear packed in the storage room." Cristian glanced at the old analog clock on the wall. "I've got to be at the Marina Piccola an hour from now."

"What? Were you just going to leave without a word?" Bruno got to his feet. "When were you going to say something?"

"Bruno, I'm sorry. I—I wasn't quite sure how to tell you. But things," Cristian pointed to the monitor, "are coming to a head."

"'Coming to a head?' Fucking right things are coming to a head! You're in charge here. You can't just desert!"

"Why not? Don't be so goddamn naïve. I'm not spending my last days in misery alone."

"But what about Carla?"

"At the hospital, I'm sure she's safer than we are." Cristian waved his hand. "What do you want from me, Bruno? Carla is a great woman, but I have a daughter—*she* needs me! My daughter comes first. What do you know about it? You don't even have a family!"

"I have my father and Carla, you arrogant prick." Bruno spoke slowly, spitting out each word. "You are a coward."

"Don't you get it? It's over! We're all going to die! And I'm going to spend my last days with my family. Like everyone else!"

Cristian took a deep breath. "Look, Carla's much safer staying here. Why don't you come with me for a while? I could use your help getting out of Naples. Then you could make your way to Nusco and your father."

Bruno sat down and leaned back in the chair. "You got enough room in your boat for my motorcycle?" Bruno shook his head. "Walk nearly one hundred kilometers from Naples? By myself? Even if I could, I need to talk to Carla first, at least." Bruno looked down at his feet as he asked what he thought was a question with no good answer. "How the hell are *you* going to get back outside Rome? That's a three-hour drive on a good day!"

Cristian responded with a quizzical look. "My car, of course. I've kept it in Naples. I haven't had to drive it in weeks, so it's got a full tank. Which is good, since I doubt I'll find any fuel on the way, not with everything that's going on."

"But—" Bruno started, thinking of everything that might stand in Cristian's path on the way back to his home, from a single blocked car choking a road, to thugs bent on nothing more than theft and murder, to mosquitoes that sometimes even this late in the year buzzed, hungry for blood.

Before Bruno could complete the thought, Cristian raised his hand. "I *will* find a way."

Bruno nodded. "All right. Leave. Go then."

Cristian put his hand on Bruno's arm. "Bruno, listen to me. The government is falling to pieces—the Carabinieri are falling apart, too. If you don't leave now, what are you going to do?"

Bruno pulled away, not angry, but simply resigned to his decision. "I can't. I need to get to Carla or—" Bruno had to admit, at least to himself, the real reason why he didn't want to go with Cristian. It was not his devotion to duty, it was not the thought of being a hero; it wasn't even Carla: Bruno stayed because he was afraid. Thoughts of that ship on the way as rescue, as salvation, as a way to somewhere safe, had already been racing through his mind. The ship would spare him the agony of facing the world; the ship would take him to comrades-in-arms; the ship meant he would live. And even if it never came, he could always stay here on the island, sheltered from the chaos. Once he and Cristian parted ways after arriving on the mainland, Bruno feared what would happen on a journey alone. That fear shamed him, it paralyzed him. For all of

Cristian's faults, bluster, and foolishness, Bruno was sure of one thing about his friend: he was the brave one, not Bruno.

Cristian began to back away. "Fine. I can't force you to come." Cristian walked with heavy feet into the storage room. When he came out, he had a bulging duffle bag slung over his shoulder and his mask covered the lower part of his face.

Bruno stood in the short hallway leading to the back entrance. "What about the weapons locker?"

"Already tried, and I couldn't get in. They must have had better things to do than update the biometric access." Cristian shrugged. "You'll have to bust it open, and I don't have time to try."

"I will, believe me."

Cristian gazed at Bruno, his eyes steady. "Watch yourself. Don't let your guard down. And tell Carla I'm sorry." Cristian offered his hand, and Bruno took it.

"Looks like *you're* the Omega Man here," said Cristian.

"Stay strong," said Bruno.

With a final wave, Cristian turned and walked out the back entrance into the now-dark alley behind the station. The door shut behind him with a clang.

The silence that followed enveloped Bruno like a lukewarm bath, and he sat in a warm stupor for an age. Minutes crawled by, and the temptation to sit there, to do nothing, almost overwhelmed him. But he clawed his way back to reality. He needed to talk to his father.

He pulled the phone from his jacket pocket. After four tries he almost gave up. Finally, on the fifth try, his father's face filled the small screen. The familiar grey-haired man looked at Bruno with evident relief. "Bruno, thank God!"

"Papà," Bruno whispered.

His father's eyes stood out in relief, bloodshot, whether from tears or lack of sleep, Bruno could not tell. His father's voice trembled. "I've been trying to call for days! I can't get through to Carla at all."

"Papà, it's good to see you, too. I can't get through to her now either. But don't worry, I know she's staying at the hospital. I'm sure she'll be safe there. It's guarded." Bruno spoke rapidly. "Look, I'm not sure how long this connection is going to last. I wanted to tell you I'm supposed to leave for Naples tomorrow."

His voice brightened with a note of false cheer. "The government's decided they need more law enforcement in the city. So, they're moving me the day after tomorrow."

"Naples!" His father shook his head. "Don't you know what's been going on in the city? People are dying, and they're trying to leave the city as fast as they can—some are even making their way here, to Nusco."

"But the orders said—"

"Do you think they told you the truth? They're lying! Whatever they're saying is a lie!" he hissed. Then his shoulders slumped. "Where will you stay?"

"They've got barracks set up."

"Barracks? No, you've got to stay where you are! If you come here, if you go to Naples, in cramped quarters with people who might be infected, you'll never make it out!"

"They're coming to get me tomorrow night. I have to—"

"Find your sister! You don't have to do anything they tell you!" his father shouted, slamming his hand on an unseen table.

"You can't leave the island—you're safer there. Find Carla, she'll know what to do. Bruno, please listen to me. Do not come back. The city is full of death."

"Maybe I can come with Carla to Nusco after—"

"No! Bruno, you know it's spreading all over. You've got to stay where you are—stay away from people—anybody! It's too late for us here, Bruno. We're not going to make it. But you—you have a chance. I want you to live. Do whatever you need to do. Please—your mother—your brother—they—they would have wanted you and Carla to live. Just live!"

Bruno nodded, not wanting to answer his father's request. Instead, he simply said, "I love you, Papà."

"I love you too Br—"

His father's voice cut off, and Bruno found himself looking into a dark screen, the words "connection failed" blinking brightly. Bruno began to weep as he tried to reestablish a connection to no avail. He sobbed until numbness replaced sorrow. His limbs felt weighed down, and it was a struggle just to move an arm, like someone fighting his way to wakefulness from a deep slumber. Pulling himself from the brink of he didn't know what, Bruno wiped his face on his sleeve and dragged himself out of the chair away from his desk. He gathered up the radio, turned it off, and made his way to the back storage room.

Bruno looked around. The room's narrow walls and lone fluorescent tube flickering overhead made him feel cramped and claustrophobic. Bruno spotted his body armor leaning against the wall in the far corner, its dark-blue shape standing out against the whitewashed wall. Bruno grabbed it, threw it over his head, and cinched the Velcro tight. The firmness across his chest comforted Bruno, made him feel stronger. Along with the radio, he began to gather anything he thought might be useful and put it in an old olive duffle bag he found on the floor. Bruno looked at the name stenciled on the bag in dark capital letters: "VERI, B." He paused briefly, then continued to rummage around the shelves in the back room, while the lights still worked. He found a flashlight, a toolbox, some paracord, a first aid kit, and a few other items that he might be able to put to use. He set the toolbox to the side, but put the other items into the duffle bag. Then he turned his attention to the storage shelf bolted into the wall.

At chest-height, a square metal box stuck out about a half-meter from the wall, looking dull under the fluorescent light. The box had a seam running down the middle, bisecting the front into two doors that opened outward. In the center, just to the right of the seam, was an indentation with a tiny glass window just the size of a thumb. Bruno stared at it a moment, then put his index finger in the indentation. A white light shone from under his finger, soon followed by a buzzing sound. Of course, his fingerprints had never been registered. That was not going to stop him, not now. He opened the toolbox, and at the bottom, his hand grasped a long, cold length of metal. The crowbar was just what he needed, as there were two 9mm submachine guns to be had.

He cursed as each blow hit the box. He labored for a long while. It was much stronger than it looked. Finally, the door buckled enough for him to insert the crowbar into the seam. He jammed the crowbar in and pulled with all his strength. The screech of rending metal filled the air as the doors gave way. Bruno peered inside, expecting weapons. But what he found was emptiness and betrayal.

CHAPTER 7

Bruno pounded the remnants of the metal shelf with his fist. The duty pistol strapped to his hip was now Bruno's only firearm. Cristian had left one box of 9mm ammo. Fifty bullets, that's it. All that bullshit about not having access—the son of a bitch! He yanked the duffle bag's zipper open, grabbed the box, and shoved it in.

"Thanks for nothing, prick liar!" Bruno shouted out loud to no one. Bruno's hands shook as he zipped the duffle bag closed. Anger like this would make him careless. He closed his eyes and breathed deeply for a time, gathering his thoughts.

Bruno sat down on the floor and removed the radio from his bag. He wanted to hear someone's voice other than his own while he thought about what to do next. He turned on the radio. It was buzzing with the voices of the same two commentators. He set the radio to scan and found the government-run radio channel. A woman's voice filled the room.

". . . rats have tested positive for HAV—I repeat—the European Centre for Disease Control and Prevention has found that rats may become infected with HAV, yet remain asymptomatic. Whether or not rats, or other mammals, may be carriers, infecting people directly, or by way of mosquito bites, is still an open question. Remember, hospitals have now reopened. If you have any signs of illness, please make your way to your nearest hospital. We—"

On a whim, Bruno tuned the radio to the end of the AM stations, close to the start of the amateur radio band where the pirate radio station had broadcast those many months ago. To his shock, through the static, Bruno heard a male voice. The pirate radio station had returned.

"For years the global elites have been watching, waiting, planning *our* extermination. You didn't believe me. You thought I was out of my mind, didn't you? But I was right! The day has finally come. They have found a way to kill us all so that they can—"

Bruno could tell by the audio quality that it was probably a low power station, so it couldn't be that far away. Maybe it was even transmitting from Capri itself, like the provincial command had suspected. But its exact location would be impossible to find without specialized equipment. Bruno turned the radio off and put it in his bag. Though he would have gladly listened for hours to any voice, just to distract himself, he couldn't stand to hear what was said. He needed to get back to his home; there was no point in lingering here any longer. Twilight had long past, and mosquitoes, if there were still any this late in the year, were gone for now. It was about an hour's walk from the station to his apartment. He resolved to make it back in less than forty minutes. As he rose from the floor, the sickly florescent light flickered and went dark. Panic leapt from his gut to his throat, but he shoved it down. Blackness blanketed the storage room, and he could barely see his hand in front of his face. "It's just the dark—it's just the dark," he mumbled. Bruno felt around inside the bag until his hands found the short metal tube of the flashlight. With a click of the button on the back end of the tube, the flashlight sprang to life, casting a bright beam of light into the darkness. He gathered up his duffle bag, slung it over his shoulder, and made his way back to the hallway and the central office.

From where he stood in the short hallway, Bruno could make out the outlines of the back entrance to his right, with its square glass portal to the outside, as well as the large reinforced glass separating the office from the waiting area. He didn't want to waste time moving all the barriers he and Cristian had placed in front of the main entrances, so he turned towards the back entrance, shining the light down the hall.

From the front of the station, the sound of breaking glass stopped Bruno short. Turning off the flashlight as he crouched down, Bruno moved carefully into the central office and took shelter behind the desk. Beyond the thick glass window separating the office from the waiting area, he saw no movement. He couldn't quite tell in the dark, but he guessed that someone had smashed the window on the door leading to the outside. Before Bruno could say for sure, something flew into the waiting room, smashed against the inner glass window, and exploded into flames. In seconds, fire engulfed the waiting area. He heard someone shout "That's what you get, pigs!" Bruno snatched up what was now his duffle bag, hoping that whoever they were hadn't discovered the back exit. He ran to the back door, checking out the window as best he could to make sure the alley was empty. Then, as flames flowed into the central office, he burst into the cold air. The damp autumn night bit into him as he looked around, trying to orient himself in the dark. The half-moon, though, provided a silvery glow, giving him some light to watch where he stepped.

The alley behind connected the station to clusters of buildings to his right and his left off the main square. To his right the alley terminated in a postage stamp parking lot; to his left, the alley wound back towards the main square. Directly in front of him, a grove of scrubby pine trees blocked his vision, as the terrain stepped down in terraced levels to houses toward the sea far below. Body armor or not, Bruno didn't dare wind around back to the square, not knowing how many attackers still lingered. He would have bet his right arm that the assailants on the station and the looters he had spared were one and the same. He should have killed them when he had the chance. The sudden anger of the thought startled Bruno, but he recognized that if he wanted to live, matter-of-fact violence would have to become second nature. But violence alone would not be enough. Bruno would have to act with the ruthlessness of a frontline soldier, not with the controlled aggression of a law enforcement officer. If he acted like a cop, he wouldn't last long.

Shaking off his anger, he plunged into the copse of pines. The soft silver light of the moon now gave way to a brighter orange glow behind him as the station burned in earnest. The flames' glow let him get a better look around. He found himself in a narrow, grassy clearing on the terrace, on the next level below the station.

He knew if he continued down in this direction he would eventually stumble on the road that wound up from the bottom of the island, starting at the Marina Grande and leading all the way to Anacapri at the top of the island. As he stood on the terraced hillside looking at the shadowy houses to his left just below, his eyes wandered across the water towards the coast. He saw orange specks dotting the arc of the coastline from the peninsula of Sorrento jutting out towards the island, all the way around the bay. Cristian's words about Naples were not just hyperbole; they were prophetic. The city was in flames.

The silent burning of Naples mesmerized Bruno, and he stood for a time before plunging down the terrace, scrambling through an open field, and ending up on a side street. He followed the side street, past darkened houses, onto the Via Marina Grande, the main road that wound up the side of the island back up toward his flat in Anacapri. But he was only going partway home. First, he needed to get to the hospital. He needed to find Carla, make sure she was all right.

Concrete buildings and stone houses crowded right up to the street's edge to his left, while to his right, a low wall punctuated by gates to private dwellings ran along the side of the island on the downward slope. There was no sidewalk to speak of. Bruno looked up the narrow road towards Anacapri. In happier times, the road would have been brightly lit, with streetlights and houses casting a glow into the night. Now, the darkness made the already narrow road feel even more claustrophobic than before. Bruno adjusted the duffle bag on his left shoulder and started up the long road. His breath billowed in a white cloud as he quickened his pace. He followed the road up and away from the station, above and behind him, then came to an intersection, and a road sloped down to his right. He continued up the road and found what he was looking for: the *traversa*, a long staircase and paved path winding up between houses and buildings. It would save him some time. Instead of following the road as it wound up the slope of the island in a long S-shape, he would take the traversa, cutting off the bend and leading directly to the higher level of the road. The danger was that the narrow staircase and landings with doors into each dwelling limited his options if anyone caught him there. But the quicker he could get to the hospital, the better, and he judged it worth the risk.

He retrieved the flashlight from the duffle bag and held it in his left hand, but then he hefted the bag onto the same side. It was awkward, but Bruno wanted to keep his right hand free, in case he needed to use his pistol. He debated even using the flashlight at all, as he didn't want to draw attention, but his fear of twisting an ankle or breaking a wrist outweighed the fear of detection. A sprained ankle in this new world might be a death sentence.

Bruno's heart pounded in time with his footfalls as he started up the stairway. He progressed as rapidly as he dared, fearing the clanking of the duffle bag would draw unwanted attention. He did not stop to pause on any of the landings, but noted the shut doors of silent apartments. They stood in mute testimony to their owners' absence, or worse. He pushed the burning in his legs and lungs aside as he bounded up the stairs, sometimes two at a time. But the duffle bag weighed him down, his pace slowed, and his footfalls became louder and heavier. Breathing heavily he finally stopped, perhaps ten steps above a landing. Looking up, Bruno saw that the stairs ended, and the path straightened and flattened out. Once he made it over this last flight of stairs he was nearly at the end and would soon be back on the street. With a sigh, Bruno started once more.

A great crash behind Bruno made him shout out loud. He whirled around, but the duffle bag unbalanced him and he fell onto his side on the hard concrete stairs with a clang. The bag took some of the force, but Bruno felt a stabbing pain shoot through the ribs on his right side as he looked down the stairs. The vest he wore had a rigid plate in front, but Bruno had fallen on his side, and the soft fabric, while bullet resistant, provided only scant protection for that kind of blow.

The door leading to the landing was flung open and in the half-moon's weak light, Bruno could see a figure standing there a few meters below him. By some fortune, he still held the flashlight clenched in his left hand, and he pointed it down the stairs.

The beam splashed onto the figure's face. The shirtless figure's long, dark hair couldn't obscure the oozing sores on her face and neck, nor could it hide the coffee-colored fluid running down from her face to her breasts. Her hands trembled as she shambled towards him.

"Please, help me!"

Bruno slithered backwards up the stairs, the pain biting into his ribs as he tore his pistol from its holster. "Stop! Don't come any closer!"

"Please don't hurt me!" she shouted, insistent. "My son, he's dead—I need help!" She shuffled toward him faster than he thought someone that sick could. He dropped the flashlight and took aim at the center of the dark figure below him as he rolled to his back. "Stop! Don't make me shoot!" he cried, and yet still she came. He yanked the trigger hard. He lost count after the third shot. He saw her stumble backwards, falling onto the landing. Ears still ringing from the shots, he held the pistol at eye level until he noticed his hands trembling. Forcing them lower, Bruno holstered his pistol and scrambled back to his feet. Pain shot through his ribs, making him wince as he gathered his flashlight from where it lay next to the duffle bag.

"Please don't kill me!" the voice below him shouted. Bruno shone the light down onto the woman. Instead of clean shots to a vital area, he must have hit her low in the gut. Her face was twisted with pain and she lay in a pool of blood.

She sobbed as she spoke, her words coming out in stutters. "P—lease, I don't want to die!" He dared not get any closer, though he may have already been exposed, for all he knew. Her sobs grew louder as she bled out below him. He knew he should end her suffering; he knew it in his bones, but he feared what more gunfire would bring. And yet, he couldn't just leave her like this, no matter what the risk. He pulled out his pistol with his right hand and aimed the flashlight towards her with his left hand. He braced the pistol over his left wrist and aimed.

By now, she had stopped writhing and was lying on her stomach, moaning. As the light fell on her, she lifted her head and looked up at Bruno. Everything else around her faded to darkness, but the light shone on her face, spotlighting her eyes. She fell silent as her eyes burned into his. Her mouth opened, dark spittle running down her chin, but she made no sound. Instead, she raised her trembling hand towards him, fingers outstretched, pleading with Bruno to spare her life with that quiet gesture. Bruno squeezed the trigger as he gazed into her eyes. This time, the bullet found its mark, shattering her forehead. He holstered his pistol and turned off his flashlight. Though shadows shrouded the bloodshed below him, his gaze stayed fixed on what he had done.

His second execution cut more deeply than his first. Wiping away tears with the back of his hand, Bruno wondered if he had made too much noise and she had heard his footfalls, or if the woman had simply wanted to find someone, anyone. Anger welled up inside him, masking his fright. Damn her, why did she have to come out? Why couldn't she have just died in her house? She was going to die anyway! His anger at the dead woman distracted him for a moment from the pain in his ribs. But as the adrenaline ebbed, every breath made him wince. He wanted to go down to her dwelling to see if there was anything he could use, but he had no doubt her body could still spread disease.

That woman was an innocent. He didn't even bother lying to himself and hope it would be the last time he ever killed anyone. Thoughts like that belonged to a civilized era, a dying era. Killing, he knew, would become second nature to the survivors of this plague, if they themselves wanted to survive.

Bruno's gaze lingered on the unseen carnage for a while before he turned and stepped up the last bits of stairs. He stepped with care, trying to jostle the duffle bag as little as possible. If his ribs were cracked, if he couldn't move with speed, his next encounter might very well be his last. After only a few minutes more, he came to the end of the traversa. Of course, after encountering what awaited him on those steps, he knew he would have been better off taking the long way. But second guessing that decision now might be a fatal distraction. Bruno pushed aside the memory of the stairs, focusing on what was in front of him. He walked with care down the last steps onto the sidewalk. He looked to his left and right. The wind gusted down this higher part of the dim and empty Via Marina Grande. In front of him, a long, stone wall ran the length of the street, slowly sloping down and fading to an end at an intersection down the road. The chill night air heightened Bruno's senses as he turned to his left, continuing as fast as he could toward the piazza ahead. He made his way down the street, hugging the wall and shuffling as fast as his hurt ribs would let him. He felt so exposed on the street that keeping close to the stone made him feel safer, irrational though the thought was. The vegetation ran along the top of the wall, but beyond the tops of the low trees, a white light shone. If anywhere still had power on the island, it would be the Capomonte Hospital. As he reached the end of the wall, he crouched down. He surveyed the piazza as best he could. Something in Carla's voice when they had last spoke made him cautious. Something *was* wrong.

As the sloping wall came to an end, multiple streets met in an open piazza. He slowly made his way around the wall and entered the area, all the while sticking to as much cover as he could find, scooting from one abandoned car to another. Two streets ran up and around the hospital, like two rivers around a narrow spit of land. The street on the right ran in front of the hospital's back entrance and then sloped down, making its way to the bottom of the island, while the one on the left ran past the main entrance, sloping upwards. That was the one Bruno wanted. Looming beyond the hospital, the jagged cliffs were barely visible shadows, the light from the hospital lights nearly blocking them out. Beyond the cliffs on the higher part of the island lay the town of Anacapri. The hospital lay between Bruno and the most direct route to his home. He took shelter behind a gas pump and an old Fiat 500 at what was left of a two-pump gas station. Putting down his duffle bag, he looked up the street towards the hospital. Light poured down from floodlights mounted on long, silver poles, providing enough illumination for Bruno to get a good look around.

The building was an irregularly shaped red brick structure. A large, olive-drab tent rose in front of stairs leading from the street up into a courtyard, where the main entrance to the hospital building lay. To the right of the tent, a railing ran along the edge of the courtyard, not more than two meters above the street.

The two figures dressed in white hooded coveralls stood out against the dull color of the tent. They had complete plastic shields covering their faces, not just masks. As one of the figures turned, Bruno saw some sort of seal on the back of the suit. Ministry of Health, maybe? He couldn't be sure without getting a closer look, but the M-16s slung across their chests made Bruno think twice about getting any closer.

As Bruno watched, a man in a paper hospital gown flapping in the wind leapt over the railing. The man landed with a smack and a shout on the sidewalk below, only a few meters in front of the guards. He rolled, but quickly got to his feet and shuffled as fast as he could away from the hospital. Even from this distance, the lesions and sores stood out like macabre tattoos. While startled, the guards recovered quickly, and pointed their weapons towards the man's back as he dragged one foot behind him.

"Halt!" shouted one guard. "You're in quarantine!" The man ignored the order, if anything attempting to speed up. Bruno watched the scene in front of him with horror. The guards made no effort to pursue the man, only shouting at him to stop. The man continued to limp in Bruno's direction. Bruno could hear him whimpering. Just as Bruno looked to find cover further away from the approaching man, they shot him twice in the back. The man dropped to the ground with a shout. He clawed his way forward on his belly while the guards looked on. They waited still as statues as the man in front of them whimpered, then put his head down on the pavement and fell silent.

Neither one of the guards approached the body. Instead, one of the guards pulled out a walkie-talkie. Soon after, two more figures walked out of the tent and conferred with the guards. The two new individuals appeared unarmed, but they wore full decontamination suits made of what looked like heavy, olive-drab plastic, with built-in respirators. One of them carried what looked like two thin poles slightly taller than a person. When they turned to the side, Bruno could see what he thought were air tanks on their backs. After talking to the guards, the two approached the man. One of them laid the poles next to the prostrate man and rolled it out, making a stretcher. Then both figures lifted the man into the stretcher and marched back into the tent, while the guards gave them a wide berth.

Bruno's mind raced. Christ, deadly force? Shooting an unarmed man in the back? What kind of guards were these? Bruno had only shot that woman because she kept coming, but they shot a man who was trying to get away. He couldn't move towards the back entrance to the hospital on the other side, they'd spot him for sure. But the men in front of him blocked the quickest way home. If whoever they were spotted him, Bruno feared they would kill him, Carabiniere or not, without a second thought. While he had the element of surprise, there were two of them. Bruno knew he wasn't a good enough shot with a pistol to take them both out before one of them would nail him or call for help.

If Bruno had to cut through houses, fields, climb walls, or make his way down to the seaside, he would do whatever he needed to avoid these men. But he needed to get to Carla. He tried to think of alternate routes, ways around the hospital, ways in the hospital, ways to try to contact Carla, while the same two figures clad in the decontamination suits emerged from the tent. Bruno caught a glimpse of some sort of grey cylinder, maybe a meter high, but the guards obscured his view, forming a semi-circle around the object. A high-pitched whine filled the air, like a gnat flying too close, as the cylinder rose into the air. One of the guards focused intently on a device in his hand, while the other looked left and right.

Bruno flattened himself against the car. Too late he realized it was some kind of drone. Bruno remembered that the Americans had been using them anywhere they could, but he had never seen one like this. Did it sense movement? Did it have infrared sensors? Was it armed? The hum of the drone's fan faded as it rose and began hovering twenty or thirty meters above the hospital tent. Bruno decided he could no longer wait to be discovered as it calibrated its sensors. He would have to make a lengthy detour, heading back down toward to the seaside and around the island to get home. He saw no option to get into the hospital without announcing himself to the guards. But if he made it home, maybe he could regroup, come up with another plan.

As he turned to retreat, the whine of the drone suddenly grew louder. Bruno looked up and for a moment the bright light blinded him. A voice boomed above him.

"Come out from behind the vehicle with your hands in the air!"

Bruno didn't think, he just grabbed his bag, turned, and ran back into the piazza, pain shooting in his side. The drone whizzed above him, keeping him in its spotlight.

He glanced back and saw the guards running towards him in a low sprint. He wasn't sure he could outrun the guards, but he knew he would never outrun the drone. He looked to his right, and just beyond the pedestrian guardrail, he could make out the bulge of a hillside stretching down into darkness.

If he jumped the railing, he might make it. The guards might be reluctant to follow him down. He might even evade the drone. That is, if he could manage not to break his neck.

Bruno jumped the railing and skidded down into darkness. Time slowed as he struggled to stop his slide and his panic. For a second, he thought he would make it. But his left foot caught some stone or root and with the weight of the duffle bag leaving him off balance, he tumbled forward; then Bruno knew nothing but darkness.

CHAPTER 8

Bruno woke with a start, images of a woman's shattered head in his mind. For an instant, he couldn't remember what had happened. The dull pain in his ribs and the ache in his head brought him back to reality. He felt exhausted, battered, and sore. He groped his own arms and legs but didn't seem to have any broken bones. Bruno recalled his last memories of falling. So much for his attempt at evasion. He rubbed his forehead and felt a bandage covering part of his head. A concussion, maybe. He considered himself damned lucky, if that was the worst of it.

Bruno looked around. Spartan would have been a generous description of the room; it had no decorations of any kind, nor did it have a TV or phone; just a chair in the corner. Diffused light from the late afternoon sky streamed in from the window to his left. He swung his legs around to his right, sat up in the bed, and groaned. Bruno's body throbbed from head to foot. The pain surprised him, and the room rolled around him. Bruno lay back down. He breathed in and out and closed his eyes, recovering his equilibrium. To the right there was a dark, wooden door with a narrow glass window running half its length. A guard wearing the mottled greys of an urban combat uniform stood with his back towards him in front of the window.

Captured and in a hospital room. No gun. No knife. No bag. No phone. Not one fucking thing. He glanced at his watch.16:03. Six and a half hours before the rescue boat arrived. He still had time, but before he would consider leaving, he needed to get to

Carla. He closed his eyes and breathed in and out in measured beats. Then, with caution, he raised himself out of the bed, shuffled over to the door, and tapped on the window. The guard turned, glared over his mask, and stepped away from the door without a word.

"Hey!" shouted Bruno as he pulled the door handle to no avail. "Come back!"

Moments later the guard reappeared, pistol drawn, and gestured for Bruno to step away from the door. As Bruno retreated to the other side of the bed, the door swung open. A squat, dark-haired woman wearing green scrubs walked in with a tray of bread and pasta, and a glass of water. The guard stood behind her, keeping his pistol drawn, but pointed down.

She placed the tray and water on the table. "There's more if you are still hungry. Just knock on the door." A respirator covered most of her face; her eyes were the only part of her he could see clearly.

The woman took a penlight out of her pocket. "Please keep your eyes on the light." She moved the light back and forth.

"That looks fine," she said. "Now lay back, I need to check your bandages. Good. The bleeding's stopped. No serious head injuries," she said as she turned to the guard. "You can proceed." She nodded to the guard and they both retreated towards the door.

The woman opened the door and left first, then as the guard's back faced into the room, Bruno wobbled to his feet. "I'm an officer in the Carabinieri! Why am I being detained?"

The guard stopped in the doorway and half-turned towards Bruno. The respirator muffled the guard's voice. "Major Battisti with the Ministry of Health is in charge here. And he will have some questions for you, very soon, I assure you."

"Dottoressa Carla Ricasso is in charge of this hospital," said Bruno, puzzled. He'd never heard of anyone in that agency using a military rank. "What are you talking about?"

"You'll find out," said the guard as he retreated into the hall and locked the door.

Bruno's head swam, and not just from the concussion. A major? In the Ministry of Health? What did that mean? Where was Carla? Bruno thought for a moment about the guard. No insignia. No unit patch. Not even rank. Whoever he worked for wanted him to stay anonymous.

Bruno's mind churned for long minutes as he forced himself to eat, until he heard the metallic sound of the lock on his door turn. Three men entered, one stocky with close-cropped black hair, flanked by two larger men. All three wore grey urban combat uniforms and carried pistols on their hips. Keeping the bed between him and the soldiers, Bruno stood up and faced them.

"Buona sera, Officer Ricasso," said the shortest man. "My name is Major Battisti." Though a respirator hid his mouth and nose, from the way the crow's-feet at his dark eyes moved, Bruno had no doubt Battisti smiled as he spoke. "Your room is comfortable, no?"

"Who do you think you are, keeping me locked up here?"

Battisti's eyes narrowed. "Ah yes. I apologize. This is for your own good, really. Have to make sure you're not infected."

"Infected? Do I look infected to you?"

"Please. Don't make things worse." Battisti shifted from one foot to another. "I also have some questions for you. I hope you will cooperate, yes?"

Bruno said nothing.

"Well, let me begin. What were you doing outside the hospital?"

"I was trying to see my sister, Dottoressa Carla Ricasso. I'm sure you know who she is."

"How long were you out there by the entrance?"

"Not long. I thought I heard gunfire, so I wanted to investigate before just running up to the area."

"Gunfire. Interesting. And—this next is a very important question for us to get to the bottom of what happened—what did you see the guards doing? Did you see what caused this alleged gunfire?"

"No," lied Bruno. "There were guards milling around the entrance, but I don't know what they were doing."

"Why didn't you just announce yourself, tell them you were a Carabiniere?"

"Like I said, I had heard gunfire. I needed to assess the situation before I ran up half-cocked."

"I see. Of course you understand the seriousness of what you're saying. Because clearly, if my guards were firing their weapons, I would need to know about that."

"Why don't you ask them," said Bruno.

Battisti stepped forward. "I have asked them, Officer Ricasso."

"So you know what they were doing. Why ask what I was—"

"My job is to protect this hospital. What I know is that you were spying on this facility."

"Spying? I was trying to get to my sister."

"Let me ask you again: did you see what caused this alleged gunfire?"

"No."

Battisti paced to and fro. "Well, unfortunately, we may be at a bit of an impasse here. Because, you see, Officer Ricasso, I'm not sure you're telling me the whole truth."

"I'm telling you what happened."

Battisti stopped pacing. "Are you really?"

Bruno swallowed. "Yes, that's exactly what happened."

"Perhaps we have different definitions of 'exactly'?"

Bruno didn't respond.

"I don't like liars, Officer Ricasso."

"I don't either," said Bruno.

"Good." Battisti studied Bruno for a moment. "Do you consider yourself to be an intelligent person?"

"Smarter than some. Not as smart as others."

Battisti laughed. "That's probably the truest thing you've said so far. If you *are* smart, then you should know what's in your best interest. So, let's start again, shall we? What did you see when—"

"I'm done answering your fucking questions," Bruno interrupted. "I've told you what happened. I want to talk to Dottoressa Ricasso, she's in charge here. She can clear everything up."

"I'm afraid not. She doesn't know you're here." Battisti looked over at the soldiers, and before Bruno could react, one of them produced a black pistol, pointed it toward Bruno, and pulled the trigger.

Bruno felt a sting in his chest, just before he seized up from the thousands of volts running through his body. He let out a muffled scream through clenched teeth as he fell forward onto the bed. The guards moved quickly to strap him down while he was stunned.

"These restraints are only used for uncooperative patients, Officer Ricasso," said Battisti, looming over Bruno. "So, what's *your* plan? Are *you* going to cooperate?" Bruno's breath came in ragged gasps as he lay there trembling. Bruno choked out one word: "Vaffanculo."

Battisti responded with a smack across Bruno's face. "Watch your mouth. I'll give you a chance to change your mind. But I hope for your sake you make the right choice." Battisti bent down closer towards the bed, his voice a low growl in Bruno's ear. "And let me explain something—in this room, your sister isn't in charge: I am."

The Taser now in Battisti's hand buzzed. Bruno gazed up at some dark fleck on the pale ceiling, his breath coming in rapid pulses.

***

Bruno didn't know what finally made them stop. Maybe they thought he was going to die. Hell, maybe the batteries on the thing just ran out. Whatever the reason, Bruno didn't really care. Every muscle in his body felt stretched, torn. The pain in his ribs as he breathed felt like a pinprick in comparison to what he had just endured. They didn't ask anything about gun confiscation; they just kept asking him what he was doing spying on the hospital and what he saw last night. He heard them mutter about something called "ICP 151." He didn't reveal having seen anything about that man's murder. But they didn't believe him, and Bruno teetered on the edge of breaking. When they came back, Bruno feared that he might say anything to make them stop.

The overhead lights were off, and his room was dark, but Bruno's watch gave off a faint glow. 23:54. Bruno squeezed his eyes shut. The speedboat was long gone. He moved carefully out of the bed, walking towards the door on quiet, bare feet. He looked through the door's narrow window. An empty chair. No guard, for now. Bruno tried the handle, hoping against hope. Locked, of course. He might try bashing through the window on the door. But what he really need was stealth, not strength. He studied the room. Hospitals had patients, not prisoners. Maybe he could take advantage of that.

Bruno returned to the bed, arranged the pillows, and pulled the sheet over them. He pulled the bandages off his head and looked in the bathroom mirror. The cut on his head was mostly hidden in his hair. Good. Next, he ransacked the bathroom and cabinets. No scalpels or probes; nothing he could use as a weapon. He did find a set of scrubs, with shoe and head coverings, as well as a surgical mask. He put them on. The elastic of the shoe coverings fit tightly around his ankles. The window was the kind that opened inward, bottom tilting towards the room. It was locked. But locked from the inside. Bruno pulled the chair under the window, stood on it, and unlocked the window at the top. He pushed open the bottom section of window. He climbed down, moved the chair back, then looked out.

The cool night made him shiver. The concrete ledge outside the window looked just wide enough to stand on. Ambient light from rooms on floors above and below bathed the outside walls in a faint glow. He looked around and saw that the window of the room on the left was tilted inward. Slightly. No light came from that room, but it was too far to just hop over to the other ledge. He would have to jump. Bruno made the mistake of looking down, and his head swam. He was at least four stories up. Porca puttana, he swore to himself. Bruno acted before the voice of doubt in his head became deafening. He ducked his head out and swung his legs outside. He thought how stupid he must look, like a nurse gone mad, hanging out of a hospital window.

The night enveloped him, and though the air swirling about him was cold, Bruno had begun to sweat. Grasping the frame and ledge, he stood up. He pushed the window shut as best as he could from the outside. His back to the cold stone of the wall, he shuffled to the leftmost edge. He looked over at the ledge, his target, and the world started to spin.

Bruno squeezed his eyes shut, willing the vertigo to pass. He took one deep breath after another. Then he opened his eyes again. He would have to get this right. Too much and he would overshoot and crash into the edge of the window. Too little and he would miss the ledge altogether. Either would probably mean death. Turning with his left shoulder to the wall, he focused on his goal, took one step back with his right leg . . . and then he jumped.

CHAPTER 9

In the long moment he was airborne, panic hit Bruno. He crashed onto the edge and lost his footing, slipping, his chest thudding against the ledge. His fingers scrabbled and he caught himself, hands grasping the ledge, then through the open window. Pain shot through his already sore ribs and his arms as they bore his entire body weight while he hung. Panting, Bruno struggled to pull himself up. He swung one leg up, then another, and rolled with a grunt and a smack onto the floor of the dark room.

He lay on the cool stone floor, not caring if there was anyone there, only caring that he was still alive. He trembled like he had fallen into a vat of cold water. But he didn't have time to savor the exhilaration of survival. Bruno forced himself up and shut the window. No one was there. The room looked just like the one he'd escaped from, except this one had a TV on the wall and a telephone by the bed. He moved the phone behind the bed and used the bed as cover from the door. Bruno picked up the phone, dialed, and waited, hoping that no matter what had happened to the hospital's external communication, internal ones still functioned.

A tired voice on the other end answered after only two rings.

"Ricasso here."

"Carla, it's Bruno," he whispered.

"You're in the hospital?"

"Some guy named Battisti had me locked up in one of the rooms. They don't know I'm out."

"Christ, that was you they captured?" Carla didn't give him a chance to answer. "Shit—all right—let me think—caller ID says you're on the fourth floor, room 432. There's an elevator just down the hall. Take it up to the seventh floor. Go to my office. I'll be there."

"Okay—I'm wearing scrubs."

"Good!" said Carla. "But be careful—it's almost shift change. If you see anyone, act like you know what you're doing. We've got enough shit going on here that they won't bother you. See you in five minutes." Carla hung up without waiting for his reply.

Bruno hung up the phone and went to the door. He looked down the hall. The guard was now sitting in front of Bruno's old room, one room away. Bruno's mind whirred. What could he do? Then from down the hall to the right, Bruno heard the faint ding of an elevator. The doors opened, and five people in scrubs and masks came out, talking with animated gestures. Two others now came from the opposite direction, heading towards Bruno from around a bend in the hallway past his old room. Here was his chance. As the groups milled past his room, obscuring the guard's view, Bruno opened the door and slipped out, walking to the right, towards the elevator at the end of the hall.

He walked just ahead of two people talking. Bruno kept his eyes forward, waiting for the shout of the guard, but none came. They caught up to Bruno just as he reached the elevator. Still talking, one of them leaned past Bruno and pushed the down button, just after Bruno pushed the up button. Unfortunately for Bruno, when the elevator stopped, it was on its way down. Not wanting to linger in the hallway, Bruno got on with the other two.

The elevator chimed as it went by each floor. Bruno tried to meld into the back corner, pretending to be preoccupied with the watch on his wrist and hoping that the two men—doctors, orderlies, or whoever they were—would leave him alone. They exited on the second floor, still talking. When they left, Bruno slumped against the back wall. Then he pushed the button for the seventh floor harder than necessary. Just as the doors began to shut, an arm reached in. The elevator dinged. The doors opened, and a man dressed exactly like Bruno's tormentors stepped in. Bruno froze, standing where he was in front of the panel.

"Four please," the guard said.

"Oh sure," responded Bruno as he hit the button. He pushed and held the "close" button, hoping that would speed up the doors. It didn't.

The elevator began to go up. Bruno looked at his feet as the guard glanced his way.

"Going to the seventh floor? That's Administration." The guard's question lingered in the air.

"Oh, procurement cocked up the last shipment of medical supplies. Not enough syringes. Ricasso called downstairs. They sent me up to deal with her."

"At midnight, huh?" The guard grunted. "I'm not surprised. I've heard she can be a real pain in the ass."

The door chimed. Fourth floor. The guard stepped out. "Still, that beats sitting around guarding some sleeping idiot, like I'm going to do for the rest of the night." He strode out with a wave. "Buona serata."

Bruno mumbled a reply as he pushed the close button. Finally, the doors shut. Bruno let out a great puff of air as the elevator arrived at the seventh floor. Although he'd only been there a few times, Bruno remembered the way to his sister's office. Right out of the elevator, then left down the hall. His footsteps were only a whisper on the floor. No one was there, but he felt exposed in the harsh fluorescent light. The door to Carla's suite was half-open. He pushed the door wider and walked in.

The reception desk was empty, but Bruno saw Carla in the next room through the glass wall at the same time she spotted him. She got up from her desk and waved him in. They embraced for a moment. She'd always been small, but now her slight frame felt almost bony. A strong wind could carry her away, he thought. She was dressed in scrubs and a white coat with her name embossed over the coat's pocket, a respirator covering the lower half of her face. There were dark circles under Carla's brown eyes.

"Carla, what the hell is going on here? I—"

"Bruno, listen, you've got to get out of here."

"I need my gear. I need my weapon."

She nodded. "I think I know where they are. Locked up on the eighth floor. It's a restricted level. Let's go."

They walked out of Carla's office back to the elevator. Carla pushed the up button. Bruno's mind churned with a thousand questions.

"Where are the guards?"

"Shift change staff meeting—for now, anyway. We should have a few minutes."

"All of them?"

"Most of them. Battisti is a little martinet," said Carla. "He has to have his staff meeting *every* shift change. Doesn't matter if the world is going to shit. And there are only seven guards for the whole hospital, counting Battisti."

The elevator door opened and they entered. Carla swiped a card on the panel and pushed "8."

Bruno felt the elevator lurch slightly as it went up.

"Why are you still here, Carla? Why don't you leave?"

"We activated the pandemic emergency plans, and I was already here when they recalled all staff." She paused. "Then ten days ago, the Ministry of Health took direct control over all hospitals. They won't let me leave."

"What do you mean they won't let you leave? And since when does the Ministry of Health kill unarmed—"

The elevator doors opened, and Carla cut him off.

"Come on," she said. "Quietly."

They exited the elevator and made a right down the hallway. To Bruno this restricted level looked no different than any other part of the hospital. They walked for what seemed like forever down a long hallway. Then it turned at a right angle and Bruno heard a voice. It sounded like he was talking on a phone.

"Cazzo," she cursed. "Here, take this key—it's a master key. Go back to the stairwell near the elevator. I'll meet you there with your gear."

"But without the key, you won't be able to—"

"I've got extra keys. Just go," she hissed.

He tiptoed down the hallway as best he could. Carla walked in the opposite direction, her shoes echoing down the hall. The sound of her footsteps faded as Bruno retraced his steps. He reached the elevator and saw the door to the stairwell on the other side. But there was another smaller hallway just before the stairs. Bruno thought he could hear muffled moaning and cursing.

Curiosity overcame his common sense, and Bruno followed the sounds down the narrow hallway. There were more rooms. The voices were louder now, and he couldn't help but look in one of the windows. He saw two figures, hospital gowns flapping as they wandered around the room, and thought he saw two more on the beds. One wandering figure turned toward him. The man's eyes widened as he saw Bruno standing at the door. He scampered over to the window. Bruno jumped back as the man approached, stifling a shout, now seeing for the first time up close the ravages of the Shakes. The wispy white hair around the old man's head framed a face covered in pustules that ran down his neck. His whole body quaked with tremors.

"Please! Let us out!" he croaked, pressing his face on the glass. Some of the pustules had burst, the pus oozing around the corners of his mouth, and he left slime on the window as he pressed his face against it. "Open the door! They've got us trapped! We're going to die here!"

The door must have been specially sealed, since it deadened the man's voice more than seemed possible. Even if he could, there was no chance of Bruno opening the door—he'd be infected for sure. He shook his head and mouthed, "I can't." Bruno took one step backwards, then turned and retreated down the hallway to the stairwell as fast as he dared. Bruno heard the old man's muffled voice call out, "They're going to kill us!"

Arriving at the stairwell, Bruno fumbled with the key and rushed through the door. Now on the landing, Bruno looked up and down the stairs. He was alone.

Fidgeting as the minutes ticked by, his mind wandered from the old man in the hospital room, to Carla, to a million other things. The loss of his gear gnawed at him. He hoped they'd stored his pistol with his gear, otherwise he might as well go back and strap himself to the mattress again. For a moment, he contemplated striking out on his own, but then he heard the metallic click of the door's latch.

"Carla!" he whispered.

She started, then came through the door with Bruno's duffel bag, talking as she moved. "Took me longer than I thought."

"How did you manage to get—"

She handed him his bag. "Don't ask. Your uniform and gear should be in there."

He rummaged through his bag and found his uniform, his gun, knife, and the rest of his gear. But something was missing.

"I had body armor. Where is it?" Without his body armor, Bruno felt soft as a slug, and just as easily squashed.

Carla shook her head. "That's all there was."

Bruno dressed as fast as he could while Carla kept a lookout through the stairwell door's window. Without turning to face him, she said one word.

"Cristian?"

"He's gone," said Bruno. "He's trying to make it back to Tivoli, back to his daughter." She nodded.

"We both tried to contact you, but couldn't get through." Then Bruno's anger at his former friend boiled over. "But when he left, that bastard took the only decent weapons at the station—he left me with nothing!"

For the first time she glanced back at him. "Hurry up!" she said. She looked back out the door's window before she responded. "They confiscated my phone and restricted Internet access. They didn't want us to have any contact with outside. I think external calls are monitored. I had no way of knowing anyone was trying to reach me." Carla exhaled loud enough for Bruno to hear. "And if he did that to you, then he really is a bastard."

Bruno said nothing and pulled on his boots.

She pointed towards the bottom of the stairwell. "Come on, down to the basement. With luck, everyone will take the elevators tonight."

Bruno followed her down the flights of stairs. At least he still had his pistol. When they arrived at the bottom of the stairwell, Carla opened the door as quietly as she could, leaning her body weight onto the metal bar. She peered into the space beyond the door, then looked back and nodded. Bruno followed.

They walked down a hallway, finally coming to a locked door, with a window that showed darkness beyond. The musty odor and cramped quarters of the tunnel reminded him of the catacombs in Rome he had visited as a boy. Both were places of death.

Carla's voice sounded loud in the narrow tunnel. "I need the key that I gave you. It's a master key. The one I used upstairs won't work."

Bruno handed her the key and kept watch while Carla fumbled, taking longer than Bruno wanted. Then with nearly no sound, the door opened, and she flipped the light switch, bathing the storage room in flickering florescent light.

The low, stone ceiling made Bruno feel shut in, but his eyes widened as they fell on the free-standing metal shelves brimming with medical supplies. He followed Carla as she walked between the shelves, the lights humming above their heads.

She walked methodically down the rows, grabbing things here and there, but didn't pause to look as she spoke. "We got a helicopter drop three days ago. Maybe the last one for a while. But there are plenty of supplies, medicines, and antibiotics."

Her arms quickly filled with supplies and she stopped so fast, Bruno ran into her.

"Here," she said, as she handed him the armload. "Put these in your bag, you'll need them. There's a real respirator in there. You might as well wear a goddamn dust mask for all the good a regular surgical mask would do."

"So, the ones that everyone's been wearing—"

"Aren't worth shit. They *might* stop someone with the disease from infecting others, but the other way around, keeping someone from *catching* the virus? Probably not."

"But the respirators will prevent infection, right?"

She paused. "Maybe. The science on that isn't good. But they're a hell of a lot better than a surgical mask."

"Fucking great," said Bruno as he stuffed the medical supplies into his duffle bag.

Carla set out again down the rows of shelves. He followed her as she wound down the aisles until they returned to the door where they had come in. Bruno dropped his bag to the ground. He wanted some answers.

"Carla, what is going on? They captured me, they killed that man . . . and those people trapped on the eighth floor—why?"

Carla looked down. "There was a secret directive adopted by the EU Ministries of Health not long after that last Ebola scare. I knew about it, but I was only briefed on the exact details a week ago. In the event of an outbreak of a previously unknown virus, certain emergency measures are authorized. Like trying to stop the spread to healthy people by concentrating the sick in hospitals." Now she looked Bruno in the eyes. "No one would be stupid enough to go to a group shelter in a pandemic, but they might go to a hospital, if they thought they could be helped."

"I heard Battisti's guards say something about ICP 151. Is that it?"

"Infection Control Protocol 151—that's the directive."

Bruno frowned. "But concentrating the sick? That doesn't make any sense, unless . . ." Bruno's eyes lit up as he remembered the old man's words. Trapped. "So, going to hospital is a death sentence, is that it? They're never going to be let out, are they? And the government is lying about it!"

Carla said nothing.

"I don't believe it! Ministry of Health? Ministry of fucking Death! They're telling people to go to the hospital when all they're doing is rounding them up to die like—like—cattle!"

Carla shook her head. "Almost all of them will die anyway. There's nothing we can do."

"Maybe they're even giving the poor bastards a push!" Bruno looked at Carla, thinking she would contradict his exaggeration. Then he saw the look in Carla's eyes.

Carla held his gaze, with no emotion. "Like I said, Protocol 151 authorizes certain emergency measures. If they've come to a hospital, they're dead already."

"But why hold me? Because I saw—"

"The Protocol authorizes detention and, if necessary, liquidation of individuals who are unauthorized witnesses to infection control."

"'Liquidation'? You mean fucking murder! Christ, you're a doctor! How could they do this? How could *you*?"

"The Protocol requires a chief hospital administrator to countersign the Ministry of Health's order before liquidation of a witness. I was waiting to hear what Battisti said you saw before—before—I—"

"Before you signed my death warrant!"

"Bruno, I didn't know it was you! He didn't tell me! I didn't ask who it was—I didn't want to know!" Then her voice hardened. "You judge me? You don't know how close we came to a real shit-storm when Ebola hit a few years back—and this is a thousand—no, ten thousand times worse!" She grabbed Bruno's arm. "Wouldn't you kill if there were a chance to stop the spread? Wouldn't you kill, if you thought you had to?"

Bruno pulled his arm away and started to speak, to tell her she was wrong. Then he stopped, the vision of that dead woman's eyes from last night freezing the retort in his throat.

"The bodies—what do you do with the bodies?" murmured Bruno.

"We have an incinerator for medical waste."

Bruno turned away from Carla. "You've turned hospitals into death camps." God only knew what was happening in places like China, Russia, or the United States. What had they resorted to, if on Capri, playground for the glitterati of Europe, the hospital facilitated government-sanctioned slaughter? He paced for a moment, then turned towards her. "They're fools if they think they can contain this. It's way too late."

"Maybe they are fools. But they needed to try something, anything. Even this."

Carla's participation in the lies and death shocked Bruno, but in his heart, he knew she was right. He was beginning to understand that in this new world, only the lucky and the ruthless would survive. Her cold-blooded attitude might keep her alive for a while. But no matter how cunning, how ruthless you were, there would always be someone more ruthless, more cunning. Maybe just more lucky.

He breathed a long breath before speaking. "The old world is dead. There's no hope to stop the Shakes."

"Who knows? You call it the Shakes. That's what the Brits call it. So many different names for the damn thing. The French call it *la grippe africaine*, the African Flu, the Irish call it the Blood Trots, and the Spanish—Brown Fever. And here, every region has its own name for it." She smiled a bit. "As usual. But I think the Americans have got the right name for it."

"Omega Plague." The words chilled Bruno even as he said them. "The Final Plague."

She nodded. "The plague that ends humanity."

"But this virus . . . this plague . . . isn't there anything that can be done to help the sick? A treatment—antivirals, something?" Bruno asked.

"There's a rumor the potent ones might, just like they do against the AIDS virus. But you'd have to stay on them the rest of your life. And there's far too many people sick, too many people dying, for there ever to be enough antivirals for everyone."

Carla took his arm. "Come on. You've got to get going. This way." She led him to the far side of the storage room. A wooden door stood in their path. Judging by the rust-coated padlock, no one had opened it for a long while. Carla's key was no use. "It's so damn old," she said. "From before the renovations."

Bruno removed the crowbar from his bag and jammed it between the lock and the door. With one motion the padlock tumbled off, taking part of the door with it.

He poked his head in and looked around. The chamber smelled of water and mold, its bricks the color of dirt. A ladder led up to a manhole. The chamber was tiny and they would have to climb one at a time.

"Do you know where it comes out?" asked Bruno.

"I think on the street beyond the hospital, up the road towards Anacapri."

"Let's get going! If we jog, it won't take that long to get to my place."

Carla shook her head.

"What's the matter?"

"They need me here," Carla answered, her gaze steady.

"Carla, you've got to come. Christ, you said they're all going to die anyway. And Battisti, he'll—"

"I'm not talking about the patients. The Ministry of Health goons need me. They'll make sure I'm well taken care of. Those are their orders. And Battisti follows orders. Healthy nurses and doctors are more valuable than gold, trust me. I'll be much safer here than running around on the island like you . . . but you need to know something."

Carla paused before continuing. "Very, very few people survive this disease—we're not sure just how few. But the ones who do, become—"

"What, vampires, zombies?"

"This isn't one of Cristian's stupid fucking movies!" She took a breath before continuing. "Look, back when the Spanish Flu hit in 1918, some people who survived had a kind of brain trauma, made some of them lethargic, almost catatonic. They called it the Sleeping Sickness. This virus also changes brain chemistry in survivors. But this one makes them dangerous."

"More contagious?"

Carla shook her head. "No, if they survive, they're not contagious any more. We think it damages parts of the brain, the ventromedial prefrontal cortex and the amygdala."

"What does that mean?"

"They're the parts of the brain that process emotion. The reports I've seen say it makes survivors highly unpredictable, almost psychopathic."

"What the hell *is* this thing?"

"We don't know. Whatever it is, one thing is for sure: it can't be natural. Some group, some country, did this deliberately. Someone made this thing. Look for jaundice in the whites of their eyes; the survivors have liver damage. But if you get that close to one, it's probably too late. They'd just as soon choke someone as talk to them." Carla glanced at her watch. "I've got to get back. Time to go."

Bruno nodded and turned his back to her as he moved into the chamber. He climbed two rungs and opened the manhole cover above him as quietly as he could. Eyes just breaking over the edge, he looked around, but saw no one in the gloom. He pushed his duffle bag through the opening and climbed the rest of the way up. Once he stood on the street, Bruno gathered his bag and turned around. There below him stood Carla in the chamber, looking up at him. Her eyes glinted in the dark, but he could barely see the rest of her, even though she stood only a meter below him.

"I love you, Bruno," said Carla. "Now, find a safe place, stay there, and don't come out."

***

Bruno found his flat cold and humid, but there was nothing for it; he had no fuel or generators, and with the power off, all he could do was bundle himself in blankets to ward off the chill. The ache in his ribs kept him awake for a long while, even after he took some meds. As he lay there, finally in his own bed, he tossed and turned. He got out of bed, threw on some clothes, and went out onto his balcony.

The autumn air, laden with moisture, wrapped Bruno like a cool blanket. Bruno could see just a few flickering flames dotting the coast.

"Concrete and stone," said a voice from the darkness.

"What?" The voice startled Bruno. He looked and saw a figure on the dark balcony to his right. "What are you talking about?"

"Naples is made of concrete and stone," said Father Tommaso. "She won't burn all the way. Even if there's no one left to put out the flames."

"That's all you've got to say, Father? No comforting words while everything crumbles to shit?"

Bruno heard a shrug in Father Tommaso's voice as he answered. "Everything in this world ends. Civilizations, cities, people. All of it. I talked about it during my sermon. You should have come. You can't fight this, Bruno. This is the end of our song."

"*You* can't fight it. Or you *won't* fight it. But I will."

"How?"

Bruno thought for a moment. "I'll live to see tomorrow."

"Someday, sooner or later, it *will* be the end—*your* end."

"But not today. I'll take one more day and call it victory." Bruno tired of this debate. "Buona notte, Father Tommaso," said Bruno as he returned to his flat. Bruno heard a response, but shut his balcony doors before Father Tommaso had finished speaking.

Bruno looked around his gloomy flat. Still restless from pain and fear, his mind raced. He began to wonder if they were going to come for him anyway, even though they were so few. He blocked the apartment door with the dresser and got back in bed. The slightest bump or creak caused him to reach for his pistol. Bruno had resolved that he'd die fighting if he had to. Images lingered in his mind, keeping him from sleep, though he was bone-tired; images of that woman's eyes fixed on his and her head shattering into bone and blood and brains. But after a long struggle against his own mind, Bruno fell asleep sitting up, with pillows propped against the headboard, his last thoughts not of murder and death, but of his sister, alone.

CHAPTER 10

November 6

The rain had stopped, but the wind still blew strong enough to rattle the balcony door. Bruno pulled blankets over his head and huddled against the cold. It was ten days since he'd set foot outside his apartment. Ten days of listening to the world fall apart on his radio and battling more fear than he'd ever known. Twelve days since he'd escaped the hospital. Twelve days since he saw Carla.

Bruno rubbed his itchy beard and looked over at the radio on his nightstand.03:43. The more he fought to sleep, the more awake he became. Not for the first time, he wondered if the ship had come the night he and Cristian were supposed to evacuate. When they didn't show up, had their colleagues looked for them? How long did they stay? As he lay there, staring at the ceiling, he thought of his father. And he thought of Carla.

Bruno gave up; there was no retuning to slumber now. After a week, the ache in his ribs had finally subsided, and the last few days he had slept on his side again. He rolled onto his back and looked around his apartment. In the dark, water-filled bottles glinted here and there from the scattered moonlight. Condensation covered the bottom halves of the glass doors to his balcony. Bruno yearned for fresh air, as the air in his apartment weighed stuffy and close on him. He knew he stank. With the grid down for so long, running water had finally gone too. And he'd been loath to waste his bottled water on bathing. But while he craved the smell of the outdoors, the cold wind dissuaded him from opening the balcony door. That, along with the plastic bags of his own feces that he'd been tossing on the balcony. He didn't know what else to do with them; he was afraid to throw them off the balcony lest someone spot the obvious sign of habitation in the alley below. Bruno figured if his own balcony got full, he could start tossing the bags onto Father Tommaso's. That would get the old bastard's attention. If he was still there. If he was still alive.

For what seemed like the hundredth time over the last few days, Bruno got up and knocked on the wall separating his apartment from Father Tommaso's.

"Father, are you there?"

He knocked a few more times and called out, but got no response.

Bruno went back to his bed and sat down. Fumbling in the darkness, he found the "on" switch on the radio. Even though extra batteries lay under his bed, Bruno rationed his radio use as much as he could stand. Can't just go to the store anymore.

When a female voice roared out, Bruno turned the volume down to almost nothing, just enough to hear over the cry of the wind.

The synthvoice was good, almost good enough to fool even Bruno, but not quite. It was too perfect to be real. She (even Bruno couldn't bring himself to think "it") spoke about safe zones, hospital openings, and checkpoints. Bruno had spent the last week listening to her lilting speech. Her voice had that same resonant ring he remembered from the recordings of his great-aunt Teresa's opera singing. But none of what the voice said impacted him here on the island. Probably all fucking lies anyway.

What he wouldn't give for a good, old-fashioned shortwave radio, now that the power grid was off-line, seemingly for good. Shortwave! Bruno almost laughed at himself for thinking such a thought. What good would it do anyway? He couldn't think of one European—or other major international broadcast radio station—that still used shortwave. Only religious nuts and right-wing propagandists used shortwave. And, of course, cranky old *radioamatori*, ham radio operators, too. Those damned pads, tablets, e-books, and most every other electronic device ever invented were no better than bricks now. Bruno wondered, if maybe—

A sound snapped him back to his musty apartment. Bruno's body tensed. Did he hear something? Was it the wind? Bruno shut off the radio and listened. Nothing but howling wind and rustling branches. His shoulders slumped. Then *tat-tat-tat-tat* again. The sound, more insistent now, came from the door to the outside hallway of his apartment building. Whatever caused the noise was just outside his front door. He reached for his pistol and holster, strapping it around his waist.

Tat-tat-tat.

He crept towards the low dresser blocking his door so that he could look through the peephole. He leaned towards the hole, pistol in his right hand. Darkness in the hallway, yet Bruno felt as much as saw a dark shape.

Tat-tat-tat.

Bruno readied his pistol. Then a whisper floated in from the outside.

"Ricasso, are you in there?"

It was a male voice.

He knows who lives here, Bruno thought. He knows who I am! Whoever was outside wasn't seeking just anyone. Bruno's thumb moved the safety up with a satisfying click and he backed off the dresser, pistol raised. He wondered how much the door's mass would affect a bullet's speed and trajectory.

"If you're in there . . . they've got Carla."

Bruno froze for a moment, then scrambled onto the dresser and pressed his eye to the peephole. The man turned on the flashlight he'd used to knock on the door and Bruno now saw him. Even though the respirator covered the bottom half of his face, Bruno recognized him instantly.

Son of a bitch!

"Battisti! Why are you here?"

"They've got Carla!"

"Who's got her?"

"Look, just let me in. I can explain—"

"Don't bullshit me! Why shouldn't I shoot you right through this door, you prick?"

"Because if you do, you'll never find her. For Christ's sake, let me in!"

Bruno stared at the pistol in his hand. He heard more than just anger in Battisti's voice; he heard fear. Bruno backed away from the dresser and holstered his pistol.

"Wait where you are," said Bruno.

He donned his uniform pants and the respirator Carla had scavenged from the hospital, then moved the dresser just far enough so the door would open halfway. Bruno unlocked the door and stepped back, a flashlight in his left hand. He aimed the pistol with his right hand and braced it over the flashlight.

The door creaked open, exposing the yawning gloom of the hallway beyond and the dark figure of Battisti. Bruno swept the flashlight up and down, taking note of the streaks of soot and blood on Battisti's wet uniform and face.

"Let me see your hands."

Battisti sidled into the doorway, hands in the air. Battisti's hands were empty. But they trembled.

"You're infected!" Bruno recoiled. "Get the fuck out of here before I shoot you!"

"Bruno, just listen, I know where you sister is—she can help me—but I need your help to get her."

Bruno gripped his pistol even tighter. He didn't know what Battisti meant, but the hope of finding his sister overcame his fear of infection.

"Take your weapon out of your holster and place it on the dresser behind you," Bruno ordered.

"But—"

"Do it *slowly* or I'll blow your head off."

"All right, take it easy." Battisti, now fully in Bruno's apartment, un-holstered his pistol and placed it on the dresser. Bruno stood by his bed, keeping his pistol trained on Battisti.

"Put your hands on your head and clasp your fingers together."

Battisti complied without a word.

"Now talk. Who's got her?"

Bruno shone the flashlight directly in Battisti's eyes and Battisti squinted. "I don't know. Raiders, looters, whatever you call them. They've got her."

"How?"

"There were only six Ministry of Health guards when you escaped. And as of a few hours ago, only three were left . . ."

Battisti exhaled loudly. "And they captured one of them. Poor bastard, DiFalco. The others are dead."

Bruno couldn't give a damn about Battisti's goons, but he wanted to know where Battisti's information came from.

"How did you find me?"

"I took a look at your records before the interrogation. That was when things were still working, more or less." Battisti paused. "Not that long ago, was it? When things were working, I mean. Couldn't remember your exact apartment number, though."

Battisti shook his head. "Took me longer that I thought it would to find you, even after I got to your building. But as you may have noticed, you seem to be the only one home, so that made finding you a little easier, at least."

Wanker, Bruno thought. "If you knew where I lived, why didn't you come get me before?"

"Couldn't spare the men. Like I said, there were only six guards and me. Seven for the whole hospital. Not nearly enough to run around to try to find you."

"So what happened?"

"What the hell do you think happened? We had a containment breach, the disease got loose, so most of the others bolted. Simple as that. I got infected. And then *they* came. Nine of them. But we didn't have a combat mission. We had to try to protect what was left of the hospital staff. Made things more difficult when the enemy doesn't care who they kill. At least now there are four less looters to deal with."

"So, we need to go back to the hospital. You must have had weapons, rifles, supplies—"

"We *did*." Battisti looked down. "The drone ran out of fuel. So we didn't have any surveillance. And before we spotted them, they dropped I don't know how many Molotov cocktails on us." Battisti met Bruno's eyes again. "They burned us out. Now it's torched. I was lucky to escape."

"And the patients, the staff?"

"Dead. All dead—all except Carla. Instead of just helping you escape, she should have gone with you."

Bruno needed a second to absorb the news. "How did you know that Carla . . ."

Battisti laughed.

"Come on! Do you think I'm an idiot? She is your sister, of course if she found out you were there, she'd help you. You couldn't have escaped without help. So, I tried to have her removed and turned onto the street, let her fend for herself, like everyone else. But the high-IQ boys at the Ministry of Health wanted all doctors treated with kid gloves, no matter what they did—Infection Control Protocol 151 said so. So, I followed orders. But I'm done following orders now."

Bruno's patience grew short and his arms tired from keeping the pistol trained on Battisti.

"How do you know where Carla is?"

"After I escaped I followed them. But there was nothing I could do. I'm one person. So I gambled. I came here, hoping I'd find you. Gamble paid off, didn't it? Still, it took me a couple hours to get back across the island."

Hours? God knows what they had done to her by now. "Where did they take her? What the hell took you so long to get here?"

"So long? I didn't know I was on a goddamn schedule. I wasn't sure where I was going, and I had to make sure I wasn't spotted. They took her to a house outside of the village of Capri. I don't know the island very well, but I think it's on that road on the way to Villa Jovis."

Bruno paused, recalling that part of the island.

"I think I know what you're talking about—that building borders on an open field, just before the path winds up to the ruins on Monte Tiberio. They'll have good sightlines, since there's not much cover until the path starts. We need to get there before dawn. It's five or six kilometers from here, but it's hardly a straight shot on the roads." Bruno holstered his pistol. "But tell me one thing. Why do *you* care about finding Carla? You've got the disease. What good does it do you to find my sister? You're going to die."

Battisti unclasped his hands from his head and lowered them. "When I told HQ that we had a containment breach, their last comm said backup or extraction would be provided as 'circumstances permit.'" Battisti scoffed. "Lies. All lies. They weren't going to save us. They cut us loose, good-bye! Except they didn't have the balls to tell us. They're liars, Bruno. And they've lied to us from day one about this Omega Plague. Antivirals *can* stop it—I heard your sister say it. I'm just at the early stages. She—

she can help me find antivirals; she can help me live. She'll know what to do—I know!"

Bruno remembered what his sister had said about the antivirals, but he wasn't about to tell Battisti that he was mistaken. Or just delusional.

"How do I know she's still alive?" said Bruno.

"They wanted information from her. They were asking her things."

Bruno's eyes narrowed. "What things?"

Battisti shook his head. "I couldn't hear exactly. She just kept screaming 'I don't know.' Until they get what they're after, they'll keep her alive. Unfortunately for her."

Alive. Screaming. The full impact of what must be happening to his sister began to burrow into his mind. He needed to hurry. "We leave now," said Bruno. "I have a motorcycle, but we'll have to go on foot. They'd hear us long before they saw us, even with this wind."

Of course, Bruno didn't trust Battisti. Battisti's irrational hope that Carla could save him showed he was becoming unhinged. A man like Battisti, desperate and egomaniacal, would do anything to save his own life. But the blood and soot on Battisti's uniform spoke more about what had happened than any words Battisti could have said. That, and the tremors in his hands. Sweat, too, beaded on Battisti's forehead. And it was not a warm night. Battisti was probably lying about how far along his infection had progressed, but what choice did Bruno have?

"Let's do this," said Bruno.

***

Light had yet not broken over the mainland to the east when they came to the point where the road became a footpath. The wind and rain from earlier that night had died down and the sky was clear, but the storm left everything moist and slick. Wearing the respirator made Bruno's breathing labored and fatigued him. Listening to Battisti's increasingly paranoid raving was almost as fatiguing. And Battisti's cough, much worse in just the last hours, made his voice hoarse.

Bruno looked down the road toward a building ahead. The moon shone in the sky, not quite full, but giving enough illumination to make their way without resorting to flashlights. The beauty of the grey stone cliffs to their right, sloping south and east toward the open sea, struck Bruno even through the netting he wore wrapped around his head. Bruno and Battisti sheltered behind two pine trees that grew together into a V-shape, each thicker than a man, with scrubby bushes at their base. Bruno hoped the vegetation would provide enough cover to keep both of them hidden from view. The cream-colored stone building stood at the end of Via Tiberio, just as the road turned into a winding path leading up to Villa Jovis, the ruins of the Roman Emperor Tiberius' summer house. A whitewashed solid stone railing, really a low wall, led from the narrow road up to the front door. While Bruno couldn't see the stairs themselves because of the railing, he knew they were there, as many houses on the island shared a similar entryway. Thick bushes grew below the window on the side of their approach. Dark wooden shutters covered the window, obscuring any view inwards. A scaffold leaned against the back of the building. To Bruno, it looked like the building had once been a residence that had been converted into a café, judging by the sign that hung over the entrance.

"That's it," Battisti muttered. As they watched, a man with a bandanna over his face walked out onto the landing, his lower body obscured by the stone railing. The man stood there, looking around. He pulled the bandanna down, took something from his pocket, and turned his back to them. When he turned around, Bruno could see the orange-red glow of a cigarette dangling from the man's mouth.

"Why would they come out this way?" said Battisti.

Bruno shook his head. "Not sure. The ruins are on a high point, the closest part of the island to Sorrento. Good views of the whole Amalfi coast, the Bay of Naples and the Gulf of Salerno. Maybe that has something to do with it."

"Probably why good old Tiberius built a villa there in the first place," said Battisti. "Maybe this lot isn't as stupid as your average lowlife."

"I don't care if they're the captains of Napoli, Milan, and fucking Juventus, they're still animals," said Bruno. "What now?"

Battisti took out his pistol and pointed it at the man. Battisti's hands trembled

"Christ, you're not going to try to shoot him from here, are you?" said Bruno.

Battisti lowered his pistol, suppressing a cough. "No, I'm not going to shoot, just sizing up the distance." He re-holstered the pistol. "I won a marksmanship competition in the States three years ago, you know. The Americans and Brits thought *they* were the best, but I showed them." Bruno couldn't see Battisti's face well, with the dark and the netting over both their heads, but he could hear the irritation in his voice.

Bruno wondered who Battisti really was, whether he belonged to some kind of Special Forces unit, and who his bosses really were. If they got out of this alive, Bruno resolved to find out.

"We need to get in closer before we do anything," said Battisti in a rasping whisper. "Scout them out first before taking any of them out. See if we can find out where they are in relation to each other." Battisti coughed softly into his respirator.

"I'm fine," said Battisti. "Must have swallowed wrong."

Bruno shifted away from Battisti. "What about the bushes under the window?" said Bruno. "I might be able to get a look through the shutters."

Battisti paused, considering the idea. "Yes—risky, though." Then he nodded. "But I don't see another option. Get to the bushes, then signal how many there are. The windows on the building are low. I see a window behind the scaffold. Once you see where they are, I'll climb the scaffold and," Battisti reached into his jacket and pulled put a canister, "I'll drop this through the back window."

"Tear gas?"

"No, better; a vapor grenade," said Battisti. "Salvaged it from our gear at the hospital."

"What is it?"

"Tear gas without the smoke, enough to gas a whole house," said Battisti.

"I've never heard of a 'vapor grenade.'"

"Yeah, because it's not usually authorized for domestic use. But who gives a shit now," said Battisti. "I can set it off in a back room and they won't know what the hell is up. Their first instinct will be to find fresh air. Then we can deal with them in an open area; take them out before they know what hit them."

Battisti turned his head toward the house. "Looks like the scaffolding is blocking the back wall and any door that might be there. Good. Means they have only one way out."

"But my sister, she—"

"We'll have to fucking aim carefully when we shoot. Signal me with the number of people and how many are armed. Once you signal, take cover across the path in those trees and bushes." Battisti pointed down the road. "Looks like they're about ten meters from the front entrance. After I drop the grenade, I'll circle round."

Battisti continued to look down the path. "Cazzo," he swore. "That's the only cover near the front entrance. I'll have to hide near you. If we were lucky, there'd be somewhere else I could hide, and we could set up a real ambush—get them from different angles. But we're not lucky."

"Not really cover, is it," said Bruno. "Just a bit of concealment. Some bushes aren't going to stop bullets."

Battisti didn't answer.

"So, this is the best we can do, eh?" said Bruno. "Flush them out and shoot?"

"You want to knock on the fucking door? This is the best plan I can think of right now, Mr. Carabiniere. So, if you have another idea, a better one, let's hear it."

"I don't."

Battisti nodded. "All right, then. We'll go as soon as he's back inside. Once I set the grenade off, it'll fully discharge in about fifty seconds. In a building that small, I'd say we have another minute before the gas reaches them. Should be plenty of time to get to the trees before they come out."

Battisti's worsening cough frayed Bruno's nerves as they waited. A glow grew across the eastern horizon, and Bruno feared the coming morning light would destroy any chance of approaching undetected. But then, after dropping his cigarette to the stairs, the man turned and entered the house.

Battisti tapped Bruno on the arm. "Let's go!" They jogged in a low crouch until they reached the side of the house. Bruno worked his way through the bush while Battisti stood at the back corner, waiting for Bruno's signals.

Bruno heard a woman's cries and men's laughter. For the first time in his life, his mother's and brother's death seemed like a blessing, not a curse. They were dead and buried, and would never have to know the sick horrors that Carla must surely have endured.

The window was just above his head, so Bruno stepped onto one of the bush's lower branches. It provided just enough height for him to get his head above the window's ledge, though it was precarious, and he leaned against the ledge. The long window had no glass, but gaps in the shutter's slats let him peer into the room. By now, the fast-approaching dawn gave enough light for Bruno to see figures in the room.

Bruno counted five men, milling around a room strewn with upturned wooden tables and chairs, looking to Bruno like what used to be a main dining area. They all wore masks or bandanas around their faces. When one of the men moved, Bruno saw her sitting on the floor. The bruises on Carla's face almost made him gasp. She stared at the floor, her green hospital scrubs stained with blood and dirt. Her hands were bound in front.

One of the five stood apart from the others, away from Carla. Bruno couldn't quite see him, his face hidden in shadows as the man spoke.

"Again!"

Another man kicked Carla in the gut.

The man in the shadows spoke in a low growl. "This is going to be a long day unless you tell us where he is. Where does he live?"

Carla's voice was quavering. "I've told you—I've told you. I don't know where he is."

The man in the shadows laughed. "Oh, I think you do! Your hospital was the only place on the island with any pigs left. All the rest are gone or dead." He moved closer to a shaft of light. "That's part of the reason we went there, right, boys? To kill pigs?" The other men laughed.

"But the Boss said to find you. And then you could help us find *him*. The guard said there was a Carabiniere at the hospital before we got there. So we know he's on the island."

He's looking for me? Bruno thought. But who—

"I know he can't be at the station 'cause I torched it myself!" Bruno began to shiver, and not from the cold.

"So," the man strode forward and turned toward Carla. "You don't want to end up like that poor guard, do you? You're his sister. So, you must know where he lives. And I think you'd better tell me . . ."

"Listen, Enzo, let me have her for a bit. I'll get her to talk," said a man with a greasy ponytail and a shotgun.

Enzo, the one who had been doing most of the talking, moved into the light, but with his back toward Bruno. He had close-cropped black hair, and the straps of a respirator covered part of his head.

"I should give you to Damiano," said Enzo. "He likes you a lot. You up for another round with the doctor?"

"Absolutely. I'll make sure there's still enough of her left for Il Serbo when we bring her back," said Damiano.

"The Boss is after the brother, not her. He's the one we want. She's just the way to find him," said Enzo. "Now Alessio here can be very persuasive, right, Doc?"

Carla whimpered. A man wearing a *chiodo* jacket, its black leather and silver zippers glinting, laughed. "Sure," said Alessio. "Let me have her—again. I'll get her to talk."

Bruno forced himself to look around. Bruno noticed a pistol on the small of Enzo's back, poking out from under his olive-drab jacket and t-shirt. He couldn't tell whether or not anyone else, other than Damiano, carried a firearm.

Bruno turned his head toward Battisti at the far corner of the house, canister in hand, waiting. Bruno gestured "five," then signed the number "two," and touched his sidearm.

Battisti nodded, and moved out of sight behind the house. Bruno extracted himself from the bush and in a crouch, scurried along the side of the house and out across the path to the stand of bushes and two trees. He crouched down, took out his pistol, and waited. A few seconds later, Battisti ran across the path to Bruno's position, pistol in hand.

Just as Bruno took aim toward the entrance, shouting erupted from inside the building. Screaming and swearing, the group stumbled out of the building, coughing and gagging as they fanned out on the path. Enzo held a pistol in one hand, and Damiano had the shotgun slung around his back. He gripped Carla by her hair as they both coughed and spit. Alessio was bent over close by, panting. The other two stumbled a little away from the rest as they struggled to breathe. Bruno and Battisti wasted no time eliminating the two that had moved off. Battisti fired two bullets in succession.

One found its mark, dropping a man, and Bruno shot another in the head, and he collapsed.

Enzo fired toward them, but not really taking aim. Battisti crouched lower in response and fired back.

Bruno grabbed Battisti's arm.

"You'll hit Carla!"

Battisti broke Bruno's grip and elbowed him in the temple with one fluid motion. Bruno fell to his knees. A kick on the back knocked him on his stomach. Bruno felt hands yanking his pistol.

"I could have got him! I know what I'm fucking doing!" shouted Battisti.

More shots rang out.

Bruno forced himself to move, rolling onto his side just in time to see Enzo, Damiano, and Alessio fleeing up the path towards the ruins. Damiano had Carla slung over his back as he bounded up the path. Enzo pointed his pistol backwards, firing without looking back, and Battisti returned fire as he ran after in hot pursuit. They rounded a bend in the path, disappearing from view behind stone columns, trees, and scrub.

"Wait!" But it was too late. Bruno struggled to his feet. He didn't care that he had no pistol now. His only thought was to find Carla. That fucking nut Battisti was going to get her killed. Bruno had to move quickly.

Bruno staggered up the path, lined by pitted stone columns and heavy scrub. He slowed down as he reached the end of the path and found himself standing amid low walls and ruined columns, the flat, red brick and grey stone construction typical of old Roman ruins. The path cut directly into the ruins, becoming long brick stairs and sloping upward between two walls that stretched well over his head. Still dizzy, Bruno crept up the stairs into Villa Jovis against the wall, one hand brushing against the crumbling stonework. Listening for any signs of a struggle, he heard nothing except the sighs of the wind and songs of birds, now that dawn had truly broken. A multi-level maze of ruins and walls, Villa Jovis lay perched on top of Monte Tiberio, and provided ample space and hiding places. Bruno thought a search would be futile at best, and he only had a passing familiarity with the ruins. So, he decided to take the path he knew best and make for the highest point in the ruins, the one place he could survey most of the ruins from above: il Salto di Tiberio, the Leap of Tiberius, the place where the old emperor cast those he disfavored down sheer cliffs into the sea.

Bruno picked his way up the stairs, winding up and through the ruins. His head swam from the blow to his temple, and he missed the comfort of anonymous dark. Every time he turned a corner or the path opened up into a once-great room now exposed to the sky, Bruno paused, peering around, before proceeding with speed to the next narrow portion in what used to be hallways.

Bruno started up the stairs that led to the Leap. He picked his way with care until he heard the sounds and shouts of men wrestling. Bruno leapt up the rest of the stairs, but just before emerging onto the flat top of the hill, he paused out of sight, trying to plan as cursing and yells rattled his concentration. Then, the blast of a shotgun followed by a scream rang in Bruno's ears. He poked his head just enough above the wall along the stairs to get a look.

Stones and weeds littered the small hilltop, some twenty meters across, that was the Leap. A low, black railing ran around the area, defining the safe zone where people could admire the views of the island and the sea without risking death on the cliffs. Some tall grass and bushes grew along parts of the railing. Bruno could not see Carla anywhere. Damiano stood with his back to Bruno, but Bruno could see he held a shotgun. Damiano stood no more than three meters from the stairs. Bruno saw Battisti on his knees, the red of his blood making a shocking contrast to the grey camouflage pattern on his shirt. For a moment, Battisti seemed suspended upright. Then, in an instant, he fell on his face in the dirt, like a puppet with its strings cut.

Bruno rushed towards the scene hoping to get a hand on the shotgun before Damiano turned and dealt Bruno the same fate. Damiano whirled, his ponytail whipping around his face, but Bruno wrapped his hands on the barrel of the shotgun just in time.

The shotgun blasted into the earth, spraying up soil and pebbles. Bruno clung to the barrel and butted his forehead against Damiano's face. Bruno pressed the advantage, pushing the shotgun toward Damiano, but Damiano tripped and fell, jerking the shotgun out of Bruno's grip. It fell, clattering over the rail and down the cliffs.

The split-second Bruno watched the falling gun gave Damiano a chance to grab Bruno's ankle and yank. Bruno fell to his back. Damiano pulled a pistol from the small of his back and Bruno kicked at his hand, knocking the pistol into the grass. Damiano turned to find the pistol, but Bruno scrambled on top of him. They struggled, rolling in the grass, looking for the pistol, but Damiano ended up on Bruno's chest. Bruno clutched at Damiano's hands as they squeezed his neck. He bore down, throttling Bruno's windpipe. Against all instinct, Bruno let his right hand off Damiano's and slid it underneath his back.

Frenzy shone in Damiano's eyes just before they flickered to his left and he saw a black blade. Bruno felt his blade nick past Damiano's ribs as he buried the knife up to its hilt. Damiano fell forward, gurgling, and Bruno's breath came in gasps as he rolled Damiano off of him. Bruno yanked the blade from Damiano's chest.

He stood and looked at his hands, the black leather of his gloves now covered in the dead man's blood.

Bruno dropped his knife and yanked off his gloves. As he fought to keep from vomiting into his respirator, he felt more than saw some shadow behind him. He ducked, but something grazed across the back of his head and knocked him forward over Damiano's body.

"Pig, you're dead!" someone shouted.

Bruno rolled to his back, next to Damiano.

Alessio held a flat red brick in one hand, its color standing out like a stain against the black leather of the chiodo jacket he wore. Alessio's shadow fell over Bruno as he tried to slither backwards, all the while feeling around for the pistol, or even his knife. Alessio simply kept stepping forward, and when he smiled, Bruno saw a mouth full of yellowed teeth. "You came back for the girl, eh? You're that cop, aren't you?" he spat. "You know, when we took turns, she screamed like a real dirty fu—"

A gunshot reverberated around the Leap. Alessio staggered forward a step, then turned. Another shot. Alessio clutched at his gut and fell forward to his knees. Chest heaving, he collapsed on his face in the stones and grass.

Bruno pushed himself up on his elbows.

"Carla!"

She stood there holding a pistol with her arms stretched forward. Her hands, still bound, shook, and she dropped the pistol to the ground.

Bruno rose to his feet with caution, staggering. He touched the back of his head; his fingers came back sticky with blood.

He wiped his hand on his pants before he spoke, then looked at Carla and smiled.

Carla smiled too, but when he approached her, she backed away, shaking her head.

"Carla?" He gathered his pistol off the ground. "What are you doing—"

By now, Carla stood dangerously close to the rail. Bruno stepped toward her. "Carla," he said, "you'll fall! Come ba—" But he heard the sound of a stone clattering on the stairs to his right. He yanked out his pistol and fired toward the sound. The crack of responding gunfire echoed in Bruno's ears.

He threw himself behind the crumbling remains of a partial wall at the top of the stairs and continued firing four or five shots without looking. Then he heard a thud. When he peeked down the stairs from behind his cover, Bruno caught a glimpse of the back of Enzo's head before he rounded a bend and disappeared into the ruins.

Bruno felt the urge to press his unlikely advantage now that Il Serbo's gang lay dead, to find Enzo and kill him. If Enzo escaped, Il Serbo would almost certainly guess that Bruno was on Capri and still lived, for who else would have tried to rescue Carla? But the pain in Bruno's head and wobbling knees forced him to rethink. That, and Carla. He couldn't leave her again. He would never leave her again, not while there was breath in his body. Bruno holstered his pistol and turned, walking toward her.

"Please," she said. "Please don't come any closer."

"Look, we've got to get out of here, to get to my place. Come on, there's no time for—"

"Bruno, look at my hands!" she screamed. "Look at my hands!" They were trembling.

"Carla, I know you're scared, but you have to come back with me to—"

Carla looked at him. "I'm infected."

He shook his head. "No, no, that isn't true, you're just nervous, you—"

"There's nothing you can do. I don't want to get you sick."

She stepped back, almost to the rocky edge. "This is the only way . . ."

"Not like this." Bruno's voice was barely above a whisper.

She smiled. "Thank you for coming back for me, Bruno. I wish . . ."

Then her lips mouthed the words, "I'm sorry," and she took her final step, tumbling backwards over the edge in complete silence.

Bruno's shouts broke over the Leap, masking the dull thud of her body as it tumbled over the rocks on the way down to the sea below. He wept like he'd never done before, not even that night when his mother and younger brother had died. When his sobs finally faded, Bruno gazed around, still in bewilderment and shock. He did not know what to do. But then his hand strayed to the ground and he felt something cold, something metal. His eyes, blurry from tears, looked down and made out the sharp lines of his knife in the grass. Its dark blade was a black shadow amid the scrub and grey stones. He grasped it, an anchor, pulling him out of his stupor and back to reality.

Bruno stood up, the handle of his knife biting into his palm. He stared at the knife before wiping it on the grass. Once he had removed most of the blood, Bruno placed the knife with care in its sheath at the small of his back. He wiped his eyes with the back of his hand. He looked around the hilltop, surveying the carnage around him, his senses slowly returning.

His gaze fell on the man Carla had shot. To Bruno's amazement, Alessio still lived. He crawled on his belly, dragging himself toward the stairs and leaving a trail of blood, like a slug leaves mucus. For a while, Bruno stared at Alessio as he inched his way over weeds and rocks towards the stairs. Then he walked over and stood beside the prostrate man. Bruno heard him suppressing gasps of pain, his whimpering growing louder. With one foot, Bruno rolled Alessio onto his back. Blood and foam oozed from the corner of the Alessio's mouth, and his dark eyes filled with fear.

Bruno retrieved his gloves. He returned to the dying man and knelt beside him on one knee. As he tried to speak, Alessio's lips trembled. Bruno took his knife from its sheath. Alessio began to sob. Holding the knife in a reverse grip, Bruno plunged his knife down into Alessio's throat. He left the knife in for a long moment, then pulled it out.

"Brutto pezzo di merda," said Bruno as he wiped his knife on the grass.

Bruno stood up and cast off his bloody gloves, their purpose fulfilled. He looked down at his naked hands. Not a trace of blood stained them. Bruno searched the area, scavenging whatever he thought he could use from the dead bodies. He found that Battisti still had Bruno's pistol stashed at the small of his back. Battisti's pistol was the one Bruno had kicked away, the one that Carla had used. A standard 9mm and the same model as Bruno's, he put it in his waistband, then dumped the bodies over the side of the cliffs down to the sea. He walked the short distance back from outside the railing to the top of the stairs. Bruno stood at the top of the stairs and started down. After a few steps he turned to his right, peering out over the ruined wall at the top of the stairs before he descended too far to see over it. He stopped just before he reached eye level to the ground.

Tiberius' Leap remained the same grassy, stony patch, just as it always had, barely scarred by the centuries or by the death on it today. The morning light bathed it in a beautiful glow, belying the horrors that had gone on there. Bruno supposed he should not have been surprised. This place had seen much death all those centuries ago. Why should these four deaths today be special? In the end, what did they really matter?

Bruno walked down the stairs, pistol in hand and senses acute, but utterly alone.

CHAPTER 11

December 15

The reds and oranges of the evening sky lightened Bruno's mood. He started through the balcony doors and over the water. But the perfect tones of the synthvoice brought him back. He laughed at the bullshit she spouted while he sat at his kitchen table, tearing sheets into wide strips.

—The following hospitals in the Province of Caserta are accepting patients: Saint Anne and Sebastian Hospital, Saint Michael's Hospital. Entrance is limited to those currently manifesting symptoms of HAV. All patients will be treated with care and dignity during in-processing—

"Care and dignity?"

—Please bring your national ID card or other form of identification—

"Why? So that you can notify next of kin when you murder them?" Bruno shook his head. "Can't they program you to sing? Something from *Aida*, maybe?"

—All individuals admitted must abide by emergency regulations or face expulsion—

"What's the matter, Teresa? You don't like opera?"

Bruno continued to tear strips down the length of the sheet. "Or just not *Aida*?" Sometimes he used his knife to get a tear started.

—Asymptomatic individuals will not be admitted under any circumstances—

"Of course; no reason to kill them, eh?"

—Asymptomatic individuals will be directed to the nearest emergency shelter for further assistance—

"Oh, I mean—no reason to kill them *yet*, right?"

—Treatment will begin as soon as possible on all those admitted—

Bruno surveyed the wide strips in a pile on his table. "There, I think that might be enough to reach from here to the ground." He sighed. "Hopefully, I'll never need to go out over my balcony, right? But, before I finish the rope, first: the door."

Teresa continued to speak as Bruno gathered up some tools and brackets scavenged from a hardware store. Bruno was tired of her lies. He knew there was one other station still operating. But he scanned the FM and AM bands hoping for something other than that station, his last alternative, his only alternative: Radio Vaticano. Finding no other, he left the radio tuned there. Its signal was crisp. Bruno sighed when the man's voice filled the room. Whatever group had taken over the Vatican after the pope died was incessant in its broadcasts. The voice hissed at Bruno as he moved to the door with his equipment.

—I am your way, your truth and your life now. Not Him—

Bruno began to screw a bracket into the wood frame on the left side of the door. Without power tools, he wasn't sure how long this would take. What did that matter? He had nothing but time. He turned the screwdriver, firmly pressing the screw. It bit into the wood. Slowly. He turned the screw again. And again.

—I am the Lord, your God. Not that carpenter from Nazareth—

As the man's voice droned on, Bruno envisioned the brackets mounted, holding a wooden beam across the door, making his apartment that much safer.

—Caesar and Pontiff, we are one—

Turn. Turn.

—Those who can hear my voice, you must know that your end approaches! Your end is—

Bruno threw down his screwdriver, stomped over to the radio, and tuned the dial in to the pirate radio frequency. The only sound that came from the speaker was a soft hiss.

He lingered for a moment over the radio. Then he picked up the screwdriver and returned to the door.

The white noise soothed him. But sometimes Bruno thought he could hear voices in the static.

CHAPTER 12

January 23

The cool winter sun shone down, making the afternoon shadows sharp and movement easy to spot. Bruno darted into the alley behind his apartment building, hoping he hadn't been seen. He heard them smashing windows, laughing. This wasn't the first group Bruno had seen, here and there. Some looked like families and friends. Others looked like people together because they had no one else. Bruno didn't go out of his way to hide, reasoning that if they spotted him hiding, they might think he was a threat. He kept weapons concealed, relying on the respirator and dark sunglasses to make him look alien, ominous. And he always moved with a purpose, never looking like he was just wandering. Even though he really was wandering, looking for some untouched shop or home, searching for food or equipment. He kept an eye out for antennas or something that would give away the location of the pirate radio broadcaster, who must have had quite a radio setup, and given his conspiracy-minded rantings, maybe other even more useful items as well, like firearms. But old antennas from another era littered the roofs of Anacapri, making the search difficult.

So far, when others saw Bruno, they avoided him. But this was the first group in Anacapri he'd seen vandalize for fun. Bruno needed to avoid them.

His pack was heavy with cans of soup and sauce and a book. A good haul. Carla would have liked that chickpea soup he found and—Bruno squeezed his eyes shut. Thoughts of her were a distraction; they would have to wait until he was safe.

When Bruno opened his eyes, the sounds of people were gone.

He crept out of the alley and around to the front of his building. The empty street stretched in both directions. That prick Battisti had broken the lock on the front door of his apartment building, so there was nothing to stop anyone from coming in. Bruno needed to find materials to fix that on his next run. He pushed the door open with one hand while he held his pistol in the other. Empty and quiet.

He took off his sunglasses and climbed the wide, flat stairs, making sure his footfalls were soft. He arrived on the third floor and walked off the landing. The light from the few windows in the stairway did little to illuminate the gloom of the hall.

He turned right and walked past poor Signora Locurto's apartment. He thought about her corpse, probably still lying where he last saw it those long months ago. Her biscotti were the best he'd ever tasted, and he never had the heart to go back there after seeing her body, twisted and naked on her kitchen floor. But as he approached the door of his own flat, he noticed a bit of light coming from Father Tommaso's door. After what happened on Tiberius' Leap, Bruno had sought the old priest's company. No one ever answered the door, no matter what time of day or night Bruno knocked, and he had given up weeks ago, assuming Father Tommaso must either be dead or gone. Now he saw that the door to the priest's flat was partially open. Was he there? Bruno crept up to the door. He could hear someone moving, rustling inside. With his free hand Bruno pushed open the door.

Father Tommaso's flat was one room, with glass doors to the balcony at the far end. The rest of the mess and disarray barely registered because Bruno saw a man rummaging around the cabinets in the small kitchen area on the right wall.

Bruno pointed his pistol at the man and shouted, "Hands up!"

He turned, stepped back from the cabinets, and retreated away from Bruno towards a small upturned table just to the left of the balcony doors.

"Don't shoot! I'm just looking for food!"

Bruno entered the hallway of the small apartment, keeping his pistol trained on the man. Bruno realized he was not a man, but a pimply faced teenage boy.

"Where is Father Tommaso?"

"Who?"

"The priest who lived here! Did you see him?"

The teenager shook his head, and his voice trembled. "I don't know him! We're just looking for food!"

Bruno paused, wondering what he was going to do, when he realized what the boy had said. We.

"Put your gun on the ground!" said a voice from behind Bruno. "And turn around slowly!" Bruno glanced over his shoulder, just enough to see the glint of a weapon. Bruno complied, gently placing his pistol on the floor. Then he turned. Another teenage kid in blue jeans with shaggy hair pointed a revolver at Bruno.

"Now kick it to me, then sit down."

Bruno did as he was told. As Bruno sat down, the boy with the revolver picked up Bruno's pistol.

"Now that's why we always move with two people!" He tossed the revolver to his partner in the kitchen and laughed. "You take mine. Now I've got the sweet gun, not some old piece of shit!"

"Hey, I wanted his gun," the first one said.

Bruno said nothing as he looked both of them over. The one who had got the drop on Bruno shut the door. This second boy stood in front of the open closet near the entrance, keeping his attention and the pistol firmly trained on Bruno.

"Take off your pack, slowly! And don't stand up."

Bruno shrugged the pack off. "What are you going to do?"

The shaggy-haired boy laughed. "If you're lucky, we'll let you live."

Bruno opened his mouth to speak, but a hand reached out of the closet behind the boy. Bruno saw a flash of steel and blood splattered everywhere. The boy dropped Bruno's pistol with a gurgling scream.

Bruno rolled, grabbed his pistol, and pumped three bullets into the kid with the revolver. The kid dropped to his knees with a cry, his revolver clattering on the stone floor. Ears ringing from the shots in such a confined space, Bruno rolled back to face the threat from the closet.

"Come out slowly, or I'll blow your fucking head off!"

Bruno scrambled to his feet as a figure stepped through the dark clothes and out of the closet. The clothes parted to reveal an old man clutching a bloody butcher's knife.

Bruno gasped. Father Tommaso, wearing an unkempt, grey beard, stepped over the twitching body of the boy.

CHAPTER 13

The priest's eyes narrowed. "Bruno? Is that you?"

Bruno holstered his own pistol and pulled his respirator down. "Yes, it's me, Father."

Father Tommaso's eyes searched Bruno's face. Then the priest nodded.

Bruno looked around at the carnage. Two teenage boys lay dead. Their blood decorated the floor and walls. Bruno put his respirator back on. If they were infected, Bruno didn't know if his respirator would be enough to protect him.

Stepping toward the boy closest to the balcony, Bruno picked up the revolver. It was a .38 Special. He opened the cylinder. Empty.

Bruno looked at the dead boy he had shot. He hadn't given the boy a chance to surrender.

"Unloaded. Why didn't you say something?" Bruno said to the dead boy.

"What did you think he was going to say? You think he would admit he didn't have any bullets?"

Bruno stepped back towards the balcony doors, away from Father Tommaso, who still held the bloody kitchen knife in his hand.

"Father, are you all right? You should cover your face with something."

"Did they follow you here?" The priest had just cut a boy's throat, yet Bruno detected not a hint of remorse in the man's voice.

What Bruno heard was anger. Father Tommaso took another step toward Bruno. The priest left bloody shoe prints behind him.

"I don't know—I think they—"

"You're fucking careless! You led them right to our building!" The priest shook his head. "Help me get these bodies out into the hallway for now."

After moving the bodies and wiping up the blood as best they could, Father Tommaso put his small table back in the kitchenette near the balcony doors. Bruno sat with his back to the cabinets, with the glass doors on his right. His respirator hung loosely around his neck. Father Tommaso had said almost nothing while they were moving the bodies. Bruno thought the killings—or whatever else the priest had been through—must have left him traumatized.

Father Tommaso stood to Bruno's left. "I don't have much to eat. I've got some prepackaged toast. You want some?" said the priest.

"Sure."

The priest rummaged around in one of the cabinets above his sink. Then Father Tommaso walked around the table and sat across from Bruno. They were so close their knees touched. Bruno's back was to the balcony doors, while Father Tommaso had his back to the exit. The priest opened the small package of toast. He handed a piece of the toast to Bruno.

"I'm glad you're still here," said Bruno. "I thought for sure you were dead or gone. What happened to you?"

The crunching of the dry bread sounded loud in Bruno's ears, as it was the only noise in the room. The priest absentmindedly drew circles on the table with his knife, the same knife the priest had used to kill the boy. He didn't look Bruno in the eye. Father Tommaso must have wiped the blade clean at some point, but Bruno could still see a smear of blood near the handle.

"I saw sin and sinners, Bruno. My faith was tested, tested like I couldn't believe. But I'm still here. Still alive. I still have my faith. Do you?"

Bruno bit the toast and chewed for a moment in silence. Then he swallowed. "How could anyone still have faith after all that's happened?"

Father Tommaso smiled. "That was always your problem, wasn't it, Bruno. Your lack of faith."

The priest continued to scratch the table as he spoke, staring at the marks. "But how could you not see what was coming? You know San Gennaro's blood didn't turn to liquid this year? You know what that means?"

Bruno put the toast down on the table. "The legend says bad things are supposed to happen to Naples."

"Legend? Look around you. Bad things did happen! So, why don't you believe?"

"Look, Father, I know it's been hard, being alone, I know because—"

"It's a lack of faith that brought about this judgment from the Lord. The lack of faith of people," Father Tommaso pointed the knife at Bruno, "like you."

"Listen, Father, you can't stay here. Why don't you come with . . ." Bruno's voice trailed off when he noticed the other man's eyes. The whites of Father Tommaso's eyes were a pale yellow.

"Father, look, you need to put down the knife. Then we can talk."

"This is your fault!"

Bruno shook his head. "No, I don't think so." He kept his voice as soothing as he could. "Just calm down and put the knife on the table." Bruno stood up slowly as his hand crept towards his back and his pistol.

Without a sound, Father Tommaso launched himself at Bruno. The knife flashed toward Bruno's gut. Bruno caught the priest's arm with both hands, pushing it to one side, but his momentum smashed them both through the balcony doors. Father Tommaso's wiry strength shocked Bruno but he clung to the priest, fighting to disarm him. If his knife hand got free, the priest would cut Bruno to shreds before he could get to his pistol. A head butt to Bruno rocked him and his knees buckled. Bruno's sudden change in level took the priest by surprise, and Father Tommaso lurched forward. Bruno took one hand off the priest's arm just long enough to yank as hard as he could at Father Tommaso's calf. Father Tommaso went backwards over the railing with a wail.

The sound of the knife hitting the ground echoed in the alley, yet Father Tommaso managed to cling to the bottom bar of the balcony's railing, his legs dangling in the air. Bruno gasped for breath.

"Help me, Bruno! Please!" the priest shouted.

Bruno stood up. He swayed back and forth, still unbalanced as he looked down at his friend. Bruno could already feel the swelling on his cheek where the priest had head-butted him.

"You're infected!" He pulled off his respirator to breathe more easily.

"I was, but I'm better now!" Father Tommaso's hands were white. "Please, I don't know how long—I can—hold . . ."

Bruno rolled his head up and looked at the sky. Father Tommaso struggled, cursing, as he tried to hoist his way back up. Bruno focused on a wisp of cloud in the blue sky. Then he looked down at his friend. Father Tommaso continued to babble.

"Help me! I don't know why I tried to hurt you, I—"

Father Tommaso tried to pull himself up, but then he fell back with a cry, gripping the lower rail, clinging for his life four stories up.

"I'm sorry! Please don't let me die," the priest pleaded.

Bruno watched as Father Tommaso's grip weakened and his hands began to slip.

Father Tommaso panted out words between breaths as his watery, jaundiced eyes focused on Bruno.

"Remember . . . someday will be *your* end."

Father Tommaso fell to the ground screaming. Bruno heard the crunch of his impact and saw the priest's broken body in the alley.

For a few heartbeats, Bruno stared down at his dead friend in silence. Then he turned away and looked back into Father Tommaso's flat. Bruno didn't want to leave these bodies so close to his own place, afraid that if a warm spell came through, the stench would become overwhelming. Bruno was sick of the smell of death. The upper floors of his apartment block had reeked for a long while, until those poor bastards had finally dried out, turned to mummies, or whatever the hell happened to people when they died in their homes with no one to bury them and no scavengers to eat them. But he didn't have the strength right then to do anything about the dead. Bruno's body ached, his face was bruised, and he could feel the blood from the cuts on his head trickling down the back of his neck. Worst of all, he realized that he had twisted his right knee.

Stepping carefully through the broken glass of the door, he shuffled back into the flat and surveyed the mess inside. One thing was clear: Bruno knew that he didn't dare risk being seen anymore. He would have to give up the daylight and move only in the dark. He considered abandoning his flat for another hideout, but he'd be damned if he'd let some teenage looters frighten him out of his home. Bruno would do his best to move in the shadows now, but if there were more, let them come, and he would take care of them, too.

Bruno scooped up his pistol and backpack and began his short journey back to his own flat next door, hoping that his knee was just strained. Anything worse would probably mean that the ultimate winner of the fight lay dead in the alley.

CHAPTER 14

June 1

"Stupid bitch," Bruno muttered as he fumbled with the radio, scanning through the bands, but hearing only hiss and crackling.

"Stupid bitch!" he yelled at the radio. He nearly threw the radio against the floor, only stopping himself at the last moment. He dropped the radio at the foot of his bed.

She was gone. The synthvoice, the last vestige of technological civilization, had disappeared from the airwaves. Teresa had signed off without so much as a farewell to her loyal listener. Bruno's anger seemed strange even to him, since he didn't believe aword she had said over the last few months—talking about safe zones, food drops, and the destruction of the Monte Bianco tunnel to stop refugees from streaming south.

But only now did Bruno realize how dependent he had become on her measured voice, on her punctuality, on the illusion of companionship she provided. Gone. He lay on his bed and rolled onto his back, staring at the ceiling. The bed stank of his own body. He tried to sleep, but though he had been out for hours the previous night, sleep would not come. In the five months since he had killed Father Tommaso, Bruno only left his sanctuary at night, prowling in the dark. He heeded Carla's advice to stay away from people, lest he, too, succumb to the Omega Plague or become the victim of a survivor's madness. Bruno last saw a person, some scavenger in the dark, three months ago, and had slipped away before that sorry figure spotted him.

Each of Bruno's long nights began the same, his rituals providing some structure to his rudderless existence. Opening a can of whatever he had, Bruno gathered his map and his pen, and sat at the table in his kitchenette. He waited for nightfall before going outside. He waited not just for twilight, but for true night. And yet, though he waited with anticipation for the dark to come, when it finally did, he ached with dread. No streetlights. No lights in houses. No one lighting up cigarettes, laughing in the street, and no gaudy lights at the entrances to the dance clubs. No brightly lit yachts plying the waters between the island and the Amalfi coast. No light anywhere, unless the moon and stars were overhead or he made his own light. But in his mind, when he prowled outside, turning on a flashlight or lighting his Zippo in that velvet blackness was a flare, advertising his presence and making him feel naked in the dark. No, he thought, better to brave the dark and remain unseen than expose himself to who knew what. Afraid that he might be followed after what had happened before, he always returned well before dawn to avoid being caught in the light or by mosquitoes.

Most of the time, Bruno now believed he survived alone on the island. But sometimes he noticed things out of place, things that made him realize others, too, may still lurk in dark places: a trash bin moved, a door open, a window shattered. Yet he saw no one. Did he think something had moved when it really hadn't? Was it paranoia? He could never be sure. Bruno wondered if loneliness had poisoned his mind. Increasingly, he had felt the gaze of someone drilling into the back of his head during his nightly runs. But every time he turned, there was, of course, no one there. Two nights ago, the surprise sound of a skeletal cat meowing as it followed him, looking for food, had nearly caused him to shoot. That cat had tasted surprisingly good for something so mangy.

But today as he lay on his bed, almost impatient for darkness to fall, Bruno decided he could stand the dark no more. The night sickened him; he had finally had enough of skulking and hiding.

Bruno got up and moved to his kitchenette, muttering to himself. He pulled open the curtains in front of the glass doors to his balcony and sat at the table. He dragged his backpack from under the table and pulled out a map of the island of Capri. All along the road, stretching into the center of Anacapri, he had placed tiny "X"s denoting the places that he had visited, almost down to the individual house. "Strange," he said out loud, at the thought that he now called what he did "visiting," despite it almost always involving a crowbar and looting. Undoubtedly, the former patrician owners would not have approved. On the bottom of the map he had made notes of anything he'd seen that was of interest.

Bruno realized that he needed an alternative location, another base of operations, in case someone discovered his apartment block or some natural event destroyed it. After killing the old priest, he had found some other places here in Anacapri, in case his own flat was ever looted. But Bruno needed a retreat on another part of the island, just in case something unexpected happened . . . like if Il Serbo came knocking. The thought shocked him. Where had Il Serbo's name come from? Il Serbo was likely long dead. Still, Bruno reasoned, there might be others as bad or worse, or maybe something could happen in Anacapri that he couldn't anticipate. So, Bruno needed to return to the village of Capri. Capri. Bruno hadn't been back that way since the day Carla died. When he had nightmares, they almost always ended with Bruno falling in Carla's place.

Bruno looked out through the glass doors of his balcony and glanced at his watch. Not even noon yet. Time enough to get to Capri and back, if he had to.

He debated whether or not to take his motorcycle. He smiled to himself. Anyone left could hear an engine's roar halfway across the island. So, on foot it would be. He threw on a battered leather jacket. The chiodo hung on him open, unzipped, to keep him from overheating. On each side of the jacket, perfectly round holes reminded Bruno every time he wore it of the fate of its previous owner. He was never really sure why he took that jacket. Maybe it was a trophy. Maybe it was guilt. Or maybe it was just a reminder of how things are. Bruno gathered his backpack and made his way out of his apartment and onto the street.

He looked around. Though grey clouds covered the sky, the light still made his eyes water, so he put on his sunglasses. The whitewashed building where he lived stood behind him. In front of him a stone wall overgrown with ivy and bushes ran along the street. He looked up Via Pagliaro to his left. The street wound east toward the center of Anacapri, and he saw Monte Solaro, a ridge running across the island, dividing Anacapri above from Capri below. That's where he needed to go. He knew he should check on his water collection contraptions on the roof. The garbage barrels, lined with plastic and covered with screens, served to gather rainwater, but he needed to make sure they stayed covered and didn't become a breeding ground for mosquitoes. He also wanted to rig up some tarps to increase the surface area collecting water. But, anxious to begin his trek, he decided it could wait.

Bruno shouldered his backpack and began his return to Capri full of trepidation. The grey afternoon, odd for this time of year, begged for silence. Only a whisper of wind ran down the narrow street. More often than he wanted, Bruno found himself glancing behind him as he half-jogged past shuttered storefronts, through empty *piazze* with their low pastel buildings quaint in their solitude, and motorini strewn about like fallen leaves after a spring storm.

Bruno made his way to Piazza Vittoria, the heart of Anacapri. He stopped and rested for a moment on a patch of rough grass with two neat rows of bushes, a tiny park in the middle of the piazza. As he sipped his bottle of water, he looked up at the bronze statue of winged Victory, sword held high. Bruno remembered the place, although he hadn't been here in months. The stores and boutiques seemed a hair's breadth from liveliness, and Bruno half-expected to see people coming out. The bushes had not yet overgrown their final trimming, but the grass had turned to hay. Bruno put away his water and slung his pack over his shoulder. Time to go.

He walked on the Via Provinciale, the main road out of Anacapri. The narrow road wound out of the village, past villas with their walls and gates, and onto the side of the ridge separating Anacapri above from Capri below. To his right, the sheer rock face stretched into the sky. To his left, a guardrail ran along the side of the road, and he could see out across the bay. The top of Vesuvius poked out from the clouds, but the shoreline of Naples could not be seen, shrouded in the grey haze.

After snaking around the side of the ridge, the road straightened. Houses now grew up along the stone wall to his right, and in front of him the lower part of the island came into view. Capri lay before him, the white stone of its dwellings still splendid even in the dull light.

Bruno lingered on the outskirts of Capri, pausing for a moment while he took another sip from his water bottle and admired the view. Before the Omega Plague, he rode his motorcycle on this street almost every day. He remembered flying down the curves of this road, and yet in all that time he had never really noticed this part of the island, the outskirts before the heart of Capri.

Thoughts from happier days played in his mind until he realized he wasn't far from the hospital. Or what was left of it now. As he surveyed the area, he shivered, the wind picking up speed. It was cool today. He thought of Carla. Then he wondered if maybe he should leave the island. Leave? But where could he go where there were no mosquitoes? The Alps? Switzerland? How would he get there? On foot? By bike? How would he find food? Could he survive the trip? The rational part of Bruno clamped down on the thought of leaving. As far as he knew, all of Europe had mosquitoes at some point during the year. And if the disease was endemic in the environment, then no place was safe. That wasn't even considering the dangers other people might pose, people like Father Tommaso, or even just some gang of scavengers. He knew the island now like an old lover. No, better to stay here.

Bruno's internal debate was interrupted when he spied something he'd never noticed before. A long metal spike stuck straight up maybe ten meters into the air. It projected from amid a red-tiled roof on a grey stone building just down the street on his left. Bruno walked closer to the two-storey building and saw small spokes jutting out in all directions from the top of the spike. He studied it for a moment. An antenna? Then he noticed something else on the roof: flat, dark panels oriented roughly south. Bruno approached the building. He could tell from the two wooden green doors at street level that the building contained two dwellings. Given what he remembered about grounding wires and lightning protection, what he sought would most likely be found on the lowest floor. He needed to find a way in.

Bruno twisted the door handles while the sea gulls called in the distance. First one door, then the other. Locked, both of them. Decorative wrought ironwork, painted green to match the doors, covered the street-level windows. Bruno looked up. Reaching the windows on the top floor was out of the question, unless he wanted to try something truly stupid. For a moment, Bruno allowed some self-pity. Never the easy way.

Bruno walked past the green doors to the far side of the building and found an alley separating his target from another building. Adjusting his backpack, he made his way down the alley, picking his way around two motorini lying on their sides. The alley ended in a concrete wall about the height of a person, connecting the two buildings. But to his left, just before the alley ended, Bruno saw four stairs leading up to a metal gate. Beyond the bars of the gate, Bruno could see outdoor furniture, tables and chairs. Glancing behind him, he tried the latch on the gate and to his surprise, the gate swung open inward. He found himself on a stone terrace littered with metal tables and chairs, the flower patterns on their cushions faded and weathered. A waist-high metal railing ran around the square terrace. From here he could see out across the Bay of Naples and down towards the Marina Grande. The terrace of these dwellings lay on the roof of the building behind and below them, so Bruno was not far above the street that ran behind this building. Bruno could see that the two dwellings shared the outdoor area, as there were two sliding glass doors leading from the terrace into the dwellings. Which was the right one?

He glanced up towards the roof and followed the wires and cable down. They penetrated the wall at the base of the glass door closest to the gate. Bruno placed his backpack on the ground, removed his crowbar, and approached the glass door. Curtains blocked any view inside.

As Bruno expected, the glass door did not slide open when he pulled the handle. He used his crowbar to pry the door open, hoping that the sound would not carry as far as the crash of breaking glass. Once the latch broke he removed his sunglasses, un-holstered his pistol, and pulled the curtain slightly as he slid the door. He peeked inside.

The musty air laced with a hint of dry meat almost made him gag. He breathed through his mouth. In the gloom he could see a bed to his right, its head against the wall, and a desk with a chair to his left, close to the glass door. The small bed jutted into the middle of the room. Bruno's eyes adjusted to the gloom and he noticed an armchair in the far corner on the other side of the bed. There was a figure sitting shrouded in the shadows.

"Hands up!" shouted Bruno.

But the figure did not move or make a sound. Bruno threw open the door and curtains. Light flooded into the room, and he saw the desiccated body of a man in the armchair, his head lolled back against the wall. It was not the first corpse Bruno had come across in his scavenging, but somehow his revulsion never diminished.

He exhaled loudly. To be sure no other occupants lurked in the shadows, he walked up the short staircase leading to the ground floor. He checked each room, but found no one, dead or alive.

Returning to the small room off the terrace, Bruno retrieved his respirator from his backpack. He had no idea if he could get the Omega Plague from someone who'd been dead this long, so he wore his respirator, hoping it would provide some protection. Maybe the respirator wasn't worth a shit, but it made him feel safer, and that was at least something.

Bruno spent the next hour in nasty work, wrapping the body in a sheet and dragging it onto the far corner of the terrace. The desiccated corpse didn't weigh as much as Bruno thought it might. He didn't really know where to put the body, but for now the far corner of the terrace would have to suffice. Then he turned his attention to the armchair. It was stained from the body's decomposition, and Bruno hoped that once he removed it the odor, too, would fade from the room.

Once Bruno completed his tasks, he turned his attention to the small room's contents. Black boxes with various buttons and knobs sat on a wooden desk arranged along the wall. A shelf ran along the wall above the desk, with binders and books neatly arrayed along its length. On the floor just to the left of the entrance, Bruno saw six batteries wired together sitting in the corner between the desk and the door. He studied the gear. Mounted on the wall were a charge controller to keep the batteries from overcharging and an inverter to change the direct current from the batteries into appliance-friendly alternating current.

This was quite the setup. Solar powered. Bruno hadn't seen this much radio equipment since his time at the provincial command HQ in Naples. There was certainly enough equipment for this to have been the source of the pirate radio broadcasts.

He examined the spines of the black binders for any clues as to what they contained. He pulled the one labeled "Documenti Importanti" off the shelf and opened it with care. A certificate issued by the Ministry of Communications, stamped in bold capital letters, caught Bruno's eye. The name on the certificate read "PALLADINO, Filippo." Immediately below the name, Bruno noted Filippo's call sign: IC8CQX. Bruno studied the color picture of Filippo attached to the certificate. If this guy had indeed been the pirate radio broadcaster, Cristian couldn't have been more wrong about the way he looked. Filippo appeared in his mid-forties, dark hair shaggy and a bit rakish, with a greying goatee. A hint of a smile played around the man's lips, and Bruno swore he could see a touch of mischief in the man's eyes.

Bruno looked up again at the radio equipment before him. Of course, even before he had found the license, Bruno surmised the equipment belonged to a ham radio operator. But even more important than the equipment itself, Bruno realized, were the solar panels on the roof and batteries on the terrace. He looked at the charge controller. It still had power, as he could see some numbers and a green LED light flashing. He didn't know what the numbers meant, but he knew one thing: this equipment might still be operational. He flipped to the next page and saw a picture of Filippo with a woman and a young boy on a beach, all smiling. Bruno wondered what happened to what must have been Filippo's wife and son, and why they weren't with him when the end came, but he knew the answer would always be a mystery.

Bruno continued to look around, but found no documents or other evidence that pointed to Filippo being the rogue broadcaster. Bruno's hopes of finding hidden weapons or other useful equipment were dashed. But he supposed that if the guy was as paranoid as he sounded, he would certainly have been careful enough not to leave any documentary evidence of his activities. And he was probably smart enough to hide any other, possibly illegal items, where no one, including Bruno, would find them. Still, Filippo may have left him gifts of incalculable value: power and communications. Grazie, Filippo, you crazy bastard, thought Bruno with affection for this man he had never known in life.

Before he tested the equipment, Bruno wanted to be sure that the batteries still worked. While he could have plugged in some random kitchen appliance, he wanted to try something else. But he needed to go back to his old apartment to find it, and that might take a while. He knew he wasn't behaving rationally, but he wanted to bring back something of the old world, the world before the infection. And he would need to bring back enough food and water to last a little while. Of course, Bruno had nothing now but time, so why he cared about wasting it was a mystery even to himself.

By the time he made it back to Filippo's place, the sun rode low in the western sky. He had thought his trip back to his apartment was going to be in vain but at last, he had found it, lying at the bottom of his closet. How his phone had ended up there he had no recollection, since it had been so long since he had used it. Now he plugged its charger into the power strip, and hoped.

When he saw the long-dead phone battery light blink he let out a shout. He turned the phone on. Of course, there was no cellular signal, and he didn't expect one. But he scrolled through its menus, finally finding what he sought. He touched the screen again. Most people his age had stored their music in the Cloud, but not Bruno. The constant ratcheting up of storage fees every year pissed him off, so he had kept all his music on his phone. At the time, he never would have imagined how well his cheapness would serve him once the world ended. Out of the small speaker a melody soared into the air. The light, cheesy pop tune filled the room. Now and again he sang out loud to the music.

While the music played, Bruno sat at the desk, flipping through each of the documents contained in plastic sleeves. The well-organized documents consisted mostly of long manuals for operating the equipment and other ham radio materials. A goldmine, though some were in English, and that would slow him down a bit. Without them, Bruno might have spent days, at least, trying to figure out how to operate this equipment by trial and error. Now at least he could start listening and scanning the bands right away. But he wouldn't transmit. Not for a while. Bruno knew full well that it wouldn't take much equipment to triangulate a radio signal. Who was out there and what might they do if they could find him? Maybe there was no one left who would care.

Bruno paused and looked up from the documents. He stared out the glass door, his gaze falling over the island and out to the sea. He had no idea who was left, eking out an existence among the detritus of the West or anywhere else. But the more Bruno thought, the more certain he became that there had to be others out there. And not just the ones who had become psychopaths. Just as a matter of sheer statistics, some people would escape exposure, maybe people living above the Arctic Circle, where the cold would keep most people and all mosquitoes out. Some percentage of the population, miniscule though it might be, had to have not just the capacity to survive the infection and be forever changed, but actual immunity. Could any disease, bioweapon or no, be absolutely, one hundred percent infectious? Bruno even remembered reading that some tiny fraction of people simply couldn't be infected by the original AIDS virus. That might be true for the Omega Plague as well. Yet, even if people were out there, scrapping and surviving, what were the chances anyone would be broadcasting? What were the chances they had equipment and power? What were the chances they could avoid being killed by others who had survived infection? Bruno returned to the documents on his lap. Survivors or not, scanning for a signal might be a fool's quest.

Bruno laughed. "Then again, it's not like I have anything better to do."

He removed the radio operating license and propped it up on the shelf over the equipment. Filippo's picture smiled down on him.

"Well, Filippo, what do you think? I guess it's time to get to work."

***

After some hours reading manuals and testing equipment, Bruno set the radio to scan up and down the bands, stopping only when it found a strong signal. All that night, Bruno sat in the desk chair, his hopes raised every time it lingered on a single frequency, the frequency blinking instantly. But each time it stopped, Bruno could hear only powerful bursts of static, maybe caused by a faraway thunderstorm or atmospheric fluctuations, fooling the radio into stopping. Bruno heard no voices or music, no digital tones, not even the simple "dit-dah" of Morse code, used by ham radio diehards. Only static and silence.

The hours crept by, and Bruno's head lolled in a half-sleep while the radio continued its scanning. As Bruno's mind wandered in the grey area between sleep and wakefulness, in the depths of night, he heard a sound, just at the edge of his hearing. In his half-dream, he thought he heard a flute. Then he came awake with a start.

Bruno looked around, still in a daze. The dim yellow light on the radio panel provided the only illumination in the room as it blinked, stopped on some frequency. The sounds came not from Bruno's mind, but wafted up from the small speaker in the radio, filling the room. The high-pitched tones came in rapid succession, with a steady knocking sound setting an underlying beat. After a few seconds, the radio went silent. Then the tones started again.

In the dark of night, the tones sent chills down Bruno's spine, their plaintive, lonely quality spooking him as he listened. But it wasn't just the sounds that made him tremble, as he realized what they meant.

Someone is out there—someone wants to make contact.

CHAPTER 15

July 25

Bruno, frozen in place, listened. He thought he heard something on the wind. He stood on the lower section of La Scala Fenicia, the Phoenician Steps, in the last stretch before reaching the environs of the Marina Grande. The sun loomed high, and its rays drilled into him. Bruno glanced up at the sky, wiping sweat off his forehead with the back of his hand. He would have to be careful about being caught out at dawn and dusk, fearing the warm summer meant mosquitoes. Bruno wondered if they could survive on the island with no humans or other large mammals, sucking the blood of birds and lizards. Whether or not they still carried the disease remained an open question in Bruno's mind. But he didn't want to find out the hard way, spending his last days bleeding out his eyeballs and puking blood.

Bruno rested his left hand on the low stone wall that served as a railing running the length of the ancient stairway. He glanced back up over his right shoulder. The narrow grey ribbon of stone meandered up the side of Monte Solaro, back up to Anacapri. No one behind him. He squeezed his eyes shut. He'd been hearing things that weren't there for the last few weeks, the solitude eating away at him. Voices, mostly, just outside of earshot, lost in the sound of the wind. But when Bruno turned, no one was ever there.

Then he heard it again. He dropped his pack to the ground and removed his binoculars from a side pocket. No hallucination could last this long. Scanning the water towards the Marina Grande, Bruno heard the low buzzing grow louder before he spotted it. A small motorboat bobbed on the water, gunning towards the island. Bruno lowered his binoculars. He raised them again almost as soon as he lowered them.

He shoved his binoculars into his pack and scooped it up. As he bounded down, the Steps became less rough-hewn stone and more regular brick. Then without any transition to speak of, the Steps simply ended as they met the asphalt of the Via Marina Grande, the road to the principal marina.

Bruno looked around, then jogged through the street towards the Marina Grande. Who were they? How many? His thoughts took a dark turn as he considered why they had come. Scavenging, of course. They would consider Bruno a threat. But he considered them an even greater threat, and they no doubt outnumbered him.

He saw the open sea before him, the street now running fifteen or so meters above the waterline. He had been so lost in thought that the road's arrival by the water took him by surprise. He looked to his right. About half a kilometer further down the road sloped gently downward, heading toward a wide cobblestone area between the water and piers on the left, and what remained of stores and shops on the right. Though he looked straight down the road, he needed to get closer. A jumble of hedges, trees, and low buildings running along the edge of the water obscured most of his view of the pier and the area in front of it. He could see a few boats bobbing, moored to the pier, but couldn't tell if anyone lingered on board.

Quickly, Bruno picked his way from doorway to doorway and from car to car, finding shadows where he could, until he crouched at the final bend in the road before it turned 180 degrees, becoming a ramp as it merged into the cobblestone of the waterfront. A concrete pad in the corner of the bend had a bench and a staircase leading directly down to the waterfront. A low wall ran from the concrete pad around the outer end of the bend, following the ramp down. Bruno crouched in front of the wall near the bench, hoping to spot them. He slung his backpack off his shoulder and looked around, peeking just above the wall.

Three men in t-shirts and jeans, with rags tied around their faces, jogged from storefront to storefront, laughing and breaking windows as they went. Bruno noticed that one carried a rifle, but a small one. Looked like a .22, but Bruno couldn't be sure. They reminded Bruno of hooligans on a tear after their home team lost.

Bruno watched as all three of them went into the remnants of a pharmacy, its green neon cross hanging dark over the short granite stairway leading inside. For a moment, the lapping of the water and wind against the island and concrete piers was all he could hear. Then, there was more shouting as the men emerged again, pulling a lanky figure along with them. They stumbled down the stairs as two of them almost lost their footing. From this distance, Bruno could see the wispy white hair of the older man as they dropped him onto the cobblestones. The one with the rifle was a Juventus supporter, a Juventino, judging by the black-and-white striped jersey he wore. The Juventino gave the old man a kick in the gut and he cried out. Another one of the thugs only had one ear, the scar tissue leaving a noticeable lump on the side of the man's head.

All this time, that old man had been here on the island with him, out of sight, tucked away in his own little spider hole down by the sea. Bruno had been down to the Marina, fishing, scavenging, yet had never seen him. He wondered if the old man had been watching him. Now, the old man lay curled up, trembling, as the others shouted and cursed, asking if he had food, fresh water, medicine, and who else was there. But the old man just lay there, trembling in the sun, the wisps of his white hair making a halo around his head.

Bruno knew the smartest thing would be to turn his back on the scene before him and leave the old man to his fate. Instead, he sat down and turned to his backpack. He pulled out his respirator and secured it to his face. He double checked the pistol on his hip and hefted his crowbar in his right hand. Then he returned to a low crouch, his eyes fixed on the men below. Bruno's anger outweighed his fear. He thought the cop in him had long ago perished, leaving only the bones of a survivor behind. Now he realized he was wrong. In this world, no one remained to provide justice. So, Bruno would deal out vengeance instead.

The Juventino and One-Ear went back into the pharmacy. The remaining thug loomed over the old man, still berating him. The way he kept after the old man made Bruno wonder if they were looking for someone. For the moment the thug stood with his back facing Bruno, and he shifted the grip on his crowbar. He would have to wait for the right moment. His hands grew slick with sweat.

Bruno stood partway up and almost on tiptoes, moving around the bench and down the stairs. Once he reached the bottom of the stairs, he took refuge behind a jumble of upturned tables and chairs. The thug shifted as he turned his head to call towards the pharmacy.

Bruno had to be careful. So close now. The man's stringy, dark hair swung as he turned back to his captive.

"So, what should I do with you?" said the man. Then he laughed.

Shooting this piece of trash would bring out the other two for sure, and Bruno had no desire to face off against a rifle, even if it was only a .22, with his pistol. At least not unless he had the element of surprise. Seconds passed. He fidgeted, wanting to shout. Then the man turned, his back again facing Bruno.

Bruno leapt forward, closing the gap in a silent run. The old man, lying on his side, opened his eyes and yelled as Bruno bore down on them. The thug whirled around just in time for Bruno's crowbar to split his forehead open with a crack that reverberated down Bruno's arm. The old man screamed as the thug collapsed on top of him. Bruno raised the crowbar up and brought it down once more on the thug's head. It made a wet, smacking sound, like a watermelon falling on cobblestone. Bruno did not linger as the old man screamed, darting toward an alley just to the right of the pharmacy entrance.

Bruno wedged himself past a man-sized three-wheeled motorino that nearly blocked the alleyway. For an instant, it pinned him against the wall, and he thought he would be trapped, stuck in the mouth of the alley, easy prey. But with a heave, Bruno shifted the vehicle just enough to let him pass, as the two men stormed out of the pharmacy.

He stood in the alley between two buildings, lurking in the shadows behind the tall motorino. Bruno flattened himself against the pharmacy wall and looked to his right, watching as the Juventino and One-Ear hauled the old man to his feet. They whirled the old man around, and his back faced Bruno as they yelled, "Who did this? Where is he?"

The old man, his face painted with the blood from Bruno's victim, muttered something Bruno couldn't hear. Whatever the old man said enraged them, and One-Ear smacked him in the face.

Leaning the blood-and-brains-streaked crowbar against the wall next to him, Bruno eased his pistol from its holster. The three men stood on the cobblestone street, not quite fifteen meters away. But the way the motorino stood wedged up against the wall gave Bruno only a narrow aiming window. Both men had their backs to him. He leaned against the stone of the building and raised his pistol, targeting the Juventino. But just as Bruno pulled the trigger, the old man decided to fight, and he pulled to one side. Bruno's shot echoed over the cobblestones and One-Ear dropped.

Bruno swore. Before he could take aim, the Juventino grabbed the old man, whirling him around. Now the thug had his back to the sea, and the old man in front of him, facing toward the buildings in the Marina.

The Juventino shoved the rifle in the old man's back as he shouted, looking wildly around. "Where are you, stronzo? I swear I'll blow his fucking heart out if you don't come out!"

Bruno didn't doubt the old man's life stood on a razor's edge. "All right! Don't hurt him, I'm coming out!" Bruno shouted. The Juventino shifted behind the old man, his attention now focused on the alley where Bruno hid.

Bruno pushed his way past the motorino, onto the cobblestone street. As he emerged from the alley, the thug spotted him. Bruno walked one step at a time, at almost a shuffle, as he carried his pistol in his right hand over his head.

"Drop it or I'll kill the old man! I'll put a bullet in his fucking back, you get it?"

"All right—stay calm!" Bruno squatted and dropped his pistol to the ground.

"Now kick it away from you!"

Bruno shoved the pistol away with his right foot and continued to move towards the two men, his hands not nearly as high over his head as they were before he dropped his pistol.

The Juventino straightened up. "Now stop where you are!"

Bruno stood with his back to the alley, now maybe less than ten meters from the two men. The thug shifted position, partially emerging from behind the old man.

Bruno said nothing, doing his best to look as defeated as the old man. The thug noticed Bruno's respirator. "Your mask? Where did you get that?"

"The hospital here on the island, before it burned."

"We need some of those in Naples. And meds."

"I have more masks and meds, but first let the old man go."

Bruno was trying to close the distance without seeming like a threat. His hands drifted lower now, palms out and still facing the two men, but now only waist height.

"No! You'll take me now or I'll kill him right here!"

Bruno could sense the Juventino's rising confidence, as he had almost fully emerged from behind the old man, but with the rifle now drifting away from against the old man's side.

"I'll take you," Bruno said, nodding, shoulders hunched, deflated. "You win. But first, tell me, why did you come here? Are you looking for someone?"

The Juventino laughed. "Maybe. But I call the shots here, stronzo! First, you tell me who *you* are, you piece of—"

Bruno dropped to one knee, yanked the second pistol from the small of his back, and pulled the trigger.

Both the Juventino and the old man fell to the ground. Bruno approached one step at a time, blood pounding in his head and ears ringing. He focused on the Juventino. Bruno kicked the rifle out of his hand and it clattered on the cobblestones. Blood from multiple bullet wounds stained his jersey and the stones beneath it. Bruno had never before fired Battisti's pistol.

Bruno thought he had hit the old man, or maybe the rifle had gone off, but when Bruno tapped him with a foot, he opened his eyes.

"You okay?" Bruno asked.

The old man sat up, panting, feeling his chest. He didn't speak, just nodded.

The sound of a motorboat cut through the wind and soft waves. It was pulling away from one of the concrete piers extending into the marina. He holstered the pistol at the small of his back, scooped up the rifle, and fired at the fleeing boat.

Bruno pulled the trigger until the dull click told him he had emptied the magazine, but the boat sped away unaffected. Bruno cursed out loud. He had been stupid. He should have known they'd leave someone with the boat. Whoever it was now would bring back word of his presence. And that *he* was a threat. Bruno looked at the rifle more closely. The weak snap of the bullets had told him for certain, even before he examined it, that the rifle was a .22. But unless any of the dead had more ammo, the rifle would now be little better than a club. Bruno threw it to the ground in frustration.

By now the old man was on his feet. They studied each other in silence. Bruno broke eye contact, saying nothing as he walked over to gather his pistol.

"Thank you," said the old man. Bruno noticed his voice sounded strange, hoarse. He probably hadn't spoken in months, making Bruno's practice of talking to himself seem at least semi-rational.

"We'll see how much you thank me if more of them come back." Bruno moved towards the bodies on the ground, patting each one of them down. None of them had any bullets.

"They must have left any extra ammo on their boat," Bruno said, speaking more to himself than the old man. Bruno looked down at the Juventino.

"And look at *this* guy. Wearing a Juventus shirt in Naples. Forza Juve, pezzo di merda." Bruno kicked the Juventino, then looked out over the Bay of Naples.

The Juventino moaned. Bruno looked down at him again. Still alive. Bruno would have to act quickly. He stood over the man, but didn't bend down.

"Why did you come here? Did someone send you?"

The Juventino's eyes opened. His lips moved. He made a sound.

"Who sent you? Tell me and I'll make it quick," said Bruno.

Bruno bent down closer. The man's lips moved again. Blood trickled at the corner of his mouth. Bruno thought he heard words that he had hoped never to hear. But the way the man was choking on his blood, he couldn't be sure. Then the man's eyes rolled back in his head.

"Figlio d'una zoccola!" Bruno swore.

The old man spoke up. "Look, you saved my life and I owe–"

Bruno turned, his pistol pointed at the man's chest.

"Stay away from me," said Bruno. "Hands. Show me your hands."

The old man held his hands out. They were as steady as could be expected after the carnage that surrounded them.

"Keep back. Even if you weren't infected, *they* might be." Bruno gestured at the corpses.

The old man nodded, dropping his hands. He moved backwards, one step at a time, away from Bruno.

Bruno lowered his pistol. But as he stared at the man, trying to see if the whites of his eyes were jaundiced, something stirred in his mind. "You—I know *you* . . ." He lifted his pistol again and the man cowered.

"Please, I'll give you whatever you want."

"Why were you hiding down here? Why here in . . ." Bruno looked up at the green cross. "A pharmacy?"

"I—I," the old man stuttered, "my—my friend owned this pharmacy after mine got . . ."

Pharmacy. Bruno stood in silence for a moment. *Pharmacy*. His eyes narrowed. Son of a bitch! "I know who you are," Bruno said. "How could I forget *you*, of all people."

The old man's brow furrowed. "I—I don't understand. Whatever you want, take it, just let me live."

"You don't remember me?" Bruno's voice grew hard. "Take a good look, old man!" Bruno pulled off his respirator.

Bruno enjoyed the look in the old man's eyes.

"Yes, it's me," Bruno said. "You remember now, don't you." It was a statement, not a question. Bruno took a step back and pointed the pistol at the old man's forehead.

"Please—I have medicines, supplies; you can have them—just don't kill me!"

"I don't want anything that *you* have. You know what I want? I want you to bring him back. Can you bring him back?"

The old man did not answer.

"I asked you a fucking question! Can you bring him back?"

"Look." The old man swallowed hard. "I know it was my fault. I was selfish. I'm supposed to help people, but I didn't. I failed him. But I-I swear I won't fail you, if you let me live. Please let me live. Please."

Bruno tightened his grip on his pistol. His finger moved on the trigger.

"Fine," said the old man, his voice cracking. "Do it, then—kill me. Just make it quick." He closed his eyes.

Tears ran down the old man's face into his scruffy beard, and he made no attempt to wipe them away. Bruno could smell the reek of sweat and piss. If there had been any others left to see the old man, they would have said his survival all alone was a miracle. But Bruno did not believe in miracles. He ascribed the old man's survival to dumb luck. Much as Bruno thought of his own survival.

Bruno lowered his pistol. The old man opened his eyes, still shaking from fear.

Bruno studied the old man before speaking. "I'll be back in three days. Gives us time to make sure both of us are still infection-free." Bruno waved his pistol at the dead men around them. "No telling where these bastards have been."

The old man let out a long sigh. "Why? Why let me live?"

"Who am I to deal out judgment and death, even if I think you deserve it?"

Calogero DeLuca nodded without a word.

CHAPTER 16

September 7

"I've patched the leaks in the trash bins on the roof. So we should have no problems gathering more water," said DeLuca.

"*If* it rains again." Bruno looked up. Thin, grey clouds covered the sky, keeping the late-summer sun from beating down on them. Still, to Bruno they didn't look like the kind of clouds that brought rain.

"Hope we've got enough bottled water," said Bruno. "Guess if we have to, we could start distilling seawater." Then he turned to his companion and said, more kindly, "Thanks."

DeLuca nodded. "What's the plan for today?" They stood on the street in front of Bruno's place on Anacapri.

"Today, I've got something to show you. Somewhere in Capri. And let's take my moto. It's around back."

"What about the engine noise?" asked DeLuca.

Bruno shrugged. "We can risk it. I haven't seen a trace of anyone else since I found you. And I want to stay a few days, so it'll at least be a little easier to bring supplies."

"A few days?"

Bruno nodded. "Yes, like I said, there's something I want to show you."

As they retrieved his motorcycle from the small garage at the back of the building and began their ride, Bruno reflected on his time with DeLuca. The old man had some skills, whipping up a disinfectant salve from baking soda and bleach and cooking up seaweed and crabs from the shore into a reasonably palatable dish. Not to mention just having another set of hands to help and another pair of eyes to observe. And another person to ease the crushing loneliness.

They pulled up in front of one of Bruno's hideaways in the village of Capri. Bruno glanced around. Everything looked exactly as it had the last time he had been there, just before he had found DeLuca. As they dismounted the motorcycle, Bruno pointed up.

"See those?" asked Bruno.

"Yes!" responded DeLuca, his voice overflowing with enthusiasm. "Solar panels!"

"And they work." Bruno waved DeLuca on. "Come on, this way." They went around to the back entrance. As they opened the gate, DeLuca stopped short, pointing to the pile of stones on the far side of the stone terrace.

"What is . . ." DeLuca started to ask, but his voice faded before he finished his question.

Bruno glanced back over his shoulder. "Former occupant. Couldn't figure out what to do with him, so just buried him as best I could."

DeLuca grew pale.

"Is he bothering you?" asked Bruno with a half-smile. "Oh, come on. He's not gonna bother anyone."

Bruno fidgeted with the handle on the sliding glass door for a moment. Then it opened, and he stepped inside. DeLuca followed close behind.

Though clouds covered the sun, the glass doors provided enough light to bathe the room in a diffuse glow. The room looked ransacked. The bed was torn up, chairs overturned, and the walled defaced with graffiti and smeared with feces and what looked like blood. The only semi-clean area was a desk. But it was covered with binders and papers, strewn here and there.

"Jesus, Bruno, this place stinks like an old toilet. What the hell happened?"

Bruno laughed. "The best way to put off anyone who might get curious, if they saw the solar panels, was to turn this place into a shithole. So, I did some redecorating. With my own crap, that is. You'll get used to the smell after a while."

"I doubt it," said DeLuca, breathing through his mouth.

"I've hidden some pieces of equipment around the house. Only things I left in place were the inverter and panel on the wall and the main batteries under the desk." Bruno pulled a sheet off them. "I was afraid if I tried to move them, I'd screw something up permanently. Now, let's get moving."

For the better part of an hour, Bruno led DeLuca through the house, pointing here and there, and having him bring out various pieces of electronic equipment hidden away in rooms that had been torn up. Some were quite heavy.

"I must say, Bruno," grunted DeLuca as he hefted a particularly heavy box, "each of these rooms is shittier than the last. Literally."

"I'll take that as a compliment."

They arranged the equipment on the desk, and finally, after another hour of assembly, Bruno stood back, surveying their work.

"Well," he said. "What do you think?"

DeLuca looked at the equipment on the desk, then back at Bruno. "Radio equipment?"

"Exactly. This guy was a radioamatore, can you believe it? And with a solar-powered station." Bruno gestured towards the terrace. "He was in some emergency communications radio club, I found his membership papers." Bruno shook his head, smiling as he did. "The poor bastard. Probably all his friends thought he was out of his head: 'Filippo is a moron, what is he doing, waiting for the Apocalypse?'"

Bruno thought about that picture of Filippo and his family. Neither of them spoke for a time. In contemplation, Bruno moved items this way and that on the desk with no seeming purpose.

Bruno moved a binder on the desk and found his phone. "Here it is," Bruno said. "I thought it was here." He plugged it into the charging cable, turned it on, and swiped his index finger on the screen.

DeLuca waved a hand around. "So, why didn't you tell me about this before?"

Bruno replied without looking up from phone. "Needed to make sure I could trust you. After what happened with Veri, I needed to be sure about you."

He held up the phone. "Listen!"

Bruno touched the screen on his phone. The bluesy African-American voice, singing in Italian but with a heavy American accent, boomed from the small speaker.

DeLuca laughed. "I don't believe you have him on your phone! I remember him—that song came out when I was a teenager, late sixties, I think! And someone your age has it on their phone?" DeLuca laughed again. "That I really don't believe!"

"I downloaded the album for my father, so I had it in my collection. Papà really loved that guy." Bruno sat in the desk chair, picked up his phone, and played with the screen. He paused the music.

"We have music again," DeLuca said.

"It's strange, you know? I used to do everything with my phone—buy things, take videos, get the news, whatever. Didn't make that many phone calls, though." Bruno shrugged. "Now, it's so useless, I don't even carry it. All it's good for is to play some songs." Bruno looked at the phone again. "Although, I'm not sure you'll like anything else in my collection," he said with a smile.

"I'm just happy to hear music again," said DeLuca. He shifted from one foot to the other. "Bruno . . ." DeLuca started, but then stopped.

"What?"

"Well, yes—is there anyone else on the radio?" Bruno heard a desperate note creep into DeLuca's voice. "Anyone playing sixties songs or old Napoli-Juventus games? Is there anyone else out there?"

Bruno swiveled the chair and looked at the equipment.

"No music. No voices. Not even some crazy ham radio operator." Bruno turned around to see DeLuca's reaction, and he saw pain in the old man's eyes. But Bruno knew his answer misled DeLuca. He could go down a path of lies and deception. Or Bruno could tell the truth. And why not tell the truth? If he wasn't going to tell DeLuca, why come back here at all? Bruno wasn't even sure what his own motivations were in taking DeLuca to this place. Maybe he wanted another opinion. Maybe he just wanted to share the sound of a melody. He did not know.

Bruno ran his fingers through his hair before continuing. "But," he said, "I did hear something. A signal that repeats. And regularly."

"A signal? What kind of signal?"

"Definitely not a commercial broadcast. Digital for sure. Military maybe? Or Interior Ministry? Who knows? Could be coming from anywhere."

"Have you tried to contact them?"

Bruno shook his head.

"Why not? When did you find this equipment?"

"July."

"And you didn't tell me? Why haven't you tried to contact anyone?"

"Look, there's no way to know who they are, or what they want. We have no idea what they will do if they find out there's someone on the island."

"Come get us, I hope! It's got to be whatever's left of the government."

Bruno shrugged. "Who knows where that signal is coming from? Even if what you think is true, why should we trust them? For Christ's sake, they were slaughtering people like cattle in hospitals, of all places!"

"But we're not infected, so—"

"So what? We're not special. If they were so interested in helping anyone who's alive, why not just broadcast in the clear so everyone can understand? Why this digital signal?"

"I don't know. Maybe they want to see if there are other survivors from the police or military, maybe they're looking for remnants of the government because—because . . "

Bruno completed the thought. "Maybe they're not sure who might be listening. Maybe *they* want something. Maybe they *need* something." He shrugged. "Doesn't matter. Even if I wanted to contact them, I can't decode the signal, and I can't transmit on that frequency. Only a certain type of radio, another law enforcement or maybe military radio, can decode it."

"What do you mean?"

Bruno shook his head. "Look, I'm pretty sure I recognize the sound of the signal. This is an ALE signal, it's got very distinctive tones. But the equipment here is for radioamatori, not for this type of signal."

"An ALE signal?"

"Stands for 'Automatic Link Establishment.'" Bruno mouthed the last English word with some difficulty. "It's a way for two radios to form a link like . . ." Bruno struggled to explain the way the ALE radios would skip around from frequency to frequency, finding the clearest one before establishing a link. He finally settled on a not-too-exact simile. "Like computers over the Internet."

"So . . ."

"So, I need an ALE radio, otherwise it won't make the link."

"You said military and law enforcement use them? Don't you have one here, on Capri?"

Bruno shook his head. "It was sometimes used for communications between regional commands and national headquarters. I think they mostly just ran test messages."

"Why just tests?"

"It's an older technology. I think that we mostly used ALE radio as a backup in case of emergency. I'm not exactly sure. Look, I spent six months working as a communications tech at the Regional Command in Naples. But that was years ago now. I could be mistaken." Bruno rubbed his chin, remembering some long-ago training session. "The beauty of radio communications is that even when infrastructure like cellular networks or the Internet fails, or even satellites, radio will still work as long as you have power from somewhere."

"Well, don't you think that's exactly what we have here?"

"Yes," responded Bruno, not rising to the bait. "Total infrastructure collapse. I've tried to fix a position with my phone, but the GPS and Galileo systems have failed. GLONASS is off-line, too. And I doubt even a real satellite phone would still work; without ground control, satellites are probably out of position now. Anyway, we didn't have that kind of setup here. We didn't even have a satphone or direct uplink. Encrypted comms over our intranet were enough for a small station like ours."

"You must have a regional headquarters—a regional command, isn't that what you call it?" said DeLuca. "In Naples, right? So, you must have an ALE radio in Naples?"

"Maybe," Bruno responded in a low voice.

"Maybe? Maybe!" DeLuca grabbed Bruno's arm. "That's all you can say? You think you know where there's a radio you can use, and you're just sitting here? What is wrong with you?"

Bruno knocked DeLuca's arm away. "Don't touch me!" he said. "There was one in Naples, yes! But it can't be there now. Not after all of this."

DeLuca backed away. "How do you know? You can't be sure," he said under his breath.

"You don't get it, do you? Don't you understand the kinds of people left out there? They're not going to help you! Why should they? What can *you* do for them? I told you what they tried to do on the island, at the hospitals! Didn't you listen? You think it's better somewhere else? Go to Naples. Find the radio yourself! You'd be dog food in a day, old man. I'm staying here. I have everything I need right here. It's safe *here.* I'm not risking everything for nothing." Bruno stepped towards the sliding glass door.

"That's it then?" DeLuca said. "Well, fucking great. We'll just sit here and hunker down like rats. What's the point? Why should we go on? After everything that's happened, what are you still afraid of?"

Bruno kept his back to DeLuca.

"Are we just supposed to live like this, alone? Just live?" said DeLuca.

For all those long months, Bruno had thought the solitude would crush him. Yet now he wanted to be rid of his only companion. Bruno remembered the words of some damned French nihilist who once wrote that people are hell, or some such self-centered drivel. He had always thought that Frenchman was an arrogant, egotistical ass. But now Bruno knew exactly what he meant.

Yet, DeLuca's final words lingered in Bruno's head. Just *live.* DeLuca reminded Bruno of his father's words, the last words his father ever spoke to him. Bruno knew in his bones that he was the last of his family. But how could it be, thought Bruno, that he had come to find *just living* enough? Why did he bother to go on? Because of his father's desperate hope that his son and daughter should live? After the death of everyone he had ever known, was Bruno still so afraid of his own death? If he were honest with himself, he would have to admit he was more afraid than ever. All that had transpired only confirmed his certainty that humanity floated adrift in the universe, without hope of deliverance. That meant faith in anything was truly absurd, and death was horribly final. After all the death he had seen and after all the terrible things he had done in the last few months, his hope had been destroyed. So Bruno chose to ignore the signal, to deny that flicker of hope that still burned inside him. Yet hope, like death itself, was insidious; it could lie dormant like an ember, only to be rekindled into a raging fire by the slightest breeze.

Bruno didn't believe in fate or destiny or powers greater than himself, but at this moment, he recognized he had a choice. He could heed the words of his father, prolonging his existence as long as he could. Or he could embrace death, the only path to hope. For in this world, even mere survival invited death, let alone embarking on a futile quest into the bowels of a once-great city. Despite, or maybe because of the inexorability of morality, Bruno knew what he would choose even before he turned to speak, for in his mind, ultimately, there could be only one choice.

Bruno exhaled. "If we're going to do more than just live, I'll need your help. I can't do this alone."

DeLuca nodded. "You know, we have that small motorboat of mine. Of course, we'll have to scavenge fuel, but I think we can find enough to get us to Naples and back." DeLuca sounded giddy with energy. Bruno felt like the old man of their duo, embittered and weary.

"Maybe you're right. Who knows? Maybe whoever it is can help us."

PART II

CHAPTER 17

September 10

Now, Bruno felt that hope had indeed died.

For what seemed like an age, Bruno stared in disbelief at bare rocks below him. He knew he wasn't in the wrong spot. He had said to DeLuca to stay here, and now both DeLuca and the motorboat were gone. Had DeLuca moved? Had they found him?

The two approaching figures sprinted faster than Bruno thought was possible with rifles strapped across their backs. Bruno's options for escape diminished with each moment. Then Bruno heard a voice.

"Ehi! Down here!" Bruno descended the stairs toward the rocks below, three at a time, nearly stumbling twice. DeLuca had pulled the motorboat further onto the rocks into the shadows, under the pier's overhang, obscuring it from sight.

There was no time for explanations. As soon as Bruno finished his descent down the stairs, he dashed over the rocks to the boat and began pulling it by the bow into the water. DeLuca lifted the stern, making sure the engine was not damaged.

When they were knee-deep into the water, Bruno clambered aboard. "Got it." That was all he said to DeLuca. They were fifty meters behind him.

"Come on, come on!" DeLuca muttered as he pulled the rip cord on the engine. On the second pull, it bellowed to life. DeLuca opened up the engine full throttle and headed for the center of the marina. Their bodies were facing away from the city, but both had craned their heads to see what was happening behind them. Though they were fast retreating, they spotted the pursuers standing on the top of the pier. One of them aimed his rifle. Bruno turned and yanked DeLuca down. Surprised, DeLuca kept his hand on the tiller, sending the boat veering to the left. They saw the kick of the rifle a split-second before they heard the rifle's report. Staying crouched, DeLuca pushed the motor to the left, and they headed out into the open bay. Swerving this way and that, they stayed in a semi-crouch long after the pursuers had faded into the haze of the shoreline.

When he couldn't stand staying in the same position any longer, Bruno turned his back toward the bow of the boat. He slid the backpack off his right shoulder and trapped it between his legs, unzipping the main pocket and peering in. He wanted to pull it out, to study it in the daylight, this thing for which he had risked his life. But he didn't dare, for fear of having it catapulted out of his hands. The waves were choppy, and DeLuca kept the engine at a high rev. The boat bounced around with enough force to rattle teeth.

Bruno slumped, back towards the bow, exhausted, in no mood for explanations or chat. Still, DeLuca felt the need to engage Bruno. "I hope it works!" shouted DeLuca over the din of the engine and the waves. Bruno turned his head and looked out over the water, pretending not to hear. The sweat on his face drying in the wind cooled him, and he didn't feel like shouting over the engine's growl or telling DeLuca to slow down. Nor did Bruno feel like saying anything to the man who had pushed him to risk their lives in the first place.

When they made it back to the island, Bruno was in a piss-poor mood. The rifle he had poached was gone. In their rush to escape, he hadn't properly secured it, and it had fallen overboard. Bruno knew himself better than to try to set up the radio that evening. So, he plugged the radio into the battery bank. It would take hours to recharge, which was just as well, since Bruno needed time to decompress. That night, they stayed in Filippo's house. Bruno had long waited for some reason to celebrate something, anything, and since merely surviving now passed for a joyous occasion, he decided he might as well drink to that. He opened an old bottle of grappa he had found in the ruins of some patrician's house. He felt better after a few drinks. They handed the bottle back and forth, laughing and talking well into the night.

DeLuca explained why he had moved the boat out of sight. "I was getting paranoid that something had happened to you." DeLuca took a swig from the bottle before continuing. "So I thought I'd move the boat where it couldn't be seen from the pier, just in case someone came looking. Then I heard the shots and knew I was right to be paranoid!"

Bruno laughed. "Well, it worked! I didn't know where the hell you had gone!"

Bruno broke eye contact, looked down, and his smile faded. He swirled the bottle around.

"Something wrong?" DeLuca asked.

"He's there, you know."

DeLuca's brow furrowed. "What are you talking about?"

"Il Serbo. He's there, in Naples. I know. You remember, when I found you, the guy I shot said his name."

DeLuca shook his head. "You said you weren't sure what he said. God knows, he was a bloody mess. And you said your sister was sick, so he must have got it too, from the one who escaped Tiberius' Leap. Il Serbo is probably long dead by now."

"No, he's not! They were organized. That gang—that bunch of thugs needs a strong hand to keep them in line."

DeLuca shrugged. "So, they need a strong hand, so what? Could be anyone."

"No, no. Only a Camorrista would know how to do that. Only someone like him."

"Yeah, a Camorrista . . . or maybe a cop," DeLuca replied, deadpanning.

For a second, Bruno stiffened. Then he chuckled. "Good point, old man." Bruno took a large gulp of grappa, and the next words out of his mouth changed the subject to more pleasant topics.

As they bantered and laughed, time passed slowly, and Bruno savored each moment, enjoying the alcohol and DeLuca's company. Hours later, DeLuca passed out face down on the bed, his snores echoing around the room. Bruno remained awake, lost in thought, long after even DeLuca's snores died down. Finally Bruno fell asleep in a lounge chair, with hope for the future raging in his mind for the first time since it all fell to pieces. Yet suffocating dreams troubled his sleep, dreams of swimming blind in murky water, dreams of clawing up out of a dark pit through rubble.

***

When Bruno woke the next morning, DeLuca was snoring again. Bruno eased his way up out of the lounge chair. While stiff from sleeping in the chair, to his surprise, his head didn't throb from the booze the previous night. I should have drank more grappa, he reflected. No impurities and no hangover.

Bruno rubbed the sleep from his eyes, moved to the desk, and studied the ALE radio. Before beginning the task of setting it up, he moved some other radio equipment around on the desk, taking care not to disconnect anything, making just enough room for the ALE radio. Unlike the ham radios in Filippo's bedroom, the ALE radio did not have a confusing number of knobs, buttons, and keys. It was simple, even sleek. The body of the unit was olive-drab plastic with two rounded metal handles jutting out from the front panel and the battery attached to the back. The front panel itself had a long, narrow screen that could display perhaps ten lines of data. Below the screen was a keypad arranged in a square. Its keys had numbers, letters, and functions listed on each key, along with volume control and various keys used to activate the functions. To the left of the screen were three ports for various types of antennas, and to the right were two ports for connecting accessories and a knob with five positions.

Bruno read through the manual with care. Satisfying himself he knew what to do, he began to connect cables. Once DeLuca awoke he hovered in the background, lending Bruno a hand when he could, but mostly just providing encouragement. They spent all morning setting up the radio, checking connections, cross-checking the manual, making sure they understood how the radio worked, and double checking everything.

By the time Bruno and DeLuca finished the setup, the sun rode high in the sky. They paused for a moment, each sitting in a chair in front of the desk, Bruno directly in front of the ALE radio, and DeLuca behind and to the right of Bruno, in a chair taken from the kitchen.

Bruno leaned back in his chair and turned towards DeLuca. "Well, everything is set, as best as I can tell. They've been broadcasting the signal every two hours." Bruno glanced at his watch. "I'm sure the date is still right, and I'm pretty sure the time still is. So we are just about due for a signal."

DeLuca patted Bruno on the shoulder. "You are quite the technician."

"Not so fast, I haven't turned it on yet," said Bruno, laughing. "But thanks for the vote of confidence."

Bruno paused, his finger lingering over the "on" knob. "Well, this is it," said Bruno.

The tiny screen blinked to life. "It works!" said DeLuca.

Bruno smiled. "I was afraid it might have been damaged from our Naples adventure."

Referring to the manual on his lap, Bruno touched the "menu" key and set the radio to search for a signal on a series of preset frequencies. Now that he was sure the radio worked, Bruno plugged in the keypad/display attachment. The display on the attachment had a full keyboard and LCD screen that was about twice the size of the one on the radio itself. The radio switched to the keypad attachment as the primary display. The words "ALE Sounding" blinked in a slow rhythm on the larger screen as the radio switched rapidly from frequency to frequency. In a regular pattern, the radio lingered on each frequency, transmitted a few seconds of audible signal, and paused for a response. Nothing.

They listened in silence. On and on the pattern repeated, and still no responding signal. DeLuca fidgeted, his leg twitching up and down. Bruno resisted the urge to swat it, and instead leaned back in his chair and closed his eyes. He had risked his life for nothing. He had—his eyes opened when he heard something else—a fainter, yet still quite audible responding signal, an echo of one they were transmitting.

"Listen! They're responding!"

The screen on the radio changed, the words "establishing link" flashing repeatedly in time with the audible signal. The word "connected" then appeared in English, steady, unblinking, in all capital letters. The word lingered for a moment, and the screen went dark.

DeLuca rose in his chair. "What happened? Did we lose the signal?"

Bruno kept his eyes on the screen. He raised his right hand.

The words "Cognome" and "Nome" flashed on the screen, followed by a blinking cursor.

Bruno looked at DeLuca. "We've got a link!"

Bruno's hands hovered over the keyboard.

"Well?" said DeLuca.

"Whoever it is will know I'm alive." Bruno typed in a fake name.

The screen cleared for a moment, and the words "Codice Fiscale" appeared, again followed by the cursor.

"What?" said DeLuca. "They want your tax ID number?"

"It's an attempt to verify identity," said Bruno. "Maybe to make sure the one answering is in the military or law enforcement."

Bruno took his eyes off the screen just long enough to glance over his shoulder at DeLuca. "Anybody might know the name of a cop or someone in the military, or even have taken his ID card with the serial number. But what are the chances they would know his tax ID number?"

Of course, Bruno realized, any number of painful, horrid methods existed that could force some poor bastard to reveal that string of numbers. Even an unwilling biometric scan could be obtained if someone were ruthless enough to remove a finger. Or an eyeball. Bruno guessed that this was the best way whoever was transmitting had to verify the identity of the person responding.

He entered a made-up tax ID number, but the words "identità non autenticata" appeared on the screen, and the screen reset back to "Cognome" and "Nome."

"Shit," said Bruno. "If we want to find out what this is, I'll have to use my real information."

"Up to you, Bruno. But we've come this far. Don't you want to know what this is?" said DeLuca.

Bruno looked at the keyboard. Then he typed in his last name and his first name.

"I want some answers," said Bruno.

At the next screen, Bruno entered his tax ID number.

The screen went blank, and Bruno thought the connection might have been broken. Then the English word "Processing" flashed multiple times on the screen, followed by the words "identitá autenticata."

"We're in!" said Bruno.

The screen began to fill with words, and Bruno used the keyboard to scroll back up and read the information. DeLuca read over Bruno's shoulder.

From the way the information appeared, at a steady rate with no typos, Bruno surmised that there was no one on the other end.

"This transmission is automated," he said, more to himself than to DeLuca.

"So, what does that mean? Is there anyone there, or is it just some computer in a bunker?"

"Who knows, really. They must still have electricity from somewhere, and access to some sort of government database. So, I would imagine there is someone or, more likely, some group, maintaining everything. But for all we know, they're all dead, and their transmitter connects to a solar-powered automated system."

"Ever the optimist, aren't you?"

Starved for so long from contact with anyone off the island, they gorged on the information all the same. Perhaps a half-hour into the transmission, DeLuca gasped.

For a second, Bruno was puzzled, but then he saw what DeLuca has seen. "I risked my life for this? I don't believe it!"

"Believe it!" DeLuca made the sign of the cross. "They want blood—the blood of San Gennaro!"

CHAPTER 18

Bruno and DeLuca spent the entire afternoon and into the evening transcribing the information from the small screen onto paper. They decided it was too risky to connect the radio to Filippo's computer to try and download the notes to a larger screen. If something went wrong, they could lose everything. Bruno's hand ached from the hours of scrawling handwriting. Once they had transcribed everything, they sat at the kitchen table in Filippo's home, poring over their notes, oblivious to the rain and wind smashing against the windows.

"Look at all of this—storage points for materiel—weapons, vehicles, fuel—it amazes me that our noble government did this kind of detailed preplanning," said Bruno.

"Just because they say something's there doesn't make it so, but still . . . sounds like the old 'Operation Gladio.'"

"What's that?"

DeLuca smiled. "How old were you when the Wall fell?"

"In 1989? I was six years old."

"That explains it! After the Berlin Wall fell, the Prime Minister at the time admitted that the CIA had set up networks to organize guerrilla groups all over Western Europe, in case the Soviets ever invaded. That way, there'd be an armed resistance already in place."

"Never heard of it."

"It was quite the story at the time—secret weapons caches all over Italy and other countries, too. Intelligence agencies with supposed ties to right-wing terrorism—like a bad Cold War spy novel, except a lot of it was true."

"Well," said Bruno, "the government probably never totally eliminated that program. Organizations like that are too useful to die."

"Yes, they keep going—until everyone in them is dead," DeLuca said, with sadness.

Bruno nodded, his thoughts turning to the death of Europe. Thoughts of loss and death had been a constant companion since the Shakes hit. Not a day went by that he didn't think of Carla. But he had become quite adept at forcing those thoughts aside. If he hadn't, he doubted he would have survived this long. When he spoke, his voice sounded more animated.

"Still, it explains why these caches exist at all and why whatever is left of the government knows about them. Hopefully, if their locations stayed secret, looters never found them."

"Yes, it does explain why they know," said DeLuca, "and it gives us a fighting chance."

"A fighting chance? At what?" Bruno asked.

"Getting the blood of San Gennaro. That's what they want us to do."

Bruno laughed as he stood up. "No. We're going to get the weapons and everything else that we can transport back to the island."

"But they told us they need the phial with his blood," said DeLuca.

"So what? I don't care what insane plots the leftover zombies from the Ministry of Defense are cooking up. Omega fried their brains. We can use those weapons and whatever else is there for the defense of Capri, or maybe to relocate somewhere else—I'm not sure yet."

"But the blood—"

"Is a fake, like—like the Shroud of Turin. Don't you know the Church was full of liars, just like the government?"

DeLuca wagged his index finger. "You're wrong. The Church never, ever, *ever* said what happened with San Gennaro's blood was a true miracle. The Church was neutral on the whole thing, just like they were on the Shroud of Turin. It was left up to the faithful to decide what to believe." DeLuca pointed at Bruno. "Now who's lying, eh?

"Fine! Then whoever sent this message must be deluding themselves—that's the only explanation." Bruno sat back down and folded his arms across his chest.

DeLuca leaned towards Bruno. "Bruno, think about what the message said: they need San Gennaro's blood because he lived before the rise of industrialized society, because it's been sealed from environmental contamination for centuries, at least. I'm not a medical doctor, but I am a pharmacist. There is a ring of truth to what they're saying. I remember an article I read that talked about how chemicals, maybe other things, could cause heritable epigenetic changes that—"

"What does that mean?"

"There were studies that said man-made chemicals, toxins, could cause permanent genetic changes that could be passed down from one generation to the next. And that these changes were factors in certain diseases.

"We've all been exposed to multiple chemicals and drugs that didn't exist in pre-industrial times—like—like . . ." DeLuca paused in thought then snapped his fingers. "Like DDT! Everyone alive on the Earth during the twenty-first century had trace amounts of chemicals like DDT in their system, even though that chemical was banned for decades before HAV hit. Sometimes even more than a trace, depending on the chemical."

"Yeah, and they tried to bring back DDT to kill the mosquitoes and stop Omega from spreading. Helluva lot of good that did."

DeLuca shook his head. "That's not the point. Think about it—the transmission said the Americans believe that a sealed, preindustrial blood sample is what they need to help find a cure, maybe that's why. Maybe we've all been exposed to some modern chemical, some toxin—or who knows what—that rendered us susceptible to the disease."

"But why here? Why don't they look in the United States for a sample?"

"The blood of San Gennaro has been sealed from outside contamination for centuries," said DeLuca. "Maybe the Americans could find a pre-industrial blood sample from somewhere on their side of the Atlantic. But even so, how would they find one that's been hermetically sealed from the environment for that long? Who in America would have thought to preserve blood like that over the centuries?"

The notion that a relic from the patron saint of Naples rested at the heart of the message struck Bruno as so utterly ridiculous that he cackled. "This whole thing sounds like a crock of shit. But I'm still listening."

"The miracle is real, Bruno, I've seen it myself. You grew up not far from Naples, right? Didn't you ever go during the feast of San Gennaro?"

Bruno's mind wandered to that day, so long ago now, when he and Cristian laughed and joked about the blood. The memory felt like something that had happened when he was a child. "I saw it on TV once. So what? Anything like that could be faked. I saw a lot of fake vids. You probably never saw that fake with the French president's ex-wife." Bruno laughed. "You could have sworn it was her!"

"I'm not talking about some sick Internet video! I'm talking about a miracle! The blood transforms from a solid to a liquid when the priest turns the ampoule in his hand. That's the miracle."

DeLuca continued, now in a reverie. "They used to say that if the blood didn't liquefy, Naples would be in for a bad year—earthquakes, Vesuvius erupting, that sort of thing. I wonder . . . you know, I think there might be another saint whose blood—"

"Well, the blood didn't liquefy this past year—have you seen Naples lately? Did they ever mention 'plague that wipes out humanity'? Was that on the Church's list?"

"We all have trace amounts of radioactive material in us from all the nuclear tests since the 1940s. That, and the meltdowns from Chernobyl and Japan, and not to mention the Koeberg meltdown after that attack." DeLuca shook his head. "Anyway, I don't know—maybe the radiation, even the small doses, affected us somehow—maybe rendering us more vulnerable to this infection, damaging our DNA. Who knows?"

"You said 'we all.'"

"So what?"

Bruno stared at DeLuca. "There is no 'we all' anymore. They're all dead! Do you understand? Everyone's fucking dead!"

"The Americans are still there!" DeLuca pounded his open hand on the table. "The message said the Americans are patching together a network of surviving governments—and that they've made progress in researching the disease. There *are* more survivors out there."

"The Americans? They couldn't even keep their own country intact after Omega spread to—"

"What's the matter? You thought you were the only one with enough balls to live through this? Does it piss you off that other people survived, too? You feel like a pussy now, is that it?"

"I don't want to listen to your bullshit." Bruno sounded weary.

"Well, you'd better listen, if you want to keep your ass intact. Get it through your head—we can't stay here forever. That bunch of animals knows we're here."

DeLuca leaned back in his chair. "You killed two of them in Naples. You killed them on their own turf. And you don't think they'll come after us? Especially if it is *him*? You're not just someone he'd like to get revenge on. You're a threat now, don't you get that? You're dumb, even for a Carabiniere!"

Bruno leaned back in his chair hard enough to make it squeal. "I'd like to see *you* do anything to stop them," Bruno said. "I'll give you credit, old man. After the way I found you, it takes balls for *you* to call *me* a pussy!" Then Bruno laughed, but it was a real laugh, not one of derision.

"So, what are we going to do?" DeLuca spoke with caution, not wanting to reignite an argument.

Bruno exhaled loudly. "Well, whatever we do, we'd better find one of those weapons caches. I think we should try Sorrento first. It's closer, and the cache there is more likely to be intact than one in Naples, don't you think?"

"Agreed. Naples got pretty bad; I could see the flames from here."

Bruno remembered watching the city burn and his own brush with death that night. Thoughts of Naples in chaos and Il Serbo made his stomach tighten, but Bruno forced those feelings down.

"Time to get started," said Bruno.

CHAPTER 19

September 18

Bruno, with DeLuca's assistance, spent the next week planning and preparing for what would have been, not long ago, a simple day trip by ferry. Now, of course, Bruno treated it like the Allied invasion of Normandy, or Caesar's invasion of Gaul, preparing and scouring parts of the island for any usable items. The day of their departure dawned cool, but with the promise of a fine summer day to come. The sun burned through the morning mist as they took supplies and made their way down to the main marina, where they again set out across the bay.

To help their memory they quizzed each other, discussing the most important parts of the message, particularly the weapons cache access codes. They took no notes or any evidence of the message with them. "In case something happens, better not to have anything that gives anything away," Bruno reasoned. "We'd better have rally points, too, in case we get separated in Sorrento."

"What about Naples?" asked DeLuca.

Bruno looked at him, puzzled. "Rally points for Naples? Why?"

DeLuca shrugged. "I know we're not going there now, but just in case, better sort it out before . . ."

"Okay, sure." Bruno nodded in agreement. "Good idea. We can't be too careful."

They were low on fuel, so they proceeded slowly, trying to conserve what they had.

Bruno rummaged in his backpack and drew out a bulky handheld radio. He was careful not to pull on the "rubber duck" antenna. In the middle, a small LCD screen lay above an alphanumeric keypad. Though somewhat thicker than a mobile phone, it could still be slipped into a vest or jacket pocket. Bruno pushed a red button and the LCD screen flashed to life. He handed the radio to DeLuca.

"So," smiled Bruno, "you remember how to use it?"

"I think so," said DeLuca as he studied the radio. "I can't believe the municipal police station still had these!"

"I tore that place apart, hoping to find some radios like this. Guess if it hadn't been for this little trip, I'd never have ransacked what was left of the local police station the way I did."

Bruno put his hand in his pack. "When it all went to shit, everything went so fast, I suppose there wasn't anyone left to take them. Not a single fucking weapon or ammo, though." Bruno started to talk to himself. "Where the hell could they all be, I wonder."

"Too bad you didn't find these before," said DeLuca.

"Why?"

"Well, wouldn't it have been convenient to have communications that—"

Bruno laughed. "Until you showed up, who the hell was I going to talk to?"

DeLuca laughed too. "Good point."

"Ah, found it," said Bruno. Turning his radio on as well, he checked both radios, keying one down and hearing the other beep in acknowledgment of the transmission.

"Charged up and ready to go, courtesy of our solar setup!" Bruno looked at the one in his hand. "They used to be part of a trunked radio network, same type as the Carabinieri used. With relays, a radio like this could get nationwide coverage. Now it's just point-to-point, radio-to-radio. Still, it's fairly powerful for a radio this size. If we're lucky, you might get a usable signal even at thirty kilometers. Important if we get separated."

Bruno noticed that their boat rode low in the water, as each of them carried a backpack with food, water, and gear. Bruno sat in the bow of the motorboat, while DeLuca sat facing Bruno, with his right hand on the tiller. When DeLuca spoke, he sounded more upbeat than he had ever been. "They said once we get the blood, to take it to Assergi in Abruzzo. You ever heard of Assergi?"

"No. Can I see the map again? Where is it?"

DeLuca gestured to the backpack just in front of him. Bruno extracted a worn map. He unfolded it and it spilled out over his lap, almost touching DeLuca's legs. Bruno studied it for some minutes and then, with a pencil, he drew a line starting in Naples and moving northeast, up a snaky path into the spine of the Italian peninsula, and circled a small dot. He folded it back so that the path he traced was on top. "That town's in the mountains of Abruzzo, near the Gran Sasso. It's just outside of L'Aquila."

"Gran Sasso," said DeLuca. "I've seen pictures of that mountain. Rugged. Beautiful. But I've never been there."

"Well, from the size of the speck on the map, this Assergi probably had less than a thousand people living there, if even that many." Bruno looked out towards the approaching shore. "I bet it was a great place to ride out the Apocalypse," he said, as he leaned forward and handed the map to DeLuca.

"No doubt," said DeLuca, taking the map and slipping it into his jacket pocket. "There were worse places for sure. Like Naples. Or any large city, for that matter." For a moment, DeLuca looked around, lost in thought. Then he looked over at Bruno.

"So, after we find the cache, we're going to Assergi?"

"Look, I never said we *should* go there! I said we should get to the cache. Then, we'll see."

"But you just drew a line on the map, so I thought—"

"You thought wrong," Bruno said. "I'm not sure what we're going to do after we find the cache, if there is even a cache at all." Bruno shook his head. "Gran Sasso! More like Gran Cazzo, for all I give a shit! I can't believe you still just want to up and leave Capri, for what? For this speck on a map? I told you about the hospitals, the exterminations. Were you listening? This is another one of their lies."

"It doesn't make any sense. Why lure people they don't even know to that place? Why—"

"Who knows? You have no idea who they are or what they want. I don't believe a damn thing they say."

"I believe them," DeLuca snapped. "I have faith."

"Oh, you believe? You have faith? Everyone's dead, the world's fallen apart, and *you*," Bruno punctuated his words with his finger, pointing at DeLuca once more, "*you* believe in them? *You* have faith, in *them*? Well, let me tell you something . . . *you*, my friend, are a bloody idiot."

After a long silence, DeLuca spoke, his voice clear. "Per chi crede, nessuna spiegazione è necessaria; per chi non crede, nessuna spiegazione è possibile."

Having attended an old-fashioned classical grammar school for a time as a kid, Bruno had heard the medieval quotation before. *For one with faith, no explanation is necessary. For one without faith, no explanation is possible.*

Bruno turned away, gazing out over the sea. They spent the remainder of the boat ride in silence as Bruno stared at the water, his mind adrift on those words from long ago.

***

They arrived more quickly than Bruno thought they would, rounding the Sorrento peninsula and making landfall mid-morning at the marina just below the town of Sorrento itself. Bruno and DeLuca surveyed the marina. Two covered boats bobbed along the dock in the strong sun. The street wound around the marina along the water. While the restaurants and shops stood shuttered, to Bruno the scene along the water looked almost peaceful. Nothing was burned, nothing looted, nothing destroyed.

DeLuca echoed Bruno's thoughts when he spoke. "It almost looks like nothing happened here, just that everyone's left, on holiday or something."

Bruno looked around. "Reminds me of Rome during Ferragosto; the city empty and everyone at the beach."

"Yeah, empty all right, except they're definitely not at the beach."

Bruno looked right and left. "We can't let our guard down, there's no telling who might still be lurking about." Bruno instinctively kept one hand rested on the butt of his pistol.

"Understood."

Bruno glanced toward the two boats. "We need to see if there's anything we can use."

As they searched the two moored boats, to their surprise, they found both had some fuel in their tanks.

"This should be enough to get us back to Capri, maybe even a little more," said DeLuca.

They moved as fast as they could to transfer fuel to their boat. As they worked, DeLuca continued to press Bruno, asking about leaving. "So, did you notice how far it is to Assergi?"

"Let me see the map," said Bruno.

DeLuca reached in his jacket and handed Bruno the map.

"Looks like about two hundred fifty or three hundred kilometers northeast of Naples. More than a few days' walk, that's for sure." Bruno returned the map to DeLuca for safekeeping.

DeLuca folded it and placed it in the pocket of his windbreaker. "Walk! You want to walk there? What about food? What about mosquitoes?"

"I know. We'd have to be careful. You're the one who's dying to go there, right? You have any better ideas? You'd like to drive? You think we can find enough fuel? Or even a car with a battery that works?" Bruno snapped his fingers. "Oh, now I get it—you want to fly, is that it? Come on, you know there's no easy way to get there."

"But walking? I'll be a walking corpse! And anyway, how will they know when we get there? Do you think anyone *will* be there?"

Bruno didn't think for one second that in the unlikely event they made it to Assergi anyone would be there to greet them. But he decided to indulge DeLuca's optimism for a change.

"Well, it would be completely foolish for them to broadcast their exact location, even using ALE. They can't be sure who we really are. No, I doubt whoever is left is actually in that village. But I think their shelter—bunker—or whatever it may be, must be somewhere in that area. And if they have enough working technology to send an ALE message, I'll bet they have some way of monitoring the area."

By the time they finished transferring the fuel, the sun had moved well past its high point. "We've got to get moving," said Bruno. "If we don't hurry up, we might not get to the cache before twilight."

"How long do you think we have?"

Bruno glanced at his watch. "A few hours. Maybe more. But I'd rather not take any chances getting caught outside with mosquitoes."

"So what's the plan?"

Bruno laughed. "The plan? Well, the plan, such as it is, is to get to the cache ASAP and find shelter. Simple, yes?" He patted DeLuca on the shoulder. "Now stop asking questions and follow me." DeLuca kept his mouth shut and fell in line behind Bruno as he moved up the winding streets towards the center of town.

Arriving at the main square, Piazza Tasso, took Bruno longer than he would have thought.

"I'd forgotten how high Sorrento was above the water."

"Well," said DeLuca between breaths, "we finally made it."

They looked up and down the piazza, taking time to drink from their bottles of water. The low, pastel-hued buildings stood in quiet, splendid loneliness in the afternoon sun. The wind moved scraps of paper here and there, but Bruno could see no evidence of fires, riots, or mayhem. Though they were tattered and fading, the ragged flags of many nations still flew over the Hotel Sorrento, right on the square. Oblong terracotta flower pots still stood in neat lines in front of the remains of restaurants, their flowering plants clinging tenaciously to life against the encroaching weeds. And the statue of St. Anthony still faced east, one hand on his shepherd's crook, the other raised in a blessing to no one. Bruno pictured all the people who once frequented this place, laughing, talking, and filling the piazza with life. But all of them were dead now. Dead and gone.

As they lingered on the edge of the piazza, DeLuca said, "Guess when people in a place with money like Sorrento died, they just went quietly. Unlike poor Naples."

Bruno shoved the bottle of water back in his backpack. "Yeah, well, good for them." He wanted to focus on the task at hand. "Follow me. And stay sharp."

Bruno crept into the piazza, with DeLuca two steps behind. Although they hugged a building, Bruno felt exposed as they gazed about. DeLuca saw their target first. "There!" he said, a little too loudly for Bruno's liking. DeLuca pointed to the only building in the square with a clock tower. The transmission had been quite specific about the clock tower.

Bruno nodded. "That's it. Let's go."

They jogged across the piazza to the light-pink building with the stopped clock. A glass-enclosed patio surrounded its base. Vines grew wild about the glass walls, climbing from the pots below into the weeds hanging from the low balcony above. Narrow streets stretched along both sides of the building into the rest of Sorrento. On one side of the patio, just where the street met the piazza, Bruno spotted double metal doors nearly flush with the asphalt of the street just in front of the building.

"I think this is it," said Bruno. "Hell of a place to put a weapons cache—right in the middle of Sorrento!"

DeLuca nodded. "Yeah, but who would have ever imagined they'd put one under a restaurant."

There was a chain and padlock wrapped around the handles. He gave the handles on the doors a tug. They moved a few centimeters, but that was all. He should have known it wouldn't be that easy.

He turned to DeLuca. "Hand me the crowbar, and keep your eyes open."

Bruno slipped the end of the crowbar into the handles on the metal doors. Leveraging the crowbar with all his bodyweight, Bruno heard the metal groan, then give way with a crack. Bruno, still huffing from his effort, tossed the chain and padlock into overgrown weeds growing out of the pots.

DeLuca raised his eyebrows. "What are you doing?"

"Don't want to leave signs of our presence," Bruno said. Bruno looked around, then motioned for DeLuca to stand behind him. He took a black metal flashlight out of his backpack with his left hand, then slung it over his back. In his right hand, Bruno held his pistol.

"I'm going down," Bruno said. "Stay outside, in case there's a problem. My radio's on; it should still work unless this place is a lot further underground than I think." He tapped the inside pocket of his jacket and felt the reassuring bump of the radio. "But I won't use it unless it's an emergency. If I'm not out in twenty minutes, it means I *am* having a problem."

"So if you're not back, what should I do?"

Bruno smiled and patted DeLuca on the shoulder.

"Don't worry. You've got the pistol I gave you, right?"

DeLuca nodded.

"Well, it's up to you. If you think it's too dangerous, run back to the boat and get back to Capri. But if I've just tripped and bumped my head, it would be nice if you came and helped. Look, old man, if you need to run, to hide, then run, hide. I understand. Do what you have to do to live."

DeLuca opened his mouth then shut it again, and simply nodded as he spoke. "All right, Bruno. Whatever you say. I'll open the door."

Bruno nodded and stepped back. DeLuca pulled back the door, but the only sign of movement was the breeze whistling down the street and the chattering sparrows. Daylight illuminated a concrete ramp stretching down into darkness. Bruno stepped onto the ramp and glanced back towards DeLuca.

"Don't worry. Worst that could happen is, it's empty." Bruno turned on his flashlight. "Remember, if I'm not back in twenty minutes, something's happened. Don't initiate radio contact. If you see anything up here, hide or come down and get me if you can. And shut the door behind me."

"And what if it *is* empty?"

Bruno shrugged. "Guess we'll try the one in Naples. What else can we do?"

Bruno walked down the steep ramp and darkness swallowed him as DeLuca lowered the door with a clang. The barest crack of daylight shone through the seam where the metal doors met. He turned around and shined his flashlight ahead as he walked.

The ramp sloped down at a steep angle, leveling out over some meters. When he looked behind and above, he could make out the seam of the doors, now two meters above and at least four meters behind him. The width of the tunnel surprised Bruno as he shined his flashlight around, looking around at the poured concrete walls and floor. He pressed forward, the beam of his flashlight cutting the gloom.

The light landed on double metal doors. His pace quickened, and he reached the wide doors in seconds. He swept his flashlight around. The metal doors stood taller than a man, unpainted, and a fine sheen of rust constituted their only decoration, except for a square metal handgrip jutting out from the overlapping door. Bruno rubbed his hand on the door, feeling the cold steel beneath his fingers. His hand strayed down to the handle. Bruno tugged on it, but the door didn't even jiggle. No key or any way to access the doors' locking mechanism could be seen.

Bruno swept the beam over the frame of the doors. On the left side of the door, between the door and the tunnel's wall, Bruno saw a black square the width of a hand. He moved closer to the square, shifting his pack to his right side, and shone his flashlight on the square.

Bruno saw the dark plastic keypad, with no visible numbers or letters. He nearly swore out loud. A scramble pad. The position of the numbers or letters moved to a different key every time it was activated, that way no one could just learn the pattern or look for wear marks on certain keys. He had assumed the code would be used on a physical device, like the combination lock on a safe, not this power-dependent lock. How could he get in? The power had to be off, and he didn't have nearly enough tools to try to force the doors.

For a moment Bruno stood there. Not sure what else to do, Bruno touched the keypad. The keys lit up, glowing red, and they beeped in acknowledgement. The keypad's response startled him. Must be battery powered. He wondered how long before the battery died, making whatever lay behind the doors forever inaccessible. Bruno looked at the keys, now a matrix of scrambled numbers glowing a dull red, with an extra row of letters underneath, and two arrow keys on either side of the letter row. He had never seen one with that extra row before. He typed in the number code and scrolled through the alphabet until he found the right letters. He had studied the complex string of letters and numbers from the transmission so much that it took him only seconds to input them. Bruno paused for a moment, then he pushed the "enter" key. He heard a buzz and a click from the door. Breathing deeply of the dusty air, he pulled the door handle.

It surprised Bruno how much of his body weight he used as he tugged on the handle. The door crept outward, with only the smallest creak.

As the door crawled open, muffled shouts, barely audible, reached Bruno's ears. The sounds drifted down from back towards the ramp. DeLuca! Bruno's mind played out his choices in microseconds—leave the door open and risk having whatever was behind the door taken from him, or close the door and risk not being able to open it again, maybe losing the opportunity forever to acquire real firepower and whatever else might lay hidden behind the steel door.

For a second he hesitated, paralyzed by the choice that might determine his fate and that of DeLuca. Then he acted. Pushing the door firmly closed, Bruno angled his flashlight toward the ground and jogged back toward the entrance. The voices grew louder, but Bruno slowed as he got closer to the entrance, fearful they might hear his steps. As Bruno approached the bottom of the ramp, he turned off his flashlight. Figures moving back and forth interrupted the crack of light that shone down.

"E con chìstu ccà, che cazzo ci facimmo?" asked a male's voice from above, speaking in the dialect of the region. "So, what are we gonna do with this one?"

Someone laughed. A boy, Bruno thought. "Dunno. Let's kill him."

A third male voice: "Screw that! We'd better take him back."

"Why? What if he's got the Bloody Shits?" asked the second voice.

"You! Show me your hands!"

"He seems clean."

"Doesn't matter, we've still got to put him in quarantine. Us, too. Three days, no less."

"We need to find out who he is, why he's here. Does he have friends? Did he come from Naples?"

There was some muttering, but Bruno couldn't make out what they said.

"Fine. We take him. Cover his eyes!"

"Hold on . . ." That was DeLuca, but a slap cut him off.

Bruno had to decide what to do. And fast. He knew if he tried to burst out from down there, guns blazing, he wouldn't have much of a chance. A thought from deep within bubbled to the surface of Bruno's mind. Bruno could abandon DeLuca. Yes, some dark part of Bruno thought, it's his fault this happened, it's his fault we're even here. DeLuca deserves this. DeLuca caused Veri's death. Why should Bruno ride to his rescue, yet again? 'Do what you have to do to live' is what he'd said to DeLuca; why should Bruno do any less himself? It would be so easy just to leave that old man, to wait until they took him away, and then slink back to the boat. Back to Capri. Safe. Back home. Bruno squeezed his eyes shut, fighting the urge to do nothing and wait all alone in the dark until they were gone for good.

He heard steps and scuffling, and then the voices faded. He walked up the ramp and pushed the door up just enough to get a look. Bruno looked at the backs of four or five figures heading out of Piazza Tasso, north onto Viale Enrico Caruso, between the tall trees lining the wide boulevard. He bided his time, and just as they rounded a bend in the road, maybe three blocks away, he pushed the metal door open, making his way onto the street. He shut the door behind him as quietly as he could.

Bruno shouldered his backpack and cinched it tight. A balancing act. Not too close, not too far. Almost on tiptoes, He stepped quickly, following the group north. He hid between cars and trees as he moved, the sinking sun casting long shadows over the silent buildings.

Bruno had made his choice. He would not just leave DeLuca to his fate. Not without a fight.

CHAPTER 20

September 19

Bruno lowered his binoculars, turned around in the cramped back seat, and rubbed his back. At least he was able to stretch out a little in the back seat overnight. Still, cat-napping in the two-door car had left him fatigued and sore, and he chafed at being confined in the back seat of the hatchback all night. But any stiffness was well worth it: the car sheltered him from any mosquitoes that might be lingering in the late summer, and its tinted windows gave him good cover from prying eyes. Still, Bruno had been on edge all night. His little cat-and-mouse game had nearly ended in disaster when he kicked that empty soda can as he followed them back through the winding, narrow street out of Sorrento into the hills to the south. After that, the group holding DeLuca took great care to be silent on the way back, and Bruno had nearly lost them more than once. But he persisted, and had found their lair.

He turned around, looked out the back window, and raised his binoculars again. The morning light splashed across high flagstone walls, flanking both sides of the barely two-lane street. About one hundred meters away, the street curved up and around to the left, wandering out of Bruno's sight and rising deeper into the wooded hills outside Sorrento. A four-level apartment building, studded with balconies, stood at the top of the curve on the left side, commanding the street stretching beneath it. The other residential buildings on this street ran along the top of the flagstone wall.

Having been in the outskirts of Sorrento many years ago, Bruno vaguely recalled that behind some of these buildings, hectares of orchards, vineyards, and olive groves lay unseen from street level.

No wonder they live here, mused Bruno. Defensible, with resources. A good spot. Bruno's thoughts turned to the grim task of what to do next. All of his options were bad. He didn't know how many there were up there, and all he had in hand was his pistol. Even if he went back to the cache and found enough weapons to start his own guerrilla war, what could he do? Shoot an RPG into the building? Kill everyone inside? If that was his best option, he might as well go back to Capri. Maybe if Bruno did nothing, DeLuca might actually stand a better chance at survival. Bruno exhaled, loud even in his own ears. For all Bruno knew, this whole damned rescue might be futile. By now, they could have changed their mind, and DeLuca's body could be rotting away in the grass under some olive tree.

Bruno gazed up the street. He couldn't just storm the building, impregnable as a castle. No, he would choose another path, one of which DeLuca would approve—one that required a bit of faith.

The crackle of his radio jolted him. Bruno had left it on just in case DeLuca managed to get a message out. But it was not DeLuca's voice that emerged from his jacket pocket.

"Show yourself or your friend is dead!"

So much for any element of surprise. Bruno exited the car and looked up the street. The sun illuminated the tops of the buildings, but the street still lay in partial shade. The morning air hovered over Bruno, still and quiet, but sweat made his t-shirt stick to his back as the temperature rose and his nerves tensed. He walked on the left side of the street, hugging the stone wall. Though willing to take a risk, Bruno preferred not to give them an easy target. He knew this rescue could end with a muzzle flash and a bullet through his skull. The voice came on the radio once more.

"You've got five minutes to answer or show yourself."

Bruno turned down the radio's volume to almost nothing before proceeding. His boots made no sound as he approached their building. He stopped not far from the door in the long flagstone wall. Judging the distance to be about right, he shouted out loud, up towards the building.

Instead of responding on the radio, Bruno shouted, "Hey! You, in the building! I want to talk!"

His voice echoed across the stones and faded into silence. The wind picked up, shooting down the street, loud in Bruno's ears for a moment, before it too died away. He forced himself to yell again. But his shouts echoed in impotent noise, met only by the wind. Bruno's unease grew. He felt the urge to hide.

"Up here!"

The male voice came from the building. It sounded like he was maybe two stories up from the ground floor. Bruno kept his left hand on the wall as he leaned towards the center of the street and responded.

"You've got my friend! I want him back!"

The man laughed. "Oh do you? Why should we give him back?" Bruno saw movement midway up the building and curtains on a balcony fluttered as a man stepped outside.

Bruno squinted, the sun now higher in the sky.

"Why should we give him back?" the man repeated.

Bruno took stock of him. Bruno guessed he was maybe twenty years old. Curly hair floated around his head like a mane, and scruffy black stubble ran down his face onto his neck. With a thin green nylon jacket hanging open over a soiled white t-shirt, he looked to Bruno like a throwback to the old *paninaro* look from the '90s. Bruno might have been amused but for the long rifle gripped in his left hand. Even from this distance, Bruno could see the wooden butt stock and black barrel. Older rife, bolt action probably. Even if it could hold more than one bullet, unless the kid was well trained, he would realistically get only one shot to kill Bruno.

"Because he's my friend. And he didn't do anything to you!" responded Bruno.

The kid shifted around on the balcony, getting a better grip on the rifle. "So, friend, tell me something. Why shouldn't I just shoot you right from here? Why not?"

Bruno knew from hostage negotiation training long ago that the longer they spoke, the better, and that the chance for violence diminished with every phrase exchanged. Yet for the thousandth time, Bruno wished for his body armor and a carbine. Then, maybe he wouldn't have to trade words with this little shit. Bruno breathed deeply before speaking, calming his anger. What Bruno was about to say might decide the fate of them all, and he couldn't afford to cock it up.

"Because you need me."

The kid laughed, as Bruno expected. But he didn't respond to Bruno's statement with an expected question.

"What's your name?"

The question took him aback and for a moment, fear gripped Bruno. He looked around, checking the street behind him. Was the little prick playing for time? Were there others around that Bruno couldn't see? Then the kid spoke again, his voice raised louder.

"Are you deaf? I said, what's your name!"

"Bruno. My name is Bruno!"

The kid on the balcony nodded. "My name is Stefano. I'm listening."

"Show me my friend and we'll talk."

Stefano glanced back over his shoulder. From inside the flat, out shuffled DeLuca, hair tousled and face pale.

Bruno called up to him. "Hello, old man! You okay?"

DeLuca nodded at Bruno. "In quarantine with these . . . young men. I'm all right! For now." DeLuca glanced sidelong at his captor.

Stefano shooed DeLuca back indoors and spoke once more.

"I've showed you he's alive and well. Now, tell me why we need you?"

"Your rifle. Bolt action, isn't it? Don't you want something better? Something better than they had in the 1800s? And how much ammo do you have? You can't have much."

"What's your point?"

"Weapons. I can get you modern weapons. And ammo." In one breath, Bruno told him about the weapon cache, the door, and even its general location.

Even from this distance, Bruno saw Stefano's eyes narrowing. "So, what do I need you for? Why shouldn't I just shoot you now and be done with you, take the weapons myself?"

Bruno laughed. "Feel free. Door's probably half-a-meter-thick steel. Something tells me you lot would never get through."

Bruno tapped his temple. "No, that combination is right here. So, listen up, picciottu: don't even think about hurting the old man. And if you take a shot at me, you'd better not miss, or I'll come for *you . . .*" Bruno paused but Stefano said nothing, so Bruno spoke again. "Well, what do you say?

Stefano shifted. "And if I don't believe a fucking word you've said? What then?"

Bruno shrugged. "Guess you can find out the hard way."

Stefano started to speak, but a voice from above cut him off.

"Enough!"

A figure stepped out onto the balcony one floor above Stefano.

Her hair was pulled back into a ponytail, mostly grey with a few black strands. A man's oversized button-down shirt hung from her shoulders. She gazed down on him in silence. Before everything fell apart, Bruno might have thought she was in her late sixties. But now, without trips to the salon and spa, Bruno wondered whether she was in her fifties, or maybe even younger. Before the world fell to pieces, Bruno would have said she was a dried-up hag. Now, he'd say she was an angel.

"We need those weapons," she stated with no emotion. "How did you know about this cache?"

"I was a Carabiniere," he said, obscuring a lie of omission in the truth and hoping it would be enough.

"Yes, I know you are," she answered, responding in the present tense. "He said you'd come for him."

Cazzo. Bruno wondered what else DeLuca had given up.

"How do you know the weapons are still there?" she called down.

Bruno shook his head. "I don't."

She took a step back and rubbed her forehead. Then she bent down and spoke in low tones to Stefano on the balcony below. Bruno couldn't hear what they said, but whatever she said agitated Stefano.

She called down. "We'll let you in! Follow the stairs up to the entrance to the apartments. Don't move until I say so. You'll stay in a ground-floor apartment in quarantine for three days. From where you are, we've got the upstairs blocked off, so don't waste your time trying to come up." Then the woman smiled. "I'm sure you're armed. So, don't leave the apartment. You try anything we don't like, and we'll put a bullet in your friend's head, then yours next, understood?"

The woman turned towards the inside of the apartment and spoke in a low voice. Then she turned back to Bruno.

"Paola. My name is Paola, in case you're wondering."

Bruno was about to respond when he heard scraping and movement from the door in the wall in front of him. He took a step forward, but Paola shook her head. Bruno waited, uncomfortably exposed in the high morning sun, until she called down to him to go ahead.

Bruno stepped forward until he reached the door in the flagstone wall and with a deep breath, he turned the door handle. Paola called down to him again.

"One of the ground floor apartments is free. The door is open. There's food and water for three days. After the quarantine, we'll come down to you. Lock the entrance door behind you before you come up."

Through the stone doorway, Bruno looked up. Flagstone stairs stretched up to the ground floor of the apartment building. No overgrown underbrush spilled onto the stairs. The browning grass on each side of the staircase and poking between the stones were the only obvious signs that this place was not what it once was. The apartment building rested at the top of the rise, to Bruno's right as he looked up the stairs.

Bruno stepped through the doorway, turned around, and threw the deadbolt lock on the door. He walked up the stairs, glancing to his right towards the building. Stefano glowered down at him in silence. Paola, too, watched him.

Cresting the top of the stairs, Bruno could feel sweat running down his back. The flat, grey stones made a large patio encircling the ground floor of the apartment building. Glass doors and windows enclosed a lobby on the ground floor. The sunlight made Bruno squint as he surveyed the area. Beyond the patio, an enclosure the size of a small park rolled down in front of him. Olive trees dotted the area, and Bruno noticed a patch of tomato plants tied to stakes.

Bruno un-holstered his pistol, approached the glass door, pushed it open with his left hand, and entered the lobby. Down the hall to his left, he spied an open door. Carefully, he approached and entered the apartment. Bruno checked each room, pistol in hand. The apartment was of modest size, with a combined kitchen and living area, a bedroom, bathroom, and a sliding door to a small patio facing into the green area beyond the building. The place had been stripped bare, and he could find no trace of the previous occupant. The only things of value were cans of food and a few bottles of water sitting on the counter near the kitchen sink. Enough for three or four days. Bruno holstered his pistol. He took a bottle of water into the bedroom and sat on the bed. Though he had no idea how many of them there were, at this point he was all in. Either they were going to kill him or they would be true to their word. He didn't see any sense in doing anything but settling in. He hoped the rest of his gear would be safe in the car. He lay down on his back, pistol on his chest, and rubbed his forehead.

The certainty of three lost days, waiting, sleeping, wasting time, lay heavy in his thoughts, but he didn't see any other way. He spotted a glossy magazine on the floor and picked it up. On its cover, the face of a smiling, almost certainly dead, celebrity stared back at Bruno. Her shining-white teeth seemed to light up the room. Bruno threw the magazine against the wall and lay back down on the bed.

***

September 23

A loud rapping startled Bruno out of a deep slumber. The glow of the early morning sun bathed the bedroom in diffused light. He threw on his pants and boots, grabbed his pistol, and made his way into the living area.

"Hey, Signor Bruno!" a man called from outside the apartment door. "You still alive?"

"Still here, and still healthy!" responded Bruno.

Bruno heard the keys clinking and the click of a bolt.

"I'm opening the door," said the voice. "Wait thirty seconds, then come out and meet us." Bruno heard footsteps, as whoever it was retreated back down the hall.

Bruno paused, with his hand on the door handle. He understood that since they had the key, they could have come in and killed him any time in the last three days. Logic told Bruno that they were hardly likely to kill him now. And yet he still hesitated.

"Well, are you fucking coming out or what?"

"Yes, yes, coming out now," answered Bruno.

He pulled the handle down, opened the door, and stepped out into the hallway.

Gentle sunlight from the lobby scattered down the hallway, giving it a dull glow. Bruno saw several figures waiting for him at the end of the hall and he walked, in no rush, in their direction.

As Bruno entered the bright open space of the lobby, he felt many pairs of eyes staring at him. Bruno hadn't seen this many people together since before the Shakes. He felt cramped and crowded, feeling as claustrophobic as he had during the press of people at a Napoli football match. But when he counted, there were only six people in the lobby, and DeLuca was among them.

They stood in silence for a moment, then DeLuca spoke.

"Thanks for coming back, Bruno." Emotion made DeLuca's voice quiver.

Bruno nodded. "You know I couldn't leave you, old man." He sized up the others gathered in the lobby as he spoke.

"Your hands," said Stefano.

Bruno held out his hands. "Steady as ever," he said.

Each of them did the same. Bruno looked at each of them, then nodded. All of them lowered their hands to their sides.

Paola and Stefano watched him, Stefano with a rifle in his right hand. Bruno noticed his fingers clenching and unclenching as he held the stock across his chest. Three others Bruno had never seen also stood in front of him.

"I'm sure you've got a gun, yes?" said Paola. "So put it on the ground, slowly, and kick it to me."

Bruno complied. The pistol skidded to Paola's feet.

"Thank you. You'll get it back once we find the cache." Paola gestured around her. "This is Saverio, Mauro, and Aldo."

Bruno nodded and looked them over. Saverio and Mauro couldn't have been more than eighteen or nineteen, their scruffy beards and long-sleeve print t-shirts making them look like hash-smokers fresh from a concert. Aldo, though, looked older, maybe in his late forties, brown hair thinning. Bruno noticed the skin around Aldo's neck hung loosely, like he had once been paunchy. Aldo nodded, his watery blue eyes making him look like a sad sack to Bruno.

Bruno spoke up. "So, how did all of you end up—"

"Cut the bullshit, cop!" interrupted Stefano. "Take us to the weapons."

Bruno threw his hands up. "Okay, okay, take it easy. I'm ready when you are."

Paola shot Stefano a look. "I'm going to go up to a balcony," he said. "To make sure no one is on the road before we leave." Then he stormed off.

The group made its way out of the lobby and started down the stairs. All of them wore long-sleeve shirts of one sort or another, despite the warming air. They hustled down the stairs, then waited near the door leading out onto the street. They watched as Stefano peered down past the wall into the street for a few moments before nodding and turning back inside the apartment. They waited a moment in silence. Then Stefano came bounding down the stairs, rifle in hand.

"All clear," Stefano announced. Paola produced a key from her pocket and unlocked the door in the flagstone wall to the street. She and Bruno were the last ones out. She turned and locked the door. Bruno lingered back with her, and they quickly caught up to the group as it began walking down the street.

"No one around?" asked Bruno as they caught up.

"No, not for a long while." Paola tossed her head back up toward the balcony where Stefano had surveyed the street. "But still, we're very careful after that bunch from Naples came up."

Bruno stiffened, and DeLuca's eyes met his. Bruno noticed Aldo, Paola, and Saverio look at him. This time Aldo spoke.

"What? What do you know?" Aldo asked.

"Wait," Bruno said, not responding to the question. They had arrived at the car where Bruno had stowed his gear. "I have some gear here."

Stefano stepped forward. "I'll get it."

Bruno gestured to the back seat. Stefano stooped into the vehicle and retrieved Bruno's backpack. Stefano unzipped it and rummaged around before handing it to Bruno. "I don't want surprises; got it, Bruno?"

"No surprises from me." Bruno slung the backpack over his shoulder and continued walking.

Aldo persisted, his voice rising, "I said: what do you know about Naples?"

Bruno answered with his own questions. "These people from Naples . . . when were they here?"

Stefano gave his opinion right away.

"Bastards!" he spat. "They came here plundering, looting, raping. They came when things got really bad. Just about the time when you cops had deserted us for good, right?"

Bruno refused to give him the satisfaction of a reaction, choosing instead to repeat the question. "So, like I said, when were they here?"

Stefano, giving up his taunting, shrugged. "Maybe eight months ago. Bunch of wankers, twenty or twenty-five of them, maybe more."

Now Mauro spoke up. "A few of us fought. That's how we found Aldo."

Aldo didn't even glance up as they talked, but continued trudging along, shoulders hunched. Bruno could see that as soon as Mauro mentioned how they found Aldo, he had treaded onto sensitive territory.

Paola spoke sotto voce. "Saverio and Mauro caught two of them by surprise. But not before they savaged Aldo's daughter and nearly beat him to death."

Stefano chimed in. "Oh, but we got a few of them good, didn't we? Those bastards got what they deserved, didn't they?"

Stefano turned towards Bruno, making a scissor's cutting motion right at crotch-level, and laughed. "Better be nice to us, cop!"

Paola said nothing.

Now even people who used to be "the good guys" were as barbarous as the bad, discussing mutilation and torture as if talking about the funny parts in a movie. Not much more than a year ago, these boys' only worry was whether their mothers would catch them sexting on their phones. Now they laughed about mutilating men. Their savagery is what passed for justice now. But Bruno wondered whether, just maybe, deep down, that's how it had always been. Maybe it just took a disease to strip off the pretense of calculating justice and lay bare what really lurked in its heart: passionate revenge.

Mauro spoke up. "That bald guy." Mauro shook his head. "I wish we could have gotten him, too! What a piece of—"

Bruno grabbed Mauro by the arm and Mauro pulled away, yanking a revolver from somewhere on his body.

"Don't touch me! I'll blow your fucking head off!"

Stefano swung his rifle towards Bruno's chest. Everyone else stopped dead. Bruno threw up his hands, letting Mauro's arm go.

"Sorry, I just need to know—" Bruno said.

"You just what?" answered Stefano. "What do you need to know?"

Bruno breathed deeply. "The bald one. What did he look like?"

Aldo spoke up for the first time. "He had a tattoo on his head. Double-headed eagle. I'll never forget it."

DeLuca took Bruno's arm, whispering, "It's all right."

Paola stepped forward. "You know who he is."

Bruno swallowed. "I think . . ." Bruno grew quiet. Then he spoke with confidence. "He's a Camorrista. And a particularly nasty one. Nickname is Il Serbo. He wants to kill me. Or worse."

"What's he got against you?" asked Stefano.

"We were on a raid back when Omega was spreading. I shot his brother." Bruno thought for a second about continuing his lie, but then realized it didn't matter anymore. "It was an accident, but when the investigators asked me, I told them the brother made a grab for my weapon." Bruno shrugged. "But he didn't."

Paola's eyes narrowed. "You're just as bad as they are."

Bruno laughed. "Oh I see, you're a saint, right?"

Paola just looked at him.

Bruno's smile faded and he turned to the group. "You've all been perfect fucking angels since it all went to shit, is that it?" No one responded. His eyes narrowed as he moved toward Paola.

"That guy was a rapist and a murderer. I shot him by accident. I fucked up, yes. But he deserved what he got, and I don't feel bad at all. Not one damn bit."

"Weren't you supposed to uphold the law, not break it?" Paola said. "And that was before the Blood Sweats really hit. What are you like now?"

Bruno didn't answer, then Mauro spoke up.

"Oh, Paola doesn't get how things are." Mauro pointed his finger at Bruno and pulled a pretend trigger. "We get it. You finished him. He deserved it."

Stefano joined in the joking, too. "Sure, don't worry. If you're lucky, maybe some other cop shot your Camorrista friend, too!"

Ignoring their derision, Bruno walked in silence near Aldo, while Mauro and Stefano lingered in the back, laughing, talking about nothing. Bruno eavesdropped as Paola and DeLuca discussed life after it all went to hell, how their group had gotten together, and the future.

"I was friends with Mauro's mother," Paola said to DeLuca. "She worked in my restaurant."

Bruno slowed, matching pace with Paola and DeLuca and interrupted their discussion with a question of his own. "How did you survive?"

Paola looked at Bruno. "How did *you*? Like any of us. Hunkering down. Scavenging. Doing things we never thought we could."

"What about Stefano and Saverio?" DeLuca asked.

"Saverio was one of Aldo's students at school. And Stefano? Just a kid, some hooligan, really, loved the Sorrento calcio team. But a real scrapper. He took down three guys. Mauro and I found him unconscious, bleeding, a real mess, and those guys—well, let's just say, they got more than they bargained for."

"So why help him then?" asked Bruno. "He could have been dangerous. Why not let him die?"

"Same reason I helped you, maybe. I've got a soft spot for someone who's a scrapper. That kind of person reminds me of my son. He never gave up, not even after . . ." Paola's gaze wandered for a moment. Then she turned back to Bruno. "My son was a local, municipal police office here in Sorrento. He always said the Carabinieri got paid double to do half."

Bruno smiled at her joke. But it was what she said next that infuriated him.

"But you're not like him—I know he would never have done what *you* did."

Bruno's anger at this woman, who judged him and found him lacking, swelled.

"You judge me? They came after me—they raped my sister! Don't you fucking *dare* judge me!"

She held his gaze as she spoke. "Guess you gave them exactly what they deserved, too, didn't you?"

Bruno felt a hand on his arm.

"Bruno, please" said DeLuca. "Enough."

Coming to his senses in a rush, Bruno backed away. Their situation was already precarious, and he didn't want to make it any worse.

Eyes still boring into Bruno, they began moving again. Drifting back, Bruno turned his observations as best he could to the group as they made their way towards Sorrento's main square. Stefano kept his rifle out and walked a few steps behind. Bruno knew Stefano wouldn't hesitate to kill him if he had another outburst. Bruno did his best to watch the others. He noticed the boys were on the lookout for anything unusual. He also noticed the confidence in their step, their causal ease as they walked. He could see they knew this area well, but he wondered if their overconfidence would someday be their undoing. Aldo, though, plodded along, mostly indifferent and quiet. Bruno studied Aldo as they walked. Aldo kept his gaze focused on the pavement just in front of him. His hunched shoulders and meek shuffle spoke of a broken man. Bruno wondered if he had any useful skills.

As they came into Sorrento's main square, Saverio and Mauro led the group. The two produced revolvers. Paola, Bruno, and DeLuca walked just behind them. Aldo brought up the rear along with Stefano, who readied his rifle. Bruno could almost feel Stefano hoping for a reason to put a bullet in his back.

"Where is it?" asked Paola.

Bruno nodded towards the light-pink building with the stopped clock and glass enclosed patio.

"There?" said Saverio, glancing back at Bruno. "Fucking hell! A restaurant? Are you joking?"

Bruno shook his head. "No joke, it's down the service entrance. Leads to what should be the basement. Who would ever think to put weapons there?"

Saverio shook his head as they crossed the square and stopped in front of the metal doors. "Well, now I know why the pizza here was always shit."

By now the sun rode high in the sky, beating down on the group. Bruno could smell sweat and anxiety clinging to them as they stood there. He pulled open the door. A puff of cool air hit him in the face. Though the sun shone brightly, it only illuminated the top of the ramp. Beyond that, the darkness was complete.

Bruno opened his backpack and took out his flashlight. "Down here."

Stefano gestured with his rifle. "You first."

Bruno nodded. "Fair enough."

"I'll stand watch up here," Mauro volunteered.

"I'll stay with you," said DeLuca.

"No," said Stefano. "He comes with us!"

Paola nodded. "I agree. Mauro stays. The rest of us are going down with you, Bruno."

Bruno shrugged. "Fine." It didn't matter if DeLuca came or stayed. If looters had gotten here first, if all that was down there was dust, Bruno knew that the cache would probably become their tomb. He looked down into the gloom, and his flashlight illuminated the area. He could see no sign of disturbance.

Paola and Aldo took out flashlights and turned them on.

"You walk in front. We'll be right next to you," said Paola.

Bruno walked between Paola and Aldo as they stepped down into the darkness. DeLuca followed on their heels, while Saverio and Stefano were in the back. The smell of dry dust filled Bruno's nose. They walked in silence, almost as if the darkness demanded it. Bruno glanced behind him. Though already dim, he could just distinguish the rifle carried by Stefano, pointing towards DeLuca's back.

After what seemed an age, they reached the dull steel doors.

"Here it is," said Bruno, his voice sounding too loud in the dark. He moved past Paola to the panel. Touching the panel, it once again flared to life. He tucked the flashlight under one armpit, and then put in the combination.

"You pull anything, and DeLuca dies, then you," said Stefano.

Ignoring the threat, Bruno heard the sharp buzz of the door's mechanism unlocking. Bruno turned back to the group. He had left the doors to the street open, so there was still some dim glow behind them. But he couldn't see anyone's face.

"This is it."

Paola responded. "You first, Bruno. We'll be right behind you."

Bruno hoped a bullet wouldn't be right behind him as well. Moving toward the door, he shifted the flashlight into his left hand and tugged on the door with his right. With some effort, the door swung outward. The darkness in the chamber seemed to creep out into the tunnel.

Bruno walked forward, swinging his flashlight around. He had the sense of a large space and his light hit the far wall dimly, maybe twenty meters from the entrance. His boots stirred up dust on the concrete floor, and the sounds from their steps echoed in the room as the rest of the group entered.

The beams from their flashlights danced all around the room, falling on bare concrete walls. Dust whirled around in the dark emptiness.

"There's nothing here," said Paola.

"Keep looking. There must be something," said Bruno. He swept his flashlight back and forth, hoping that the signal was not an empty lie, empty like the space before him.

The group moved deeper into the room, their flashlights probing the darkness.

"I still don't see anything," said Saverio.

"Keep looking, for Christ's sake!" said Bruno.

While looking towards what he thought was the far end of the room, Bruno heard a grunt and a thud behind him. Swinging around, his flashlight fell on Stefano towering over DeLuca, who was lying on the floor. Stefano pointed his rifle at DeLuca's head.

"I said you were dead!" shouted Stefano.

"Let him up!" Bruno shouted. Light splashed around as Paola and Saverio aimed their pistols and shined their flashlights at Bruno.

The two flashlights weren't powerful enough to blind him, but he squinted as he shouted again. "Let him up! I told you there were no guarantees!"

"I said that—" started Stefano, then a voice from across the room cut him off.

"Wait!" cried Aldo from across the dark room. "Over here! I found something!"

Bruno could see Paola looking at him, but couldn't see her eyes as she spoke. "We're all going to lower our weapons."

Paola and Saverio lowered their weapons and aimed their flashlights at the ground. Though pointed down, they illuminated the gloom enough for Bruno to see Stefano still pointing his rifle at a prostrate DeLuca.

"Sure, we'll do it your way then, Paola," said Stefano, his voice taut. Stefano stepped back and DeLuca scrambled to his feet.

"Look at this!" shouted Aldo across the dark room.

The rest of them made their way over to Aldo's voice. He pulled aside a tarp and tossed it to the floor. Their flashlights shone on what was underneath, illuminating the lines of a motorcycle, with an attached side car. The motorcycle shielded most of the sidecar from view, as the sidecar butted up against the stone wall.

"That's it?" said Stefano. "A motorcycle?"

"Keep going," said Bruno. "There might be something else here."

The group fanned out, beams of light bobbing around. But after a few minutes they ended up back at the motorcycle.

"What the hell are we going to do with this?" asked Stefano.

Bruno approached the motorcycle, flashlight in hand, starting at the front and walking toward the back.

"Key's in the ignition, at least," he said. "Maybe it still has fuel."

Aldo grunted. "Lovely. Maybe we could take turns riding the scenic road along the coast."

Bruno ran one hand along the body and moved the flashlight beam along its length. "I think I recognize the model," said Bruno. "It's unmarked, got a diesel engine."

Bruno remembered that diesel fuel lasted longer than gasoline, so he hoped it might still run. He half-mounted the motorcycle and looked in the sidecar. Shining his flashlight into it, Bruno saw a long barrel. He grasped it and pulled it out. The group's flashlights converged on Bruno.

Bruno studied the long lines of the weapon.

"One fucking rifle? That's all? What can we do with this?" said Stefano.

Bruno looked closely at the scope on top. The rifle had a shorter, somewhat "bull-pup" design, not as lean as an M-16. He adjusted the stock, shorter, longer, then he saw that it folded. A detachable bipod dangled from near the end of the barrel, making it top-heavy.

"Nice," Bruno said under his breath. Then he raised his voice. "I've never seen one of these before, but I've heard of it. They were just starting to issue this rifle when everything went to hell. Certain army units got it first."

He looked again at the scope mounted along the top of the rifle.

"Must be a laser scope of some sort," he said.

The scope was obviously designed to be quickly detached, judging by the levers at its base. But it seemed unusually large and bulky. There was an on/off button, and other buttons, black rubber, running flush along the base.

He pushed the on button and looked in the scope. He had never seen anything like it. What he saw reminded him of a heads-up display in a fighter plane. As he looked into it, he remembered an article he'd read on a military website describing a scope like this. He remembered now reading about this scope and what it could do. Bruno leaned over and looked in the sidecar, shining his flashlight. There was an ammo can and a magazine. Bruno turned toward the group, smiling.

"It's an ARX-160. And with this scope and enough ammo, maybe we can start an empire."

Aldo spoke up first.

"With one rifle? What the hell are we going to do with one rifle?"

Bruno stuffed the extra magazine in his pants pocket. He grabbed the ammo can with one hand while he held the rifle.

"Don't worry, lads," said Bruno. "It's empty! Here!"

Bruno handed the rifle to Paola.

Paola took the rifle and Bruno strode through the middle of the group, walking back toward the entrance.

They stood there in the semi-dark, waiting for some explanation. Bruno nodded back toward where they had come in.

"Come on. Let me show you what this thing can do."

CHAPTER 21

October 7

The sound of a single gunshot broke the morning silence.

The summer, lingering on past its prime, clinging to life like a sour old man, made Bruno sweat. Bruno wiped his brow with his sleeve and squinted into the distance, shielding his eyes from the sun.

"Good shot, Aldo!" he shouted.

From his position on one knee, Aldo stood and hoisted the rifle up from the ledge. Bruno stood behind, slightly to Aldo's right. Far down the street towards the heart of Sorrento, on the top of another nondescript apartment building, Bruno could just make out a row of terracotta flower pots along the roofline. But the line of pots now had a gap. Aldo shielded his eyes and looked downrange. After admiring his handiwork for a moment, he turned around, smiling, and handed the rifle to Bruno. Bruno could see a change in Aldo from when they'd first met. Aldo now had a spark in his eye. He had a purpose.

The group stood behind Aldo on the roof of the apartment building where they made their home. Stefano huddled by Saverio and Mauro, while Paola and DeLuca stood in their own group a little apart from the others.

After making sure the rifle chamber was empty, Bruno glanced around. The group made quite a sight, ears plugged with random scraps of cloth dangling along the sides of their heads.

Bruno pulled the cloth from his ears with one hand, and the rest of the group followed his lead.

"Good shot," he repeated. "I think we're done. You hit that pot dead-center!"

Saverio laughed. "He never misses, does he?"

Aldo shook his head, smiling. "Almost never."

Bruno smiled. "That pot must be over six hundred meters away."

"Actually," answered Aldo, "it was six hundred thirty-four meters, to be exact."

Bruno nodded. "The distance calculator is a great feature, huh?"

"So is the targeting function," laughed Aldo.

Bruno knelt down on one knee, resting the rifle's bipod on the ledge. He aimed the rifle towards the pot next to the one Aldo had obliterated. He looked in the scope and saw the now-familiar green dot. Then he pushed the button on the side of the scope with his right thumb. After a second or so delay, bullet drop compensators with a flashing red dot appeared a little above and to the right of the pot. Bruno raised the rifle ever so slightly, matching the green dot over the red. When the dots matched, they blinked on and off as one. Bruno stood back up, shaking his head as he handed the rifle back to Aldo.

"Incredible," Bruno said.

Aldo nodded. "Just activate target designation function, and move the green dot onto the red dot, then, BANG, it's over."

"Well," said Bruno. "You still have to worry about shooting fundamentals: breath control, a stable platform, flinching, trigger pull, and all that."

"Understood."

Bruno continued, wanting to make sure they all heard him. "But you've got the best technique of anyone here." He moved towards the rest of the group. "And that means that Aldo here should carry the rifle." Everyone nodded their agreement. Even Stefano.

"I wonder why they left it there?" said Aldo.

Bruno shrugged. "Who knows? I wouldn't shoot much farther than six hundred meters. The bullet is running out of punch by that distance. And 5.56 mm is not the ideal caliber for a sniper. Maybe the scope belonged on another rifle. Maybe they meant to come back for it."

"Good thing they never did."

Saverio spoke up. "Shall we get off the roof before we fry?"

Stefano looked up at the sky. "Yeah, still feels more like summer than fall." Fair-weather clouds drifted in front of the sun, giving them a moment of shade. Stefano looked down, then looked up at Bruno before he spoke.

"We hate to see you go."

Bruno smiled. Quite a change from the belligerence Stefano displayed not long ago. "We don't want to go, either. But you know what we're trying to do."

Stefano nodded.

Bruno looked at the group. "It's time."

They made their way off the roof through a doorway that led downstairs to the ground floor of Paola's lair. Bruno smiled to himself as he scooped up his backpack along with another from the glass entryway. "Paola's lair" is what DeLuca called their hideout. Sounded like the name of some hip club in Milan. From the ground floor, they made their way back out through the courtyard, down the steps and to the street. The group spoke in low voices, talking but saying little. Out of the corner of his eye, Bruno watched Paola and DeLuca whispering together. DeLuca's hand rested on her elbow as they spoke. The way DeLuca moved around Paola told Bruno everything he needed to know.

They assembled on the cobblestone street just outside the entrance to the group's home. The motorcycle from the weapons cache stood gleaming black in the sun. Bruno loaded up the side car with his gear and DeLuca, tearing himself away from Paola, did the same. He would have to ride behind Bruno, since their backpacks took up most of the room in the sidecar.

DeLuca looked at Bruno as he arranged his gear. "Give me a second."

"Sure." Bruno watched as DeLuca moved off up the street a few meters, just out of earshot of the group, and Paola followed. Bruno stopped what he was doing and walked over to Saverio, Mauro, Stefano, and Aldo.

Bruno shook hands with each of them, smiling as he did so. Then he turned to Aldo, clapping him on the arm that held the rifle. Bruno glanced down as he spoke.

"Watch the ammo, Aldo. Remember, when the bullets run out, it's back to clubs and knives."

Aldo grasped Bruno's own shoulder in response, his gaze serious as he spoke. "Thank you for teaching us how to use this."

"Just watch your fundamentals."

Bruno pulled the radio out of his jacket pocket and handed it to Stefano.

Stefano studied the radio for a moment. "I wrote down the transmission schedule. I'll turn it on every time like you said."

"Just make sure you turn it off after ten minutes. Don't want to run down the charge," said Bruno. "We'll probably have to get on top of a building to get a signal out, so don't worry if you don't hear from us. We'll just text—no voice unless we have a serious problem."

Bruno looked at Stefano's wrist. "Please tell me you have a watch."

"Oh yeah," laughed Stefano, tugging on his sleeve, revealing an analog watch. "I'm old-school like you, Bruno." Stefano looked down at his watch and shrugged. "No telling how long the battery will last, though."

"Hopefully long enough for this adventure." Bruno looked up at the sky. "Shall we call this 10:00?" The exact time no longer had any meaning. All that mattered was that they agreed to some arbitrary time so that they would turn on their radios at the same moment.

"Works for me."

Bruno looked down. "I wish one of you would come. You know what this is about. Paola, she doesn't—"

The group looked at Bruno, then at each other. Mauro spoke first.

"We want to come," said Mauro. "But Paola, she . . ."

Saverio chimed in when Mauro faltered. "She thinks what you're doing is crazy. And she doesn't trust you, not after what you told her you did."

"We think she's wrong," said Stefano. "But we're alive because of her judgment. I'm alive because of her, and we can't just—"

"Right, I get it," said Bruno, cutting Stefano off. Bruno realized even in this world, speaking the truth had consequences, and maybe lies were preferable after all.

"Hey, Bruno!" said DeLuca. Bruno turned and saw DeLuca sitting on the motorcycle. He seemed oddly eager to leave, but Bruno heard tension in his voice as he asked, "Are we ready?"

Bruno noticed that Paola still stood apart from the group. He walked over to her and spoke softly, so only she could hear.

"You know what we're trying to do. Just let one of them come. We could use help."

"DeLuca trusts you. That says something. But I don't. And the signal? The blood? Even if you were my son, I'd tell you this is crazy."

Bruno knew nothing he could say would change her mind, so he stayed silent while she spoke again.

"I'm trying to keep them safe, Bruno. Not send them on some stupid chase that might get them killed. Or risk revealing to people who would kill us that we're here. And you? You're reckless, volatile. You don't give a goddamn about killing anymore, if you ever did." She gestured toward the group. "You see how they are already. Imagine what they might have to do, how much worse things could be for them if they did go with you. Do you get that?"

Bruno opened his mouth to speak. Part of him wanted to fight, to justify all of what he'd done so that she would understand. Then he decided to stop making excuses to himself. He had stopped counting the people he had killed. And what would she think if she knew all that he had done on Tiberius' Leap? To Father Tommaso? To the innocent woman he had killed for just getting near him? Maybe she was right after all.

"You could at least wish us luck."

Paola nodded. "Good luck then, Bruno."

He plodded back to the motorcycle, but he did not get on. Keeping his back to the group as he spoke, Bruno muttered, "Look, old man, I think you should stay."

"Stay?" whispered DeLuca. "No, I'm going with you."

"But Paola—"

DeLuca did not look over at Paola. "I know, Bruno, I know. She thinks this is insane. She thinks you . . ." DeLuca's voice fell into silence. Then he continued. "You didn't abandon me, Bruno, and I will never abandon you."

Bruno looked down, fiddling with the ignition key on the motorcycle. He frowned. Then he nodded. Without looking up at DeLuca, Bruno said, "I hope you won't regret coming with me."

DeLuca rested his hand on Bruno's arm. "Believe me, no matter what happens, I won't."

Bruno nodded. "Let's go before this gets any harder."

He mounted the bike, putting on his dark sunglasses as he settled in. The motorcycle growled to life. With a wave, Bruno shot down the street. He felt DeLuca's grip around his waist tighten as they sped off.

Bruno did not look back, but he wondered if DeLuca did.

CHAPTER 22

Bruno glanced behind him. Grim, Soviet-style apartment buildings now blocked any view of Vesuvius to the southeast. Turning the engine off, Bruno dismounted the motorcycle. DeLuca followed.

They surveyed the area. "Porca troia!" muttered Bruno as he pulled off his sunglasses. "Fucking hell! I should have known this would happen."

The A3 Autostrada ran right into the heart of Naples. But now instead of ending in an intersection that flowed in and out of the city, as Bruno remembered, military trucks parked length-wise blocked both lanes and the narrow median. In front of the small space that wasn't blocked by the trucks, thick tangles of barbed wire and metal barriers that looked like large jacks painted yellow barred the way. Bruno could see the nondescript apartment buildings and billboards of this part of Naples that lay behind the barrier. Apart from some ragged posters, half-stuck on streetlamps, flapping in the wind, Bruno saw no movement.

Motioning to DeLuca to stay back, he approached one of the trucks with one hand on the pistol at his back. Bruno looked in the cab. Empty. He scrambled in, looking for anything of use. To his surprise, he found the keys, put them in the ignition and turned. But to no avail. The engine didn't even turn over.

Bruno put his head back on the seat and sighed. He kept his sunglasses off. A sheet of clouds had rolled in, blotting out the sun, but the still oddly warm temperature for this time of year made him sweat. Bruno wondered exactly what day or even what month it was. October he thought, or maybe the end of September? He glanced at his watch. October, if the thing was still right. Amazing how little something like the date meant anymore.

He walked back toward DeLuca.

"Strange," DeLuca said. "Less than an hour's ride from Sorrento to Naples, but it feels like we're on another planet."

Bruno grunted in acknowledgement, wiping his forehead with his sleeve. Noticing his watch as he raised his hand, Bruno unhooked it.

"Here," said Bruno. "You've got the radio. You need the watch, too."

As DeLuca fastened the watch on his wrist, they both looked around, each seeking a way through. On their right, a high brick wall topped by a metal fence separated the road from what Bruno thought must be railroad tracks, the once-electrified wires running in the air a telltale sign. To their left, a shorter vertical fence made of metal slats ran along the side of the road. Bruno glanced behind them. Both ran for kilometers back in the distance from whence they had come.

DeLuca followed Bruno's gaze. "We'll have to backtrack. Take the last off-ramp."

Bruno shook his head. "No. We'll go on foot from here."

"On foot? Why?"

Bruno looked around. "The military probably blocked all the roads in and out of the city at the end, trying to keep Omega from spreading into or out of the city. We might run out of fuel long before we could find some side road that they forgot. Not to mention the noise of this thing would wake the dead." Bruno looked back up the road from where they had come. "If we find the blood, we should go back to Sorrento, regroup before we decide what to do next. So, we need to leave the moto here. I'll move it close to the truck so that it'll be harder to spot."

Without turning on the engine, Bruno rolled the motorcycle closer to the truck. As he did so, he nodded towards central Naples. "Check the map. We're not that far from the cache now; I don't think."

DeLuca pulled the map out of his jacket pocket and unfurled it. He turned it over from the side that had the whole of the boot of Italy to the one with a focus on the major urban areas. He folded it again, leaving central Naples the only square exposed.

"Yes, two kilometers or so. Can you believe it's in a church, let alone *that* church?"

Bruno maneuvered the bike parallel to the part of the truck just behind the passenger cab. Then he glanced about, his eyes focusing on the low rooftops beyond the trucks in front of them, while DeLuca folded up the map. "We'd better get a move on. This used to be a key access point to the city from the south. They might have patrols here."

DeLuca frowned. "Patrols? But aren't they just savages, they can't have—"

"They can," interrupted Bruno. "Don't you remember the last time we were here? They called it *organized* crime for a reason."

Bruno rummaged through the backpacks, took some things out, and left them at the bottom of the passenger side of the truck, hidden under the mat. He hoped his things would still be there if he ever managed to come back.

"We've got to travel light," said Bruno. "Some food, water. A couple of tools. That's it."

He tightened the straps on his backpack, handed DeLuca's to him, and checked his pistol. Safety on and a round in the chamber. Bruno was ready. "We've wasted enough time already. Come on."

He clambered into the truck with the open door and DeLuca followed. Bruno moved over to the driver's side and looked out the window. The bright sun illuminated the open intersection. In the middle stood a stop sign amid a triangle overgrown with brown grass, the only remnant of nature. Harsh right angles of five- and six-storey grey concrete buildings dominated the area. A low stone wall festooned with faded billboards ran on the other side of the intersection, perpendicular to them, maybe a hundred meters away, until it reached the end of the block.

"Make for the wall and stick close to it. That'll make us harder to hit." Bruno pointed at what looked like a parking garage and some apartment buildings looming on the other side of the wall. "See those buildings beyond the wall? If someone is up there, they'll have a clear shot at the whole area, so we've got to move fast."

DeLuca moved forward a bit, tightening the pack on his back. "Ready when you are."

Bruno put his hand on the driver's side door handle. He peered out the window one last time, but saw nothing except the bones of an empty city. He turned to DeLuca.

"Stay low."

Bruno threw open the door and jumped out. Without looking back, he ran in a crouch across the asphalt, his breath loud in his own ears. Bruno fixed his eyes on the wall. Though his feet churned beneath him, his backpack slowed him down and the wall seemed only to creep closer. As he approached the wall, Bruno almost felt like a fool as he ran, crouched, like a thousand eyes were watching. He knew Il Serbo couldn't be everywhere. He could hear DeLuca's footfalls just behind him, but then the sound of gunfire filled the air. Between bursts of gunfire, sounds of a nearby referee's whistle filled the air. More whistles answered it. A grim realization swept over Bruno. They are coming.

Struggling through what felt like spider webs, Bruno lurched into the wall, with DeLuca next to him. Bruno yanked his pistol out and DeLuca followed suit.

The shots stopped once they reached the wall, but those goddamned whistles wouldn't stop. Bruno crouched down and spoke to DeLuca, his voice struggling to contain his rising panic. "I can't tell where it's coming from. We've got to find cover!"

"But how could they know? How could they—"

"No time for that now! Follow me!"

They hurried to the end of the wall, and Bruno risked peeking his head beyond it. The street moved into the heart of Naples. The dingy parking garage dominated the newer buildings at this end of the street. Bruno saw a flash of movement at the top of the garage. He pulled back, put his back against the wall and looked up at the overcast sky. He knew more were on their way, converging on this area and coming for them.

"Bruno," hissed DeLuca. "What now?"

For the first time in a long while, Bruno's confidence faltered. He had no answers and did not know what to do. Still, Bruno understood they needed to move quickly, or they would surely be found and killed, or worse. If they escaped back to Sorrento, they might never find the blood, the cache, or any chance of destroying Omega. And if the gang had a working vehicle and could follow, they might lead this bunch of murdering thugs back to Paola and their new friends.

For long seconds, Bruno struggled with himself. Then he turned to DeLuca.

"Come on," said Bruno. "We're heading for the garage. Sniper's on the top. Stay low, and follow me, as fast as you can."

Bruno holstered his own pistol, then put his hand on the barrel of DeLuca's. "Put it away—won't do much good if you drop it. Once we're in, he can't shoot us. We'll have to get out the other side, and hope we can lose them in the narrower streets."

Bruno knew that not many people could hit a moving target from a distance like the top of the garage to the street. He hoped that the bullets to come held to the law of averages, since he was risking not just his life, but that of DeLuca as well.

"There's a door, I think it's open. That's where we're going."

DeLuca nodded. "I'll be right behind you."

Bruno took two breaths and emerged running from behind the wall in a semi-crouch. Shots echoed around as they ran toward their goal. His heart in his throat, Bruno blasted into the entrance bar on the door, almost knocking it off its hinges.

The sound of DeLuca's huffing filled Bruno's ears as he shut the door behind him and looked around.

"Find something to block the door!"

DeLuca and Bruno both scrambled around the small area. They stood in a narrow room at the bottom of a staircase that led up to the other levels of the garage.

"There's nothing here!"

Bruno glanced around, searching as much for an idea as for something to block the entrance. Going up the stairs would be suicide. They'd end up trapped on a higher level with no escape. Bruno peered into the semi-gloom of the lower level of the garage, just opposite the door they had used to enter. It was half-filled with cars coated in grey dust, but at least the inside offered the hope of an alternate exit.

"Come on, maybe there's an exit back there!" hissed Bruno.

Bruno burst out of the room and hurried along a row of vehicles, heading towards the far side of the garage. He darted between a van and a car, just as he heard the metallic smack of a door being thrown open.

Bruno crouched behind the van, taking care to make sure the tires hid his feet as best he could manage.

Bruno realized DeLuca was missing. He looked across the aisle where cars used to meander to find parking. A long row of abandoned cars stretched the length of the garage. There he spotted DeLuca, squatting between two cars, making himself as small as he could.

He and DeLuca locked eyes, but before they could even mouth any words, the sound of many footsteps echoed from the cold concrete walls. Bruno couldn't tell how many pursuers followed, but he knew there were more than enough to take both of them out.

Though they were on the ground floor, concrete slats running above the wall were too narrow for anyone to fit through.

He glanced behind him. In the back corner of the garage, he could just make out the once-illuminated green lettering of an exit sign. But Bruno's row of cars ended not far from where he stood, at least fifty meters before the exit. DeLuca's row of cars extended all the way to the back wall. Bruno had no chance to escape without being seen. He couldn't make a run for it without completely exposing his back to these thugs. With any luck, though, if DeLuca stayed between the wall and the cars, he could use his row of cars as cover all the way to the back exit, but only if he acted quickly.

DeLuca had a chance for escape, but everything rested on Bruno. He had to do something, to create a distraction and give DeLuca a chance. Voices wafted over the vehicles and footsteps approached. Bruno gritted his teeth and tears of anger welled in his eyes. Bruno's random act of darting behind this row had doomed him. His heart sank and he bowed his head as the realization washed over him: today his luck ran out—today, there would be no escape. But while he could not escape, Bruno knew he still had a choice to make: he could end it all now. He could fight and die, killing as many as he could before they killed him, and give DeLuca the time he needed. Or Bruno could choose another way: he could choose life and suffering, and maybe give DeLuca even more time to escape.

Bruno turned his head towards DeLuca. Jerking his thumb towards the back, he mouthed the words: "You-Go-Exit." DeLuca's eyes widened in silent protest, but Bruno shook his head slowly, his eyes fixed on DeLuca.

The footsteps grew closer. Bruno closed his eyes and took a breath. Then he spoke.

"Don't shoot! I'm coming out! I give up!"

The footsteps stopped, then Bruno heard scrambling.

A man's voice responded. "Come out with your hands up, and we won't shoot!"

Bruno responded, "I'm coming out now!"

He stood up straight, coming out from behind the van, his hands at shoulder height. As he did, he looked across to the other row. DeLuca was gone. At least he made it.

Bruno walked in the middle of the two rows of vehicles. Completely exposed, he spotted his pursuers. In the semi-light of the garage, Bruno saw seven, maybe eight figures, ten or fifteen meters away. Three of them approached. One had a rifle, and the other pointed a revolver. The third had no visible weapon. Veils, fabric, and other makeshift materials hid their faces.

Bruno focused on the coverings over their faces. He never wore one, feeling that the impairment to his vision outweighed the risk of a bite. But though they approached, Bruno still could not see their eyes in the twilight, and the odd coverings over their faces rendered them alien, travelers from a world that knew only torture and death.

They stopped a few arms' lengths from where Bruno stood. In silence, they looked at Bruno. Two of them kept their weapons trained on Bruno. Then the tallest one, the one without a weapon spoke, breaking the silence with a bark.

"Turn around and put your hands on your neck."

Bruno complied without a word. Then the man spoke again.

"Kneel!"

Bruno shifted first down to one knee, then the other. His breathing slowed as he knelt. He hoped that the end would be quick, a bullet to the back of the head. He closed his eyes, and his thoughts swam. Soon, so soon, all would end, it would be over. Bruno's last thoughts raced. Strange thoughts surfaced—the last woman he'd slept with, the last dinner he'd had with Carla, the last gelato he'd eaten—was it blackberry or raspberry? Would the end be quick? Then another man spoke.

"Il Serbo wants to talk to you."

The man's accent . . . he's not from Naples. Bruno opened his eyes. The voice—something about it was familiar. He started to rise, to turn for a better look at his murderers, but a strike to the side of his head knocked him on his chest and his face scraped across cement. The man's voice echoed in Bruno's mind as he slipped down into darkness.

CHAPTER 23

October 11

Bruno rolled off the plastic gym mat onto the grey concrete floor, shivering in the dampness. Streaks of rain ran down the small window near the ceiling. A feeble light cast down, giving some illumination to the stark scene. As he lay on his back, Bruno looked up at the bars on the other side of that window, just out of reach. Three days of staring at the bare walls of what looked like an old storage room had numbed his brain. He figured he must be in some kind of basement. Unfortunately, while Bruno could tell the window stood at street level, about knee-height off the pavement, he had nothing to climb on to get a view. Fighting to sit up, his head throbbed and his limbs felt tied down. Three days of quarantine with only crackers and water had left him tired and weak. His room stank, his only toilet a plastic bucket that started off filled with only sawdust and dirt that now reeked of feces, urine, and vomit. For the first day and a half, Bruno's eyes had felt like they were going to pop out of his head as he threw up and dry heaved into that bucket, the symptoms of a concussion, he knew.

Now he simply felt empty, void inside. He'd nibbled on the crackers and drank the water they'd left for him. Of course, it was not enough, and he could feel his strength ebbing every day. His quarantine would soon end. Only a matter of time now until they came for him, now that he had spent three days in his cell. His hand strayed behind his back, and Bruno fingered the emptiness where his knife's handle had once been. He pondered what to do. Bruno's thoughts wandered to the man's voice from the garage. Something about his voice continued to gnaw at Bruno, troubling his mind, but Bruno was at a loss to figure out why.

The sounds of the lock being thrown and the door handle turning shocked Bruno out of his own head. He scrambled to his feet as the door swung open with a piercing creak. A man walked in, his head covered with a ski mask. The man stood there looking at Bruno, his dark eyes reflecting the soft light in the room. Then, without taking his eyes off Bruno, he reached behind him and pulled the door closed.

They stared at each other; neither man spoke. Then the man peeled the mask off his head with one hand.

His face was gaunt, angular, and a scar ran down in a vertical slash from the forehead, cleaved his left eyebrow in two and restarted on his cheek, only to disappear in his scruffy beard.

With a snap, everything fell into place—the voice from the garage, the accent, the face. Bruno launched himself at the man, slamming him up against the door. He breathed up into the man's face, his fingernails digging into the soft tissue of the other's neck.

"Cristian!" Bruno hissed. "Tell me why I shouldn't rip out your throat!"

Cristian croaked in a whisper. "Because you need me."

"I need *you*?" Bruno said, squeezing Cristian's throat with greater force. "I don't fucking need you! You abandoned your post, you abandoned me, Carla, and everything else!" Bruno spoke through clenched teeth. "You left me with nothing! But I made it without you, without anyone!" Bruno squeezed Cristian's throat for another second, then dropped his hands and stepped back.

Cristian smiled weakly as he rubbed the thin red gouges from Bruno's fingernails on his throat. "Still a self-righteous bastard, right, Bruno? Not to mention a hypocrite as well. You didn't take the ship they sent either."

"Yeah, I stayed. No thanks to you. I survived with my pistol and the clothes on my back." Bruno wanted to spit in Cristian's face. The betrayal bit deep. "You had the weapons, so, why didn't you go back to Tivoli, back to your daughter? Why are you with this scum?"

"Doesn't matter now, does it?" Cristian's face darkened. "I never made it back. The weapons are gone. I was stupid, I . . ."

Cristian didn't finish the thought. He moved back towards the door, glanced out the small portal, and turned back towards Bruno. "We don't have much time. Why are you here, Bruno? Why didn't you stay on Capri?"

Bruno ignored his questions. "Did you know that animal and his crew came back to the island? That they captured Carla? Do you know what they did to my sister?"

Cristian stood mute, stony. His silence infuriated Bruno even more. "She'd been beaten so bad . . . her face . . . she . . ." Bruno's voice caught.

Bruno grabbed Cristian's shirt and pulled him down to his level. "Do you understand? What *else* do you think they did to her? Take a fucking guess!" Bruno's eyes welled up, but his voice stayed filled with rage, not sorrow.

Cristian's gaze finally met Bruno's. "So, is that why you're here, Bruno? Revenge? On Il Serbo? Or on me?"

Bruno unclenched his grip and stepped back. "No. I'd be happy to gut him and you along with him. But that is not why I'm here."

"Then tell me why you're here."

Bruno turned his back to Cristian and stepped away. "I'm done talking to you. Tell your master whatever you want."

"You have to trust me if you want to live." Cristian let out a long breath before continuing. "I told him I'd spent a few years in the army, that's why I know weapons. Which was true, you know that. But let me tell you something he doesn't know: he doesn't know I was a Carabiniere. If he did, he'd cut my liver out for all of them to watch. So now you have something you could use against me."

"Bugger off!"

"Look, I'm your only hope to get out of here. You're not here for revenge. You wouldn't come here unless you had a very good reason. And if you want to live, you'd better talk."

This time Bruno stood mute. Cristian spoke again, gazing directly at him, his voice tense. "We don't have much time—they'll be back soon. Seeing you again—it—it makes me think that maybe there is hope—hope that I can get out of here. Help me, Bruno. Help us."

Bruno turned around. "So, just leave then! You don't need my help! Why do you stay?"

Cristian shrugged, his eyes downcast. He stepped back, away from Bruno before he spoke. "Fear, I guess. I'm afraid there's nothing left—nothing but . . . this." Cristian looked at Bruno. "But you've come here for a reason. I want to have a reason, something to fight for."

Bruno turned away from his former friend, cursing in his mind his decision to come back to Naples. But the die had been cast, Bruno thought ruefully, and his decision set him down a track that he could not change. Once again, Bruno's choices were no choices at all. Cristian's mention of hope reminded Bruno of his own seduction by the prospect of hope. Yet even after hope's betrayal, Bruno felt its siren call. By all rights, Bruno should not trust a single word Cristian said. But what were his alternatives? What choice did he have?

Bruno turned back toward Cristian and their eyes met.

"Help me," Cristian repeated. "Help both of us."

Making his choice, Bruno told him everything without hesitation, pouring everything out as fast as he could.

When he'd finished, Cristian didn't react, except to nod. Then he looked out the small window of the door into the hallway. "I've got to get out before they come back. I'll come up with something. But I won't lie to you, it's going to get bad. Really bad. You've got to hang on. And no matter what it looks like, you've got to trust me."

Bruno nodded and was about to speak, but Cristian was already through the door, locking it behind him. Bruno stared at the space that Cristian had just occupied, his mind racing at the thought of what may come. Then Bruno sighed, turning back toward his mat.

Just as he took a step, the door burst open. Three hooded figures rushed in, grabbed him, and bound his wrists in front of him. Bruno offered no resistance as they yanked him by the arms, hustling him out the door, through a narrow passage, and up a flight of stone stairs.

He blinked as they burst out into a large, open room. His eyes watered in the brighter light. He realized that he was standing where the priest would have emerged and was looking out into a church. Looking up and around, Bruno drank in the scene before him. Built in a time long before the electrical grid or even the discovery of electricity itself, the neatly spaced windows above the marble columns that ran the length of the nave let in abundant late-morning sun. The alabaster and the soft pink and grey tones of the stonework reflected and enhanced the glow. Bruno's eyes fell on a marble altar, its white tones gleaming under a vaulted dome. The clean lines and understated decorative work on the ceiling gave the place a simple beauty. Bruno had visited a few churches in Naples, but never this one. It looked big enough to be a basilica. In better days, its effortless magnificence would have touched even Bruno's skeptical heart.

But now, the ugliness of a group gathered around the altar in a semi-circle captivated Bruno even more than the church's beauty. They stood on the far side of the altar, all faced towards him. Arrayed in shabby, dark clothing, with their faces covered, they seemed to suck all the light from the building like wraiths. Bruno could not see one pair of eyes, but he could feel their gaze fixed on him. He counted fifteen dark figures, not including the three who held him.

The men holding Bruno moved him closer to the altar. One of the figures on the other side stirred, stepping around the altar towards Bruno. As the figure moved, the others removed their head coverings. Bruno saw a scruffy grey council, all men. Then Bruno's eyes fell on Cristian, but he stared forward, refusing eye contact, as expressionless as the stone columns that surrounded them.

The still-hooded figure approached Bruno, stopping directly in front of him. The knot in Bruno's stomach tightened as Bruno looked up into the other's dark eyes, the only part of his face exposed. The man stared down at Bruno, then reached up and pulled at his hood.

Bruno watched with a strange detachment as it slithered down across the man's face. Il Serbo stared at Bruno expressionless, with an almost blank look. Unlike Cristian, Il Serbo looked the same as Bruno remembered him on the night they had met, in a jail cell, in a world so different it felt like another dimension.

Bruno said nothing, but Il Serbo spoke, still holding Bruno's gaze.

"Did you find his friend yet?"

One of the group spoke. "Not yet."

"Keep looking. You eight will patrol in pairs. You'll find him."

Bruno counted in his head. If eight go, still ten left. Too many. Bruno knew he didn't have a prayer of escape.

One of the group spoke up. "Boss, it's a fucking waste of time, don't you think? Bet the other one's long gone by now."

Il Serbo shook his head. "Oh, I don't think he'd leave poor Signor Bruno to the likes of me, now would he? No, he's close. We'll find him."

Bruno knew Cristian would be on patrol with the others on Il Serbo's errand to find DeLuca, but he didn't know if this should give him hope or tear at his heart.

Il Serbo turned back to Bruno. "But before you boys go off searching for Signor Bruno's friend, I want you to watch this."

He walked around Bruno one pace at a time, footfalls so soft they barely caused an echo, even on the stone.

"You've been a pain in my ass a long time."

Bruno stayed silent.

Il Serbo stopped in front of Bruno and laughed. "What's the matter? Nothing to say?"

Before another thought registered in Bruno's mind, fury twisted Il Serbo's face and he punched Bruno in the gut.

Bruno fell to his knees, coughing and gasping.

"Still, we could use someone with your skills here. If you prove yourself, who knows? Maybe we'll let him stay, right, lads?" Il Serbo turned to the group. They grunted and nodded in acknowledgement.

Il Serbo crouched down closer to Bruno as if to have words only with him, but he spoke loudly enough for all of them to hear.

"Well, Signor Bruno, what do you say?"

Bruno felt the cold stone of the altar's steps sucking the warmth from his blood, and his knees ached. He looked up at Il Serbo. The soft light of the church did nothing to hide the queer gleam in the man's eyes. Bruno knew as soon as he met his gaze that nothing he could say could spare him whatever agonies Il Serbo had dreamt up for him. He knew Il Serbo would never let him stay, except as a rotting carcass. That thought should have left him paralyzed. But instead, the certainty of agony and death freed him to speak the truth. And though he rested on his knees, Bruno's voice was strong, and it reverberated against the walls of the basilica as he replied, laughing.

"You are a liar!" Bruno looked past Il Serbo. "Is this what all of you want? Is this how you want to live? Under the thumb of this piece of garbage? Cowards!"

Before the echo of Bruno's voice died away, Il Serbo backhanded Bruno, knocking him off his knees and onto the steps of the altar. Bruno fell on his side, his face pressed against the steps. He felt the salty taste of blood in his mouth and rolled on his back with a groan.

"Listen to that! He calls us cowards? Calls me a liar! Now you see, that's what I hate about you pigs—you think you're better than everyone else." Il Serbo's voice echoed in the church.

"While you were holed up on your island, the rest of us had to survive. When everything crumbled to shit, none of you cops did a damn thing. Deserters and thieves, just like everyone else, that's what you lot really are. You're no better than anyone! But you know that already, don't you, Bruno?"

He leaned forward and spat on Bruno as he lay on his back. The drool splattered on Bruno's face and ran down his cheek, mixing with his blood. "You call *me* a liar? Did you forget about murdering my brother? You're the lying piece of trash! And a cold-blooded murderer!"

Bruno stayed on his back. The stone stairs bit into him while Il Serbo gestured here and there as he loomed, a great, bald figure in the dim light.

"And while you cops were looking out for your own asses, I did something! We did something! This isn't all there is. We have women outside the city, storing food, growing crops. We rotate men in and out of our base here, scavenging what we need in the city. We're starting over."

Il Serbo strutted around. "And what happens when one of the women disobeys?" A low chuckle went up from the group. Someone said, "We take turns!"

Il Serbo nodded. "That's right! Keeps everyone in order, doesn't it, lads? It sure kept your sister in line, Bruno." Not for the first time, Bruno gave thanks that his parents and little brother never knew that Carla had suffered for this man's pleasure.

He turned back towards Bruno. "Whatever happened to her, anyway? I heard she kind of liked my last group of friends."

"She's dead."

"Now that's a shame. We could have used a doctor. But after what you did to my brother, I hope she died in pain."

Il Serbo laughed. "Enzo told me all about her, all the things they did to her. Good thing we quarantined poor Enzo when he got back. Before he died, he told me all about what happened, how two men attacked them. I knew it was you, Bruno. I knew you were on the island. So close to us.

"And of course, I've been waiting for you. We've been watching the main roads and the docks since your last visit. We were getting ready to come over and burn you out of your little island paradise, for real this time, when you came back, just like I thought you would!"

As his tirade went on, the seductive thought that Cristian could help somehow, that he'd stop this, coursed through Bruno's mind. But the last rational filaments in his brain knew that there was nothing Cristian could do for him. Hoping for a quick death was all he had now, and that meant provoking Il Serbo.

"You're a real fucking humanitarian, aren't you?" Bruno said. "Like your piece-of-shit dead little brother. Shame I blew his brains to jelly. Should have shot him in the balls and let him live like a neutered little bitch!"

"Get him up on the altar," said Il Serbo.

When he tried to roll away, Bruno ended up on his stomach and saw his own blood in streaks on the steps of the altar. He froze, and two men on each arm yanked him up and dropped him face-down on the altar, knocking the wind out of him.

Bruno tried to get up, to fight them off, but soon two more joined them. With wrists bound in front of him and each of his limbs held by two men apiece, he was no match for their combined strength. But it didn't matter. He continued to fight, even as they lifted him and dropped him face-down on the altar again. Then a seventh man, the largest one, ran up and sat on his back, crushing the air from his lungs.

"Untie his wrists and spread out his arms," said Il Serbo.

Bruno dreaded the interrogation that would start.

"Why are you here, Bruno? Why have you come to Naples?"

Bruno felt the weight of the man crushing his chest into the hard stone. The lower half of his body hung off the edge of the altar and its edge bit into Bruno's abdomen. Two men squashed his arms against the altar, and Bruno instinctively gripped the edge of the altar with all his might.

Bruno's mind raced. "We needed supplies . . . we . . . "

"Don't lie to me! I'm sure there's enough on Capri. Why come here?"

Bruno said nothing.

Il Serbo pressed. "Or maybe I should say, why are you going to Assergi?"

Even Bruno couldn't stop a flicker of surprise from showing through the fear on his face. How could he know?

Il Serbo laughed. "Got you!" Yanking a folded map from his back pocket, Il Serbo shouted and waved it in Bruno's face.

"They found this in the parking garage. Now tell me, why Naples, and why Assergi?"

Bruno searched for a lie. "My—mother's—family—from—there," Bruno grunted.

Il Serbo laughed. "Please! The way you talk? You're not from there, and neither was your mother!"

Bruno didn't respond.

"Don't worry, Bruno, we'll find out the truth." He spoke louder now, his voice echoing in the church.

"Pull his pants down!"

The words jolted Bruno into action. He struggled, screaming and cursing to no avail. The light feeling of liberation he had felt only a short while ago drained from Bruno's body.

Bruno felt someone tug at his belt, then yank his pants and underwear down around his boots in one sharp motion. He ached with fear, and nothing in his life had prepared him for the horror of the helplessness that coursed through his veins: not the merciless solitude of the island, not the times he had killed or been close to death himself, not even the death of his mother and brother and Carla. Bruno's breath came in small gasps. The only thing that kept him from telling Il Serbo the truth of why he had come was the other truth that Bruno clung to like a mother clutched her baby: that no matter what he said, he would die anyway.

"We found this knife on you," said Il Serbo from behind Bruno. "I can find plenty of uses for a knife—it can be a tool or a weapon. That's what makes it beautiful."

Bruno could still raise his head up off the altar. He looked about in vain for Il Serbo. But then Bruno heard his voice, just behind him.

"I'll give you another chance, my friend!" shouted Il Serbo. "Tell me why you're here!"

"I—told—you," responded Bruno between gasps.

Bruno felt more than heard movement behind him. Cold, sharp steel pressed into his left buttock. Bruno stifled a cry as Il Serbo gradually pressed the point until it just broke Bruno's skin. Il Serbo dragged it down the back of Bruno's thigh, almost gently. Bruno cried out as the knife tip crept down towards his knee. Amid the pain, he felt the trickle of blood dribbling down his thigh.

Then the knife tip pushed up between his legs.

Bruno's entire body seized. "Please!" cried Bruno. "We're on our way to Abruzzi—my family is there—please—" Bruno's voice dissolved into a sob.

"Maybe you'd better pray to San Gennaro for help!"

Bruno choked out a reply between gasps of breath. "I—don't—believe—in—him—"

Bruno felt Il Serbo bend over him from his left side. He whispered, his breath caressing Bruno's ear.

"Good. Then we have something in common, don't we?"

Without warning, Il Serbo retreated. For an instant, Bruno's body relaxed. Bruno heard whispering behind him.

Then Il Serbo whirled in front of Bruno. The weight on Bruno lifted as the man on his back moved off. Bruno raised his head. Il Serbo held the knife by the blade, offering it to someone outside Bruno's vision.

"Here, you do it," Il Serbo said.

Bruno heard a voice from behind him. "No, I don't—you know I don't like this kind of . . ." The voice trailed off. It was Cristian.

Il Serbo chuckled. "Come on, don't be such a pussy! He's got be to taught a lesson!"

Bruno heard footsteps as Cristian walked around the altar. Il Serbo and Cristian both looked down at him. Cristian took the knife from Il Serbo's grasp.

"Please, please don't do this!" Bruno pleaded.

Cristian looked into Bruno's eyes, but Bruno saw nothing in them but a blank stare.

"Make sure you keep him down," said Cristian as he looked at Bruno.

"No!" Bruno screamed, and bucked against the crushing weight on him, but there were too many, and they crushed the breath out of him. Someone pounded on his left hand until he opened his fingers. He felt pressure and sharpness, and Cristian brought his fist down with a shout.

The crunch of bone against stone rang in Bruno's ears. For a microsecond, the shock of the sound robbed him of feeling. Then pain shot through his hand. Blood squirted onto the white stone of the altar. Parts of two fingers fell to the ground, and Bruno screamed. All the goons moved off, knowing Bruno wasn't going anywhere.

Il Serbo bellowed over Bruno's screams. "Next time it won't be fingers!"

Bruno writhed, half-naked on the cold stones of the church, his blood staining everything around him. Huddled in a ball, he wailed until his throat could make no more sound, and no one moved to help him.

CHAPTER 24

October 19

Bruno's head bounced on the stone floor, but what made him scream was the pain from his fingers as his hand scraped the floor.

"Get up," growled someone above him.

Using his good hand, Bruno tugged at the stone altar, raising himself up off the floor, and shambled to his feet. Bruno glanced down, noticing the dried blood on the altar, another reminder of his maiming. Part of his pinky and ring fingers were missing. But they had no signs of infection. He had been carefully pissing on them and drying them off every day in an attempt to sterilize them as best he could, and because of that, or maybe just dumb luck, it seemed to have staved off infection. But three more days in the basement, subsisting on crackers and water, had sapped Bruno's strength, leaving him dreading whatever was to come. He wondered for a second what he must look like: sunken eyes, ratty beard, pasty skin, fingernails caked with shit and dirt, more like a prisoner from a medieval dungeon than someone born to antibiotics and running water. They thought him so useless, they didn't even bind his hands. And they'd be right. Bruno's own hopelessness caught him by surprise.

The morning sun brightened the church, but Bruno could feel a damp chill in the air. He shivered where he stood, not just from the cold. He didn't know why they had dragged him out of his hole into the church this morning until his eyes fell on one particular figure that stood out from that ragged, grey group.

Bruno had promised himself not to show any emotion in front of them, no matter what, but when he realized the identity of that forlorn person, he gasped.

"DeLuca!"

Il Serbo glanced at Bruno, laughing. "I told you we'd find your friend. Didn't you believe me?"

The group moved toward Bruno, pushing DeLuca along until he tripped on a flagstone near Bruno's feet.

DeLuca raised himself on one arm, looking up at Bruno. DeLuca's battered face showed no emotion as their eyes met.

One of the group piped up. "Old bastard must be tougher than he looks. Cristian told me he took out our Vetrano."

"What happened?" said Il Serbo, stepping toward Cristian.

"Vetrano had tied him to a chair when we thought we heard someone clattering around outside. I went to take a look around. Vetrano said he had him under control. It was just a fucking cat." Cristian sighed. "The old man bashed his skull in with a lamp. He must have gotten loose somehow. I'm sorry I let you down."

Il Serbo nodded. "There will be time to mourn Vetrano. He was a loyal soldier."

"I was going to send Vetrano back here to tell you to meet us, but . . . Vetrano . . ." Cristian looked down, rubbing his scabbed knuckles. "But I took it out on the old man's head—I was afraid I broke my hand on his fucking face!"

"What about quarantine?" one of the group asked.

Il Serbo shook his head. "Oh, I don't think that's necessary." He waved his hand towards DeLuca. "Look at him—the only other person this guy's seen in a long while is our friend Bruno."

"How did you find him?" another one shouted.

Cristian laughed. "Found him wandering towards Sorrento north of here, a day and a half ago. Fucking knob was walking out of town in the middle of the day back towards the highway."

Bruno didn't know what kind of game Cristian was playing, with his half-truths and omissions. All Bruno knew was that Cristian's smile made him want to smash it, to crush it. Drawing on some well of strength he didn't know he had, Bruno pulled away from his captors and bolted full speed into Cristian, knocking him to the floor.

"Brutto stronzo!" screamed Bruno as he pounded Cristian. One or two punches were all he could get before the goons yanked him off. But Bruno's sharp knuckles were enough to open a gash on Cristian's forehead that covered his face in blood.

The melee filled the church with cursing and shouting that echoed off the stone. Bruno tried to shout over the din, "Cristian, you filthy liar!" But a swift punch to the gut knocked Bruno's voice out of his throat after he screamed, and someone grabbed his head from behind. Il Serbo's voice broke over the noise: "Shut him up!"

Bruno tried to shout, but they stuffed a filthy rag into his mouth until he gagged. He wretched and stopped struggling, afraid he would vomit and choke. They bound his hands behind his back, the cord cutting into his wrists. Bruno kneeled on one knee, breathing hard through his nose, spit running down his chin. He tried to look at Cristian, who now stood looking down at him. Then Bruno glanced toward DeLuca. No one but Bruno observed DeLuca, so preoccupied were the rest by discussions about they were going to do. But to Bruno, their speech was like static. DeLuca shook his head, just enough for Bruno alone to see and mouthed the word "no." What did that mean? Did DeLuca know something? What?

Cristian kept one hand pressing a rag to his head as he spoke. "I know why they're here."

Silence fell, and all eyes fell on Cristian. Then Cristian spoke words that burned any hope that DeLuca's gesture might have given Bruno.

"They came for the blood of San Gennaro in the Duomo. I've got it right here." As Cristian spoke, he produced a phial of blood from the inside of his jacket pocket. For a moment, Bruno stared at the aged glass. Part of him wondered if the blood would turn to liquid. But as Cristian told them about the transmissions, the blood, the weapons cache, everything, Bruno's head rolled back, and he looked up at the vaulted ceiling above him. Cristian's voice faded to a drone in Bruno's head. He stared at the white inlay patterns until his eyes watered. Not praying to a higher power, not begging for help from something in which he did not believe, Bruno made a simple promise to himself: he swore that today, somehow, before the day was done, before he died, he would kill Cristian.

Two of the group yanked Bruno to his feet. Bruno saw Il Serbo pull DeLuca up by his shirt.

Il Serbo shook his head. "What a pair of fools!" He raised his voice, speaking to the group. "Time to take a trip, boys. We're going to the cache." Il Serbo dragged DeLuca out the front door of the church while Cristian followed. The rest of the group followed and hustled Bruno through the great wooden doors of the church and out into the street.

The bright sun blinded Bruno and tears ran down his face. He tripped over a misplaced cobblestone, but they dragged him up again and kept going. His eyes adjusted as he walked. Though the sun shone and the temperature climbed to a pleasant level, Bruno felt cold to the bone. The wind whistling down the street cut through him and he shivered. Bruno's eyes shifted back and forth as they made their way through the empty streets towards the church and the cache.

Cristian walked not ten meters in front of Bruno, but he might as well have been across the Bay of Naples. If he could have spoken, Bruno would have told them all about Cristian's past as a cop and would have been glad to see them gut his former friend before his own demise. But the gag allowed Bruno only grunts and wails, and when he tried to talk, someone smacked him in the head. As Bruno's mind churned, the grey buildings of the city passed quickly, time slipped by, and before Bruno had a plan for vengeance, he looked up and found the great church looming over all of them.

The group came to a halt as the street opened into a small rectangular piazza. Cars and trucks blocked the street across the way in, so much so that they had to squeeze their way through, this way and that, through gaps or crawling underneath the now useless vehicles. Bruno knew that once they were in this piazza, they wouldn't be getting out quickly. Once through, Bruno looked around. Even the other end of the piazza looked blocked. But while there were cars strewn here and there in the piazza itself, around the steps leading to the great church's entrance, the way was clear. Its grey and white façade loomed over all of them to the right, the abandoned city oblivious to its decorative stonework. Bruno remembered it had more than one name, but everyone called it the Duomo di Napoli, the place where the blood of San Gennaro once rested. The cool sun reflected off the façade, making Bruno squint. The ornate stonework drew Bruno's eye upward to the steeple at the top. As he stared, Bruno wondered how many centuries this cathedral would stand and, when it finally crumbled, if anyone would be around to care. Bruno felt more than saw Cristian now standing near on his left. He glanced towards him, saw Cristian looking at the buildings around them, glancing up at the roofs. Il Serbo strode forward, now taking DeLuca by the arm with another one of his thugs by his side.

"Come on, old man," he said.

They filtered around the cars like droplets of water winding their way down to the ground. Time was running out as they approached the bottom of the long steps to the Duomo's entrance. Desperation made Bruno sweat. Hands still bound, Bruno had no plan. He wanted to rip Cristian's neck with his teeth and hope the wound would be fatal, but he couldn't even do that. The gag, now soaked with spit, prevented even such a desperate move. But no matter what, he would try something. Bruno couldn't care less if his own death was imminent. He just wanted it all to end and take Cristian with him. The only thing that gave him pause was what would happen to DeLuca. But there wasn't anything Bruno could do to help him anyway, so he shoved his thoughts about the old man aside.

Cristian now stood just to Bruno's left. Bruno gathered the last shreds of will, ready to strike what would be his final blow. His body tensed, and for the first time since his capture, he felt strong. The rest of Il Serbo's gang stood in between the cars strewn in the piazza. Now was Bruno's final chance. But just in front of them Il Serbo stopped. Bruno watched him stiffen. Then Il Serbo whirled back, like a soldier performing an about-face, and marched right up to Cristian, with a curly-haired thug two steps behind, just to Il Serbo's left.

Il Serbo stared at Cristian, almost nose-to-nose. The rest of Il Serbo's crew looked around, scratching their asses, muttering among themselves, waiting for their master to do something. Finally Cristian spoke.

"What?"

"How did he know?" murmured Il Serbo.

Cristian looked puzzled. "What?"

Bruno noticed Cristian slip one hand into his front jacket pocket.

Out of nowhere Il Serbo roared, pointing at Bruno.

"How did he know? How the fuck did *he* know your name! When they punched him, he said your name!" Spit flew out of his mouth, and his voice echoed off the stone and asphalt.

Cristian and Bruno both took a step back. Cristian chuckled a little, but Bruno could hear something in his voice he hadn't heard before.

"What? I don't know . . . someone must have said it. Who the fuck knows?"

With his free hand, Il Serbo yanked his pistol and pointed it at Cristian's head.

"Take your hand out of your pocket and answer me! Or I'll blow your fucking skull open!"

Cristian held his hand out at his waist, palms up. He inhaled, opened his mouth to speak, but before a sound came out of his mouth, a sharp crack reverberated across the square and brains splattered everywhere.

CHAPTER 25

For an eternal instant, the scene froze in Bruno's mind. But what his eyes saw made no sense. The curly-haired man, a gaping hole in his head, seemed suspended for a long moment before toppling into Il Serbo, now stained with the dead man's blood and brains. Il Serbo flinched to one side, taking DeLuca with him. Before anyone else could react, Cristian dove, hauling Bruno with him behind a car. Bruno's damaged hand hit something as they fell and he shouted in pain.

More shots ripped through the air, and Bruno heard the screams of Il Serbo's men. Bruno and Cristian scrambled back, weaving their way between cars as bullets flew. They hunkered behind a car while screams and chaos erupted around them. Cristian yanked his pistol out, peeked out to the left of the car's front bumper, and fired in rapid succession. Bruno heard a man scream not five meters away as bullets ripped the air from above. Crouching behind the car, Cristian pulled a knife from the inside of his jacket and cut Bruno's gag and bonds. With no time for words, Cristian dropped the knife and sheath into Bruno's hands and, producing a pistol from the small of his back, handed it to Bruno. Cristian continued to trade fire with his own gang. A few of them tried to take shelter in the buildings bordering the piazza, but the doors were locked or blocked from the inside, and they perished, shot from above, while scrabbling on unyielding wood and stone.

Bruno's new freedom stunned him more than the gunshots and screams echoing around him. He saw that it was his own knife.

The knife that his father had given him and that had taken part of his fingers. He stowed the knife and checked the pistol. Full magazine.

Bullets shattered one of the car's windows, showering Bruno with glass. "Porca troia!" Cristian swore as he dropped next to Bruno. Cristian pulled the radio out of his jacket pocket, shouting, "Keep shooting—we're pinned down!"

Forcing down the pain in his still-throbbing fingers, Bruno peeked over the hood of the car and found a clear shot at one of Il Serbo's gang. With a single shot, Bruno dropped him, then followed up with another to make sure he wouldn't get up. Bruno scanned the scene, looking for DeLuca and Il Serbo. Near the entrance to the church, Bruno saw movement, but a bullet zinged past his arm and he dropped down. Before he could get a good look, Bruno heard another shot and a scream. There was more gunfire from above and answering gunfire from in front of him. But with every shot from above, the responding fire grew less, until silence fell over the scene. Bruno smelled the stinging gunpowder lingering in the air.

"How many left?" Cristian hissed into the radio.

"Not sure, six I think, they're in the church now! And he's got DeLuca!" a voice crackled on the radio. The voice was Stefano's.

"Why didn't you shoot *him*, for Christ's sake?" Bruno knew who Cristian meant.

Stefano's voice buzzed. "Because he had DeLuca in front of him! We couldn't get a clear shot, even from up here!"

Bruno peeked over the hood of the car. He saw bodies strewn around cars and on the steps of the church. The red stains on the white marble flowed slowly like ink blots seeping onto paper. No more bullets flew. The silence made Bruno even more nervous than the gunshots; he knew better than to think he was safe, so he stayed well concealed behind the car.

Cristian put his mouth almost onto the radio as he spoke. "Leave the radio with Mauro, get down here, and be careful!"

"On our way," responded Stefano.

Bruno looked at Cristian as he slumped against side of the car. He put the radio back in the inside pocket of his windbreaker and looked at Bruno.

"Didn't go exactly as I'd planned. We're on Plan B now. You should have trusted me," said Cristian.

"What was I supposed to think, after what you did to me on Capri?"

"You should have trusted me! Your bloody outburst nearly got us both killed!"

"Trust you after this?" said Bruno, holding up his hand. "And what the bloody hell did you plan, exactly?"

"Blame that fucking psychopath, not me! Did it look like I had a choice? We don't have time for this!"

Cristian leaned toward Bruno. "After I found DeLuca at your rally point, we got rid of Vetrano. Then we contacted your friends with DeLuca's radio. They managed to scavenge a working truck in Sorrento and came to the cache here in the Duomo. There wasn't much here." Cristian smiled. "We found the blood. There were only two automatic rifles and some ammo, but we found enough C-4 to blow the roof off the church and then some. Your friends and I spent the last three days wiring it up and blocking off the piazza as best we could." Cristian reached into his jacket and pulled out a metal box the size of a deck of cards.

"A remote detonator?"

Cristian nodded. Then, he shifted positions to a nearby car as Bruno saw familiar faces approach.

Stefano and Saverio appeared from behind a corner of a building, followed quickly by Paola. Jogging low, they took cover behind two cars just to the right of Bruno and Cristian. Bruno saw that Stefano and Saverio each had an AR-70/90, the predecessor of the ARX, slung around their chest. Paola had a pistol in her hand. Aldo, with his rifle and its sniper scope, and Mauro, his spotter, must still be looking down on them from one of the nearby buildings.

Bruno wanted to ask many things, but now was not the time. "What if they get out a back way?"

"We blocked off the exits. Would take them God knows how long to get out," said Stefano.

"Don't underestimate them, they could find a way," said Bruno. "How are we going to get DeLuca?"

Cristian shook his head.

Bruno insisted. "What's the plan?"

"Bruno, I've still got the blood." He patted the bulge in his jacket. "And we can end it with *this*." Cristian held up the detonator.

"What the hell?" said Bruno. His eyes narrowed. He looked at Paola. "We have to help DeLuca!"

"Bruno, listen," Paola said, her voice quavering. "He said that no matter what, the blood must be saved, and that he was willing to die to stop them."

"But you can't—"

"Enough talk! Take cover!" Cristian said. He flipped the switch on the detonator. "It's over!"

Nothing happened. No explosion rocked the square. Only the wind made a sound.

"The bloody battery must be dead!" He threw it to the ground. "There was no way to test it!"

"Bastard!" said Bruno.

Cristian grabbed Bruno's shirt. "I made a choice! Just like your friend did! He's willing to sacrifice himself for us—for you!"

Cristian let Bruno go with a push and leaned with his back against the car's fender. "There's still a way to end this. We've got to hurry."

Paola answered this time. "Manual detonation?"

Cristian nodded. "The detonator is Velcro'd under the lip of the right corner of the altar. We ran a wire to it, hidden in the seams of the stonework. In case the remote didn't work."

"We'd bloody well better hurry," said Paola. "They could spot the wire any time."

"Someone's got to go in and set it off," said Stefano. He looked up at Bruno. "Someone's got to die."

"I'll trade myself for DeLuca," said Bruno. "He wants me, not you. That's how I'll get in."

Cristian shook his head. "Do you know what he'll do to you? He will—"

"I'm out of ideas, and you don't have any better ones," interrupted Bruno. "We've got to move now!"

Bruno sprang forward, running in a crouch over to the last car before the steps up to the church. Cristian followed Bruno to the car. He looked at him with a hint of a half-smile.

"You know, your plan's not such a smart idea, is it?"

Bruno clapped him on the shoulder with his good hand. Bruno met his eyes. "It's the only way I can try to save him."

Bruno poked part of his head over the top of the car and shouted. "It's me—Bruno! I'll come to you, if you give us DeLuca!" His voice echoed over the square, but no one answered.

Bruno shouted again. This time, he heard a dull thud and saw the door to the Duomo swing open.

"Remember," said Cristian, "it's under the far right corner of the altar, as you're looking at it when you walk up to it."

Bruno nodded. "Understood." He handed Cristian his knife in its sheath. "I won't need this anymore. You keep it."

Cristian accepted the knife. "I'm sorry, Bruno. For everything." Despite all Cristian had done, Bruno admired Cristian's decisiveness. Bruno knew Cristian could survive in this world.

"Help them—Paola and the others. Free the women outside of the city."

"We will."

Shadowed in the Duomo's door, Bruno could make out three figures: DeLuca, flanked by two of Il Serbo's gang. Bruno had his hand on his pistol to hand over to Cristian when he heard a voice echo out of that dark doorway. "The boss says he wants the blood and you, then we'll give you DeLuca!"

Cristian pulled Bruno back behind the car. "You can't give it to him! It's what we came for—DeLuca would rather die!"

Bruno pulled out his pistol and pointed it at Cristian's head.

"The blood is a lie—give it to me!"

Cristian stared at him in silence.

Bruno insisted. "It's a *fucking* lie—if he wants it he can have it! Give it to me or you're dead, and I'll take it anyway!"

Bruno risked a glance toward Paola and the others. Cristian slowly put his hand in his jacket and produced the phial of the saint's blood.

"Put it down and turn the other direction. Then put your hands on your head," Bruno commanded.

Cristian did so without a word. Bruno picked up the vial, shuffled towards the back end of the car, and put his weapon to the ground. They could always use another pistol, Bruno reasoned. He knew that where he was going, he would never need a pistol again.

He dashed to another car parallel to Cristian and shouted, "I've got it! I'm coming out!"

Bruno watched as Cristian scooped up Bruno's pistol, and their eyes met. He could see the pain in Cristian's eyes as he put Bruno's pistol at the small of his back.

Now Bruno pulled his gaze away from Cristian to the figures who had moved onto the cathedral door's threshold and stepped into the daylight. The massive stonework dwarfed the three of them. Two of Il Serbo's gang stood on each side of DeLuca, clenching his arms in a vice grip. They stood just behind DeLuca, preventing a clear shot at them.

Bruno stood up from behind his cover and walked forward. Wind whipped through the square as he took plodding steps toward the wide stairs leading to the cathedral doors. Exposed to the wind, he shivered with cold fear. As he came closer to the men, he could see sweat running down DeLuca's pallid face. His hands were bound in front. Bruno could see pain in DeLuca's eyes too, but his face looked no worse than before. DeLuca tried to speak, but the gag made his words unintelligible. Now Bruno glanced over his shoulder and saw his own group peeping out here and there, sheltering behind cars in the square. His eyes fell on the only partially visible Cristian, crouching with his pistol ready. Bruno could sense Cristian just waiting for some trigger to send him into action.

One of the men growled as Bruno approached. "Put the blood down at DeLuca's feet and turn around!"

Bruno knelt down at DeLuca's feet. He lingered for a moment as he placed the phial on the steps. Something caught his eye. A red drop marred the white marble of the cathedral's steps. Bruno jumped to his feet. But one of the men pushed DeLuca down the stairs, while the other pounced on Bruno. DeLuca tumbled forward, falling down the stairs face first, with a knife jutting out of his lower back. Bruno yelled, but he knew he couldn't run or fight. He needed to get inside.

Cristian and Stefano emerged from behind cover, pistols pointed in toward the cathedral, but the two men hustled Bruno over the threshold, threw him on the flagstones, and shut the door with a thud.

Bruno was yanked to his feet and pulled down the middle of the church. The basilica had lost none of its beauty since its abandonment. The stained glass colored the incoming sunlight, just as it had for countless mornings. The pews stood as they had always done, in neat rows, just waiting for a priest to give his homily. But the men who awaited Bruno in front of the altar were no priests.

The group parted as Bruno approached. The two men tossed Bruno onto the altar, knocking the wind out of him. He groaned, rolling from his back to his stomach. One of the men handed Il Serbo the phial. Il Serbo, his shirt stained with congealing blood and brains, regarded the phial with narrow eyes.

"You thought this would save the world? This?"

He smashed the phial next to Bruno's head. Bruno flinched as the thick fluid and glass shards splashed his face. Bruno could smell the musty scent of the blood as he inched his way backward on the altar. He wondered now if he might have been wrong, if the blood really was their salvation. But it was too late for that. Bruno's last hope lay in a small box somewhere just out of reach. His good hand moved, seeking the far corner of the altar.

"What do we do now?" asked one of the men.

"I should kill you now," Il Serbo said, ignoring the question. "I should kill you now," he repeated, "but we need to know some things: are there still weapons here? The exits are blocked. How do we get out?"

Bruno lay still. Too many eyes were on him now. His right hand lay just over the corner of the altar. Still too far.

Il Serbo shrugged, staring at Bruno while he spoke. "He won't want to tell us anything. We've got time. There aren't enough of them to try and get us in here, even if they have better weapons now. Maybe he doesn't know about the weapons. Maybe he doesn't know the way out. Doesn't matter. We'll make him pay all the same!"

They turned Bruno over on his stomach. He yelled as they slammed him on the cold stone. His mangled left hand hung over the right side of the altar now.

"You like movies, Bruno? Remember that old American movie where they gutted that Scottish guy, right at the end. Remember that? That's what I'm going to do to you. I'll start with your balls and work my way up!"

"Go to hell," Bruno answered.

Il Serbo laughed. "You'll beg for death before your friends can help you!"

Bruno smiled. Death hovered over them both, but only Bruno could sense it. Bruno tasted its cold bitterness as he spoke. It was close now. "Go to hell!"

"I don't believe in hell, Bruno."

"You will," said Bruno, the remaining fingers on his mangled hand finding the switch. "You will." He smiled to himself one last time.

The blast wave broke over Bruno as he rolled off the altar, and a wave of debris cascaded down in a dark mass. The last thing he saw was Il Serbo's face, contorted with rage, falling towards him. But the debris caught up before Il Serbo could reach him and all went silent and dark. Bruno's mind faded into shadows. His last thoughts were of Carla, his mother, his brother, and his father.

EPILOGUE

The man awoke parched, with the taste of blood and ash on his tongue. He didn't know where he was or even who he was. But in an instant, memories came flooding back to him, memories of explosions and darkness. He lay in a fetal position, forced to one side by a heavy weight, squeezing him against hard, cold rock. He turned his head. A ray of light not much thicker than a hair shone down to his left. Rubble and rock surrounded him, entombed him, and he couldn't stand up. The cold, white stone of the altar bore the brunt of force from the collapse; the altar had cracked, but still held true against the strain. He realized he was pressed up against the altar. The man's head throbbed, and with the fingers of his right hand, he felt the gash and congealed blood where stone had struck him. He had no doubt the altar had saved his life.

His eyes adjusted to the dim light. Looking towards his feet, he saw a bloody arm. The rest of the body lay squashed under tons of rubble. He reveled in his own survival and in the other's death, and thought that now, now it would be so easy to sleep, to surrender to darkness and rest.

Yet something stirred in him. The urge to escape, to be free of this place, overwhelmed him. He tried to move, but his right arm was pinned. Pain stabbed into his shoulder, making him shout as he freed his arm from the rubble. The pain focused him, bringing him out of his daze and sharpening his mind. He couldn't see much, but he knew which way was up. With the remnants of a once-great cathedral threatening to crush him into nonexistence, he dug, using pieces of rubble as leverage, one rock at a time.

***

By the time he broke through, the dust and soot had nearly choked him, and the man's tongue stuck to the roof of his mouth. Even if he had wanted to speak he couldn't have. Pushing his way through the last bits of debris, he gasped as he lay on top of the rubble heap. Cut and battered, but reborn into the world, he could hardly see; the dust and tears made him half-blind. Yet he knew he could not rest here. The debris was unstable, and he could hear the shifts and groans of stone and cement. He scrambled down over the rubble pile of the once-great cathedral and out through a huge gap in what was left of its front. At the bottom of the pile he stood, staring at nothing, dizzy and disorientated. Then he looked back up at the grey ruins.

The twilight—or dawn, he didn't know which—made the scene around him blurry and indistinct. He realized that he was standing on rubble well past what used to be the steps leading to the front door of the cathedral. Three sides of the cathedral still stood, jagged, but the façade and roof were obliterated. He stumbled over the final pieces of debris and found himself now well into the middle of the piazza, still fearing that what was left of the structure could collapse at any moment. The abandoned cars—red, green, white—stood out more than the grey corpses that lay strewn about the area, the last remnants of a battle that now seemed part of another century. Out of the corner of his eye, the man spotted concrete chunks arranged in a neat circle not far from where he stood. In the middle of the circle was a backpack. He stumbled over and grabbed it, and almost tore the zippers as he fumbled it open, ignoring the pain in his shoulder.

He guzzled the water, only stopping when he thought he might vomit. Panting and nauseous from having drunk too fast, he sat on the ground and took inventory of the backpack. Not much: some packets of crackers and cookies, the water bottle, now empty, and a plastic bottle of insect repellant. He would have to make do with what he had.

Then his hand touched something soft. He rummaged around and pulled out a wrinkled map, folded into a rectangle. He unfolded it across his lap. Scrawled handwriting in smudged blue ink drew the man's attention.

He drank in the words with almost as much eagerness as he had the water. Dehydration slowed his mind, and the smeared words made it difficult to understand the note. But it emerged, word by word.

Waited as long as we could. DeLuca said to try to find you and dig you out. We tried, but the rubble nearly collapsed. He made me promise to leave something behind in case you lived. Before he died, he said that at Ravello, they kept the blood of another saint at the cathedral. Pagans, the lot of you! That's where I'm going, then on to Assergi. Good luck. (Not that you'll ever read this.)

Cristian

He crumpled the map and shoved it into the backpack. His eyes wandered. The man wobbled to his feet. There was a pile of rubble the length of a coffin close by. Thoughts of death left him colder than the chill wind whipping his face. He turned and looked down the grey, empty streets.

The man, whose name no longer mattered, stood with tears running down his cheeks, though from the wind or something else he could not tell.

ACKNOWLEDGEMENTS

After the witching hour on some nondescript night, when staring at a blank screen, writing seems a most lonely way to spend an evening. And yet, while writing itself can feel solitary, no book, including this one, could ever be completed without collaboration and assistance. In my case, I was fortunate to have help spanning Europe and the United States. Thanks to Andy G. in London, my wife, Anne, and my parents, Alfredo and Mary. Their support and suggestions were vital in the completion of this book. I am deeply indebted to Becky J. in Seattle, who graciously read my manuscript chapter by chapter as I wrote it, while it was still very raw. Thanks also to Moe G. in Washington, DC, whose late-night banter provided the seeds of an idea that became this book. I am grateful, as well, for T. Fisher's insight into law enforcement tactics and procedures.

Ivan Zanchetta's unique flair, coupled with an understanding of the images of Naples, gave the cover a distinctive "look" that only an Italian cover artist could have done. Finally, huge thanks to my editors, Trevor Byrne and M. J. Hyland. Their (always gentle) prodding made this book much better than it otherwise would have been without their outstanding guidance and creative advice.

ABOUT THE AUTHOR

P. R. Principe has served on active duty as a commissioned U.S. Air Force officer and has lived in Italy, France, and the United States. In between writing and contemplating civilization's collapse, he spent time in Glastonbury, England, learning to forge a broadsword, and obtained his amateur radio license. Visit him at www.prprincipe.com.

Made in the USA
Charleston, SC
02 August 2015